Canis Ictus in Exsilium

(Dog Bite in Exile):

Translated from the Sermo Vulgaris

In Four Parts

By

Carlo 'Ubatz' Parcelli and Harald Comus Earwicker

Country Valley Press/Flashpoint

ISBN-13: 978-0-9820196-5-8

COUNTRY VALLEY PRESS
1308 W. Washington St.
Carson City, NV 89703

FLASHPØINT
5703 36th Ave.
Hyattsville, MD 20782

Dedicated to my wife, Rosalie

CONTENTS

FOREWORD

The autobiographical epic, *Canis Ictus In Exsilium (Dog Bite in Exile),*
by the Roman Cynic philosopher and rhetorician Canis Bilius
Augustus Ictus, was 'discovered' in manuscript form by Dr. Harald
C. Earwicker in the library of the Benedictine Monastery at Subiaco
in Central Italy in 1984. The work, which was considered of no
interest or merit by literary scholars, poets, philologists, stone
masons, clinical psychologists, epidemiologists, clerics, sous chefs,
undertakers, CPAs, pipe fitters and philosophers alike, had lain
undisturbed in a discarded chamber pot for 1300 years. The text
consists of 441 rectangular vellum sheets dating from about 700CE.
Though most of the sheets are quite well-preserved, some show signs
of having been used as bibs, aprons, throw rugs, tourniquets, cleaning
rags, undergarments, insulation, dart boards, archery practice, fish
wrap, battle flags or lining for the many canary cages that adorn the
monastery.

Nothing is known of the work's author, Canis Ictus, and no other
works of this peculiar classical mind are extant. It is generally
assumed from examining the contents of the text that Canis lived
sometime between the First Century BC and the First Century CE,
straddling the new millennium, and may have suffered from palsy of
the ball sack, goat foot, duck mouth, an inverted scrotum,
toonophilia, male pattern baldness and canine halitosis.

In 819CE, while ministering in the Abruzzi region, a young priest
named Giuseppe Rastus was accused by the Church in Rome of
stealing chickens, poaching eggs, discounting indulgences, stabbing
mimes, purloining parsnips, skimming the papal tax, disemboweling
wine barrels, sampling barmaids, refusing to stab mimes, bear baiting
on the Sabbath and celebrating Mass wearing only a wine barrel and a
cockscomb hat. As a penance, he was given the task of transcribing
Canis's text, a punishment assigned directly from the Vatican by

Pope Sergius I, one of only 9 known hermaphroditic Popes. Presumably after the transcription was completed, the original was destroyed, probably by Father Rastus himself, of whom it was said was subject to violent fits.

Little is known of Father Rastus's subsequent years at the monastery. But that the priest loathed his penance is evident by the voluminous marginalia he scribbled at the borders of Canis's text. Despising his task and its author, Rastus wrote such niceties in reference to Canis's work as "quod culus" (what an asshole), "insipientiore" (simpleton), "pato pro cerebro" (shit for brains), "caput stercore" (shithead), "putidum pila sacci" (stinking ball sack), "asinus labia" (donkey lips) etc. Further, all of the priest's illustrated initials, rather than decorous illuminations, were of crude stick figures resembling Roman graffiti usually of Jesus performing cunninglingus on a nun or a priest performing sodomy on a goose or other waterfowl.

Originally intended for oral presentation, Canis's text was transcribed into a colloquial Latin known as Sermo Vulgaris. In 1998, Mr. Earwicker contacted Carlo 'Ubatz' Parcelli, a leading authority on vulgar tongues, for aid in translating the Canis text which E. had managed to spirit away from Subiaco. For the past 16 years both gentlemen have worked assiduously to bring this warrantless manuscript before the public.

The epic poem is presented in its entirety below in English translation.

Translator's Note: The translators have attempted to maintain the clumsy rhythms, mixed tenses, awkward rhymes, confounding inversions, unremitting scatology, and dull, ponderous wit of the original. As a result less inebriated readers may find the translation of Canis abstruse and brutish. For those readers allow us to invert Dr. Rabelais' bon mots, "Go there and drink". We say 'Drink. Then go there'.

Further Note: On occasion Ictus refers to himself in the third person for no discernable reason other than a surfeit of drink and drugs.

Part I: The Bum's Rush

Canis Ictus is exiled to an uncharted insula

What the bloody writ read
    'Canis Ictus Publicum Est Nocere',
     Signatores, Licinius Crassus, Julius Caesar
        And Gnaeus Pompeius.
  What this Ictus be remove a the bounds a Rome
To a barren insul heretofore ta be known as Canis Isle,
  What Crassus in his infinite good will
And interest in maintainin' the public weal provide
    50 silver denaries for immediate transport
A said Cynic philosopher Canis Bilius Augustus Ictus
    By Crassus' aide de camp, Captain Hilarus.
A writ, from what the Emperor Augustus abstain,
    Ta avoid some unseen insult
  Or godly disfavor ta the Empire,
      What this fool's exile be, I suspect,
    Received as some portent or omen
      A his excellency at his mornin' stool,
And curtail his passion ta feed this Ictus dog
  Ta the lions, lest these foul semblances he apes
Be such, what be want a blood sacrifice,
     His malicious japes findin' favor wif the gods.

So what be this exile ta me
     But I be thrice honored?
First, what be said a fame ta throw this dog a bone
    If it warrant such.
       And this be a labor a shites as I be pleased
  Ta be a bug in their blankets;
    A fly in their wine.
    A mote in their eye.
A louse in their beard.
    A canker a their bum and
A palsy ta that slumlord Crassus
     And the pocky pricks
    What stroll the bloody Palatine.

Second that this be a quarantine a what
        Be ta show me metal a what I
Be swayed by naught but the gods. And
        As No Man be archetype
    I flatter no man me idol,
        Greek or Roman, not even the Sinope,
    What be truf and tenor a me current folly
        For what be most foul ta them
Be but me mind's stink.
        As Pungius' Tractatus Bombulum writes
    "Farts please but their maker,"
And his tutelage
    Be but a double down a me thoughts,
A foul odor a ideas what wooze the patricians
    As it woo the plebes.

And third be no recourse a retreat a me honor
    Nor treaties or truce a theirs,
        No contract, bloody writ or handshake.
        For I be a solace out a earshot a those shites
As gladly they be free a me prates and japes
        About the Vicus Platea and Vicus Comici.
And what now me audience be crabs and snakes,
        And me lamps be moonlight
And me book, waves what dash the rock.

And all this talk o'ertake me stomach
        What growls as I be fresh ta peckish exile.
Now be sentiment a me temper and a the spartina
    What hiss and the sea roar
        What be more a testament a me word
Than the whole a the bloody polis
    As I be but a wrinkle upon the aether
        What not frequent human ear,
    Or but two dimensions when three
Bespeak me false ta varnish me survival.
    A barren insula be a cynic's tableau.
        What a tub berth the flesh,
    A gentle hillock be me final ceil,

2

And I be king
What bear orbit a me own crown.

Canis Ictus compares his plight to that of the Greek hero, Philoctectes

What so?! The plutocrats disguise it a quarantine
            As I be ta abase the air like Philoctetes
What me mouf be foot to foul rupture
            What shape me breaf a fouler thoughts
And words what gentle coaxed be ample
            Over despite and claims a me perdition.
What wound the archer and I suffer common
            As occlude as me foot be free,
                    But what say these be swaddled in me mouf.
            And what pus but the hiss and spittle a me despair.
            I not be on the blab.
            Wise Asclepius hisself
Dropped outta his dead muvver what be shanked
            Taint ta bowel.
            He spill out wif her chitlins, du'n he now,
And be caught in a pisspot
            Saved be he by biles' cure
Such that yet no more earnest healer
            A wounds and rheums there be.

Note: Here in the margin appears a caricature of presumably a
newborn Asclepius held upside down probably by a midwife while
the other hand rears back to spank the baby's ass. The infant
Ascelpius wails with tears springing from his eyes. The words
"Generattio Medicamentum" (The Birth of Medicine) are scribbled
next to the image.

Not Hippocrates what fathered the asp itself
            What slither up a barber's pole
            What these be any pedagogue's staff.
And none shy a Aristoteles declare him 'great'
            What be abide not be confound

3

Wif the great beasts and winds
Or the great thems what pave a field wif corpses
    What already be tilled a their paps and nunks,
            There begets and their begats.
        Or sage Callicroton and
                His prohibitions a stumblin' donkeys,
And clear fountain water
            What preserve a man as good as a pint,
        And ta speak ill not a that man
Though wif Lord Barley he but stumble
            Ere a donkey's foot be forestalled.
        Yea, speak ill a no man his honks and brays
And there but man be donkey and donkey man
        But as me betters what quarantine me tongue
Be hoof ta stomp and kick.
            And said Serapion what bore Hippocrates be a fraud.
            And Pausanias what be Empedocles ginger
What On Nature be as natural as its time's tellin'.

And let blame fall upon no man
        What say this account be brute and redact
What this Semite Jesus say be infinite wisdom saw fit
            Ta void the papyri babel a Alexandria,
                Where in youth me be wont ta sit and study.
Pyro be the purgation most mortally tendered a his ilk.
        What he see healin' by herb and suture and knife
            Be a bit rube and common,
What appear layin' on a hands
            And incant in our guinea tongue scratched
            From the Septuagint
What be most rare and occult
        So's ta be worvy a da fee.
And what blame the Christian lord what scorch
    The books a Peseshet and Merit Ptah,
            Egypt cunnie what school the midwives
        Where hirsute man behind wooden dockets
            Be provident a deliverance
And a masih's omniscience be made spittoon
        Whipped and beat and hanged a his own intent

4

What power be but ta rule out any ovver mystery.

Note: Here in the margin appears a crude image of a bare foot with wavy lines coming off of it signifying a foul odor.

And what this Philoctectes be stink foot
    By gore and pus upon the cess
What cause rags be harbored at the nose.
    So be I a sort,
        But they be wax and rags upon the ears
    What oar passed me?
And the stench be that a Hipponax,
        Though me art cast nay a thought a Hades.
And not one sir hanged
        But many portly purses
As Pluto be stride the polis
    And fickle Tyche there too ta abide,
While I be cast upon this feral shore,
    What not hanged be me crown's share a fortune.
For well I know, pigs finish what the dogs don't do.
  If this be quarantine where be me sores and nubs
But the blows me escorts rain.
    Where be me cough
        But dragged, a lead rope about me neck.
The rheum and lesions
      About me boxed and bloodied mouf.
Me fever but for their poultice a hot wax and crimson iron.
  This be exile clear what false lazaretto
Be those what cherish me swipes bid tears
      And fond ado's as me netherparts rot.
Thus the good becomes bawd and the bawd myth
    And even a knobby myth warrant a tear and a toast
        Even a that toke be taken
    A some bunter a Bow Bells.

Canis Ictus further bemoans his exile and denies putting fatal spells on prominent Romans

So's I suspect not quarantine but mean exile

At the brass a me betters what I be snufflin' about
Those what by mere sinecure 'sposed to cork me mouf
      Wif bread and barley.
Exile be reserved a bit a stature and station
      Aforesaid likes a Hipponax and most lovely Agrippa.
I must be a right burr under the saddle
   Ta be cast wif the likes a Ovidius or Marius or Vernacchio,
      Or proud Orestes, or Marius or Spartacus and his
         Cohorts a escaped cons.
Me what sought not damage a human soul
         But for naught but the good graces a the whole.
Nor exile for me estate what be a pisspot for roof
      In what me wash me cabbage and yams.
Thus must me disease be sized lower than a leper.
      I be short.
Does this not portend a rodent like nature?
      And bald conveying a slippery pate
Adorned wif a scheming dew
         And creases a cunnin' bile.
And thin as the worm in me stool
         At his candy ere the grave.
I be no Agrippa
      What banish be at an Emperor's strike
But to reappear like this wank Jesus precise,
      Wif resurrect be one twin Thoma
         Sold into slavery by his masih bruvver,
      What Agrippa's slave Clemens be his second comin'
Sorted out quite by nails and transom
         What some give up the teachers
      A saviors and spirits and all what hew ta such frauds.
Or Metellus, liar and cheat,
            A fuckin' fief adored by the citizenry
      Such as they what be not in service or breach or bofe,
So's a democrat might blush at soup set before by such.
         And he ta exile what not expel Appuleius
      A Marius's clique in turn ta be packed off ta Rhodes.
         Even noble Cicero what be brought low
      By a blasphemer as he be not so aloof
         And hard ta tether

6

As the 'holier than thou' fucks and shites he defend.
But what be this ta me in such desolation
    Much less the listener feel deserted by sense or meanin'
        Besides all but Agrippa returned in triumph
And so I what crawl up a bow line
      And hide among sacks a meal
  May 'bout me own way do the same.
I suspect we all feel a bit a Socrates,
      Wronged and in all the world to be wronged
  So a neck bespeak an island and its waters a noose.
Mind ya, I not diddle the minnows like our dear Tiberius
  Or be instruct a bofe Plato and Plato's bung'.
    I likes me puss and well past the due date,
      And a proper discount for da trade.
And not much about so's I be a bit cordial
    Wif warm sand and ripe fruit.
Like Odysseus forbear a all a us. Moved ta
    Shag a sow and the sow's mistress
And flingin' his crew like altoids ta Neptune and his minions.

Be it as they say, good arise a me 'quarantine'
    Though none I know be infected a me stench
Whevver a thought or rot.
  I mean there do be me public howlin'
    'Bout blotto money owed
And that skit what I wrote,
    Played down the Bijou
'Bout a fraud a Ovidius by one Vilis Maximus
  What owes me a few piasters for a mended fence.
But no Midas, this Vilis what court a sack a gold
  By name a Tullia, Cicero's daughter no less,
What elude the lech for she be smit by a Gallic boxer.
    But no hangman be I,
What be a his own hand debts a dice,
    And spreadin' the broads and bettin' the prads
What not by me words nor deeds
    Be his Sonny Boy.

Take Locusta, the same what poisoned Britannicas

And a thousand,
           What I share a daffy at behest a Lucullus,
An apertif what advents a bellows a me bowel,
           Farts ta make her footman declare a holiday,
And bleed and burn a goat
           While me guts twist and contort in pain.
Lucullus bid ta make a me a Socrates sure.
       So I tol' this tale in the style of Plautus
A royal shite all tragic over his vineyard
       What grapes be the horse's piss
His business what turn verily sour,
           And certain the seasons be dry
       And his grapes pucker
As what was once ta make the maids lips so.
               But that be chance as his bath be red.
       And Locusta? Nero begged death a his secretary,
And Galba order Locusta be mounted by Jove,
           What on said eve fancied hisself a giraffe.

Canis Ictus conjures

I be happenstance a these deaths
       As ta put me pen down be me own.
What me grunts and gripes be so smeared ubiquite
       That Hannibal and Dido be abashed,
For no Socrates be I, what drive his angry inch
       Into the bums a Athens privileged snipes
Whilst he direct a ten penny Platonic nail into their heads.
           Or Archimedes a dozen fortnights betwixt baths
What by the orbit a his filth gauge mass
           What be the heft a his rank, the Sicilian ass.
       Aye, as when Herakles clean the Augean stalls
       By his labor he foresaw a demigod's pedestal.
Be countenanced we a the fallen Democritus
           Or Leucippus what say
   Atoms by all account rough out a world.
Say we the Semites' Moses, this Mochus,
       What wif knots and beads come forth
               Ta count his tribe back to Eden?

8

Blind ta the touch these 'nonymous things.
Dark. As mankind be a most desperate lot
What confound heaven with his confound thought.
Be but digits and stones after the fall
To account a heaven, a garden, or an atom at all.
Or Aristoteles what gazin' upon the Parthenon
Mutters all Nature be but flutes and gutters.
Or Ptolomaeus observe our dear earf
Be at the core a thought
What wif Galileo came ta naught
And naught for naught what bein'our Great Chain
And the wee atomic world unseen
What confect man at the center
Of a Cosmic Anthropic Principality,
A benightedy reduct a our slink Machiavelli.
What I tol' me betters what curry
Be the bloke a letters.
And if the polis I so offend
Upon me sloth and drift they must size again.
For what in idleness be a threat
Na more ta bet upon this Favel
Than ta incur through this phantom race a debt.
And dun I say freat for threat and muvver for mother
Such lack a discernment be ta exile me
As likes a me be ta be like any other.
More cursed than I be exiled wif canards a quarantine
Not that postures do not afflict,
And what so ill suit so many
Where once the imposture dispense wif the critic
Wif circuses and combats where
The vox populi howl for his entrails
Be dragged about the dirt arena,
Wif the truf be left ta rot in place
Under the floating spheres', dolce carmina.
And the sun rises and sets. The stars shift and shape.
A crib toy of a some Gargantuan race.
The ironic topiary of some occult force.
And me be but a mote what tumble in space,
And by irons and oars

Chanced ta moor upon this place.

The Dog barks his Cynic's pedigree

       Sage Agregius be me guide,
Same what be prentice a him
    What sniff the clotted flanks a the Sinopean Dog;
 A flightless pupa behind an aromatic pedagogue.
   For by such extremes what cheek be Aristoteles and Ovid
Wif they's monads a smoove and rough.
     I ask, be the master's rank but creamy stool
    The stuff what consort a ragged, rural molecule?
What by compare a his master's stench
    A field of rotted corpses be but a single rose
Where a Arawat a roses be not consequent a the nose.
    Me said master, the aforementioned Agregius
What trace the fall a man by the toke a
     What the bugger took tool to hand.
The prosthetic of a hammer or trowel
    Where no handicap be manifest before,
What mates by naught a proximity or emptiness
  What once by Eden now by need becomes a chore.
     But what oceans and planets do transgress
Require but angstroms, na more, to spud the well of loneliness.
    What buggered cripples be us all
Wif false appendage a ear and eye and leg,
    A poon and paw and pelf and pud.
    What? Be next Hephaistos at his forge beget a bronze savant
Displeased be he with what his banished ball sack made?
  And counter many a vain inventor what in himself
    Be fractious toward creation
  And envy to be proxy a creation itself.
What, god's Adam be but a widget.
    Or credit Hephaistos his two gold concubines
Or giant Talus' his ironic embrace.
    Be the forge our home and hearth.
A Brownian career what cannot ken bit ta bit
  What iterate a masque to crib an ape's.
    To say to be not like me is to be unlikely.

The razor what cut short Pico's plot
    What trace the shortest path
        From ear ta ear or ungentle reaps fur from flesh,
    And the acreage so mowed be reasoned bare a art.
    What truth be merely bald
While shaggy wit tack bile wif guile
       And regard truth, bald or hirsute as truth befit?
    Hera banished Hephaistos to Lemnos isle.
For shriveled foot and unfavored face
    What augered rank Philoctetes a such a place.
And now me be grant a lame hideous beast,
    Eden's last cankered so
       What I be first a some new race.
Some seer reality what prophet a happenstance
    Though quite sure of foot as it be whole
Follow gods and heroes so entailed
    What my name be of no repute but for bit a ill
Bouyed only by the pedigree of me punishment.
    Does isolate art like a beast adapt when confined so.
Commerce wif the pain a Cassandra
      Conjure me potion a Hipponax.
Does this not speak a husband a Polis
    As it be an oxen a none other?
Who in the Senatus would smell a Cicero in me
      Unbanished not be the humble banished from thought?
Removed by force as be any Epicurean by desire
    Disposed as ta what pols and partisan in error conceive
    As be that what I despise
What I love as want by any a Gaia's brood
    As the Tiber be ta choke Ostia
  Like the flux what rose upon Willie's wild Ethiop
    Jealousy, rage, pride, all the offspring a love
And wif what knowledge peace be recompense
    What stay vengeance no more than a lamb.
Thus I be heaven's kernel but by me own propose
    What not shun pedigree as a none be me bred.

Canis Ictus recalls his old orange hirsute friend, Velius Cesinus

Dim grows light's accord and pitiable Erebus descends
    And swells the cries a the beasts therein.
Such agony pervades the night. Chaos such
      That all malevolence is unleashed
    As free to roam as the monsters
      That herein concealed make their home.
Fearful I recall one who must thrive.
    Withal an hairy man ta shame Esau.
Shag the color a rust and naked, furry foot to pate
    Palms bare, black padded feet unshod,
  And fingers long, more four hands than two
From a distant isle wise Pausanias knew.
      A satyr so randy Philo kept his ward in chains
Lest he propagate his race amongst the county's cooze
    And evince they swing among the trees
As it be but a knotted rope gird about a branching larch.
    But no, no tail as be Pliny's wont
And just a beastly wee chut
      What be bare a snug bit a any cunt.
    This shaggy man, what be called Velius,
  Silent, forlorn in his gaze
      But what be an occasional grunt or howl at his lot,
What I suspect he be a Budai sect
    What joys possessed be long a duress,
A good mate and lovin' what no ovver than Strabo relates
    Such a creature torched hisself
    At the mere sight a the Greeks.
And all a Athens for a moment was slack wif awe
    At the blackened bloke what saw no honor in it.
And Velius thus for flingin' shite and bitin' slaves
      Be removed to a cage
Furnished wif a rug what be the skin of a lion,
      Goblets and plates, two fine tunics and chairs
  A what me friend cared naught,
Hurling the wares, breakin' furnishin's, strippin' the drapes
    And whirlin' about in their ripple and folds.

Shite all about, Velius wrapped in a mangy mat
	Shunnin' all mortal things as a Budai is want.
Better what he be bathin' in the atrium and
	What stink a his bladder and rotten pomegranate.

Canis Ictus and Velius attend the games at the behest of Marcus Licinius Crassus, the richest man in Rome, And Pater Familias of AurumHomoSaccos

And bofe distal for don't Velius be all alien kinks and pranks
	And me, his dear Canis be crank and imperial burr.
	On circus days be privy we a Licinius's box
Wif his menagerie a charming twinks and monstrums
	What be ta the mobs delect.
And what me wif these
	But me book bedwarfed by Lici's freak counsel Pumilius,
Deride me, d'un he, wif his base japes and pranks.
	Velius in his lion's rag,
		Foreswore he did mounds a grapes and figs,
		Grim silent upon the slaughter a the beasts
A what drunk wif blood all Rome marvel.
	Will not perforce but so candied in death's taint,
		Rule a wealth be not suasion but coax a savage will.
Indeed so many butchered beasts by our guinea elite
	What need I fear these dark woods about
	After what surpassing terror contrive a those arenas?
More the brutes fear me me Dionysian stink.
	And Lici at some twink's bung
	Above the arena's blood and dung.
		Be we deny Nature her vengeance?
	Hold her ill if torn by claw and fang.
And Velius rock and moan
	After such as they be his own,
	What entrails litter the sand
To be cooked in stalls
	And consumed about the coliseum walls.
This killin' in the theater be ta mock the hunt
	What be enough a blood labors wif nets and hooks
	What not ta mock courage

But ta stock this mockery a blood wif blood.
Nature what be unfaced wif a masque,
      Urged by point a pilum onto the sand.

And as Licinius does violence a nature,
    He does double, nay treble or ten-fold a man,
      What Cacus doth reign,
What by gold or spice or mere paper
      Be undone. Lent at rates what Licinius fix
Beyond the fruits the land will bare
    Or sweat a brow a any honest work
      There be but unpaid rent
Where a his counsel seize any object a the fruits a labor
      Whereupon that labor be spent,
And the land, or tools or hostelry be turned back.
    Or have his agents burn a tenement
      What be no Stata Mater,
The blighted landlord accept denariis pro pupa
      And Crassus's peculium a 500 slaves
Rebuild on the cheap as it be the public weal
    Ta be huzzahed and favored by the people
For pageants a slaughter, some blood, some pantomime,
    Some by mere writ and courts,
Any tort or raid or murder
      What lets the world as an arena.

Velius and Canis are invited to a feast at Apicius's table,
The Empire's richest and most renowned gourmand
And cook book author

And Velius and I what be buskin'
    About the Empire come upon
  Minturnæ, a city a Campania renown a its puddings,
Me lanky friend mentoring wealfy twats
    In his cryptic gymnos what be called joga
      Wif its gangles and jerky gawks,
    What by gossip he get an invite a Apicius.
  This Apicius be bloke what spent such a fortune on his belly
No less Athenaeus what be a bit of a gourmand hisself take note,

14

Bein' his Deipnosophistae or, what be known ta likes a yous,
        He be the Chop House Socrates
Be it a fugitive's beacon ta many a good feed.
            This Apicius wif a table what surpass all sense
    Though sense be victuals' very portal.
What smell and taste, and some much a sight and touch
        Gather the huzzahs a the guests.
And me wif me Bodai friend attend
        Though like Livy care I not for such luxury
    But have not the luxury ta offend the gods
    Nor taste in a good sausage or libum the world's end.
Ta fail ta account be me host's lean and bias
        What I place no value be ta vex Empanda
Whose soup kitchen on the Capitoline
            See me often pack me bony glutes,
        Hunger what urge us on
            Like the Sabine regs up Saturnine Hill
    And what be ta me person what for the likes a Apicius
        To curb creed for food,
Though this sense aright provision me solitude
        By its nulling power ta give offense
    Though at a great distance do loom its berm.
Like Eumolpus what by Encolpius' grace
        Be at bath and table at Trimalchio's place.
And such be it as at the time our Cassandras
            See such as Nero or Heliogabalus,
    What Apicius cook, Batalius, be so coveted
What sacks a riches or a sack upon his head
        Be oft employed to evince his service.
What that he were a such proportion what be moved
    Pullied and levered about the Pyrenees
Or by girth hoist the planet
        Like a instrument a sage Archimedes
Not some gluttonous mogul and his earfly baggage.
    He be learned a Flaius and Glaucus,
Diocles and Gordianus what for the Mobius pretzel
        He be reknown and thereby a much wealf abide.
As one might expect of any large snake,
        An army marches on its belly.

15

And thus an empire brings the world ta such
As what bake a juicy kidney or oft baste a brace a doves
     Savored in melted swine's fat,
         Be held aloft a Caesar
    What command one's own estate and slaves.
Thus chefs be heroes what salt a Minatour
     Or boil the Nemean Lion
       And their pans glint what they be shields
    What the kidney's and sweet breads a giants fry in.
Or a general bivouacked before his cooking fire
  Wif his enemies a brace of hares
      Turned slowly upon their pyre.
   And his own Incitatus what be dined on golden barley,
Draped in purple blankets and a collar of precious stones,
    What no doubt dour Livy smell the Fall a Rome.
    And when his derby days be foregone
Our equine heroes seasoned wif with garlic and garum
    Become the stuff a myth
      On crackers, diced to a gourmand's tartar
The sweat, the straining at the reins, the race,
  The neck and neck preserved in its dogged taste.
   Say sage Apicius 'the gastronomer be artist,
      Metaphysican. philosopher, argonaut'
   What as we all know such gents
     Constant be at bouts wif all manner a
A kettles and ovens and sharp and cunning implements.
And Apicius's table be heavy wif gold plates
  Raised wif reliefs a huntin' scenes a the goddess, Diana,
Her bow, her quiver and arrows, her bare breast and muff,
  What the juice runnel a many a goddesses twat and
     And boar grease clot the thighs a heroes.
And presently a fine ragout a ostrich brains and bacon.
     Eggs boiled in buzzards' urine, braised parrot,
  And a cold porridge a larks' tongues and leeks.
   Rice seasoned wif pearls and garum,
  Honeyed mice with sesame on toast, deep fried ficedula,
And eels corpulent wif the flesh a Christians,
    And a bear what that very noon
     Dined on a counterfeiter and a solicitor.

A roast sow and six sucklings
　　　Sewn into a poached python.
Stewed hippo hooves wif garlic, marsh grass and garum.
　　　The boiled septums of a dozen Lucanian Cows
　　　　　Baffled on ivory pikes.
And smoked camel heels. Flanks and organs a five giraffes
　　　Scorched over an open pit.
Sows wombs in brine and the pickled eyes a the striges
　　　What nocturnal omen be balked
　　　　　In fish sauce and clam bukkake,
Where Pyriphlegethon coils in the belly
　　　And the viscera erupts a the AM
From Vulcan partake a too much ichor
　　　　　Before napping under Vesuvius
　　　Or a plebe what eats too many clams.

Apicius's toast before dining on his horse

Before we sup upon fleet Incitatus tonight
　　　And engorged wif meat and wine
　　　You, my dear friends, take homeward flight,
I wish ta raise a fulsome cup
　　　Ta me prized poached equine friend
What even fallen on this sticky track
　　　A garlic, raw honey and tangy garum;
Stuffed wif grapes, almonds, pheasant and fat back
　　　And boiled and braised upon the rack;
Even in succulent death, he has the bearing
　　　What declare he distance himself from the pack.
　　　For a season he provide me a ready stipend.
Thus from stable ta table, if thy fortune be
　　　　　Ta dine upon his keen eye,
　　　His sedulous brain or firm hind end…

Whereupon our host swoon wif grief
　　　As he cut and bore aloft
The nags poached nads from underneaf.

17

Note: Marginalia believed to be in the hand of the transcriber of the Ictus text itself, Father Rastus, appears at this point in the margins. It depicts the monastery's abbot, Padre Carlo de Porcaro, seated before a large ornate table straining under a mountain of braised game birds while the prelate gnaws on a stork's leg and swills wine from a gold goblet. Under the table a young monk can be seen performing fellatio on the abbot as he eats. Above the abbot's head can be seen a cross with an emaciated Christ sagging down from it like warm sealing wax. An inscription above reads, "In nomine tuo" ('In your name.')

Velius suffers a bout of indigestion and shits in his host's wine goblet

Contrary much ta agita Velius Cesinus inclines
      What he sit erect and brood and mull
Wif his hands cupped up what he be a beggar
          What his thumb oppose as be a teacup
     A transit what be most exposed.
For he by Bodai riddle know
      If guinea meet the master on the road
He dispatch such wif knowledge a Bodai say so or no.
        Most likely 'no' for such be guinea sport.
     And what opulence be ta a beggar Bodai
       What sort live on aefer.
While a follower a this Paul a Tongues
       Live on the scraps a his masih's bung.
    And our cynic? He be upturned in a prelate's bin.
But Bodai do profane as he be what spoon wif celebrity. And
      These Paulites do con the rich and poor alike
    Wif palavers a afterlife what not sport
       The heart nor soul a any holy bloke's Epicurean delight
         But by inconstant promises and foretokenin's,
     Where but obstinate and contrary the cynic be.
His riddles not dodge or glance at truf but air it inside out.
      Still me Velius need relief but by guinea custom
What exit the table be naught as grief and censure upon the host.
     So Velius's guts slosh wif meat and wine
      Be it ta ape by grunt and growl an Affluvian tumbler

A lime and gravel, water and clay.
He what defrutum and spiced pears make a soupy mix.
So after much grumble and viscerous dismay,
The gates a Acratopotes burst away,
And Velius drops a deuce in Apicius's cup
A rather fulsome load I must say.
As our hirsute harpy from the rafters swings
What be his gangly limbs as they be wings
And spew afore and shite behind
He spin as a pinwheel about its axis as
Aloft a buffet a few what cater equal to
What cranky Zeus put on display.
The same what befoul wif Snatcher shite
Take the breaf a blinded Phineus away
A bloke what saw much and jabbered more
By what Argonauts be return ta the Thessalian shore.
Or awful coils, winding ziggurats a filf what Scatalogus ascribes,
Titan stool still steaming at the brink
Noxious such stink what knock the Harpies from the sky
And gack wif vile excrement
What be a foul frescoe a Sodom's slutty cultae,
Etched at our dear Pompeii.
Vesuvio rear his arse
What the Plinys regard from across the bay
And wiser than his uncle,
The nephew demurred and stayed away
For the Younger heed the words a sage Loquatious what say,
"Objects fall what seek their lawful destiny"
And far be it such a promisin' augur
As fledge Pliny stand in Decima's way.
For Pluto broil a right spicy buffet
What as wise Varro say Vulcan's one-eyed minions
Devour in stews, casseroles and cakes
Laced apparent wif ghost peppers and onions
Such be the souls a what depart dispense
What be a nosey foretaste before we cast 'em inta holes.
As wise Scatalogus prescribe,
At birf we be but a honeyed goose,
What ripe rejoice the leavin's

19

What exit our Jordan bound caboose.
As be our Gallic Queen Gargamelle
    Once relieved a vat a its tripey smell
Want the more be shed a her babe, Gargantua,
    Her wailing, wanton heir,
Who desperate a drink deposit from his queen mum's ear
    What her bum plugged so severe it occlude her cooch
Wif herbs a some drunken midwife
    An ironic cork what keep our Sprig from his hooch.

Canis Ictus discusses the influence of exotic customs

And in defense some such austere and lawful minds say,
    Perhaps, now remain upon me train, perhaps,
In Velius's native land from what he be reft by hunger and storm.
    So stripped and torn a proper custom and far away
What prescribe the guest seek the host's goblet
    And joy a such comity doth toilet his delight
As the house's master might, nay, has presented this very night.
    For many a custom be ta Roman foul
What be fair a his guest and clash nay more than foreign fare
    As it be ta tax the acids and biles of an emissary's gut.
Doth not the Imperium Rome recoil a Nazarite folly
    What gnaw the bloody gore a their jinn
And swill his blood in Bacchic fury.
    Or Semite what trim the tarp from their pricks.
And yogis what swill fresh urine
    From the morning wood a their masters.
Tutor Galleanus at his dear wife Cornelia's bitsy spout
    Tutelage a sage Plotinus.
    And don't Aristaeus suffer the aroma
Of a fuller's shop but ta be resurrect
    By counsel a the same's fumes.
This Preconnesus what seven years dead
    The Arimaspi writ in a Bacchic fury,
What lost be bof ta Roman eyes as two be one
    And such be Plotinus one be all
As one be heno and heno be Greek,
    And ordain the Aramaspi and the sons of Uranus

Samadhi bodi what false eyes be solved behind the true.
　　Or Aurelian what be saltin' his couscous and so ire
Queen Zenobia's cook that there be words, and a siege
　　　　What end when spit and chaff be Palmyra's daily lot.
For what be custom but ta rube our senses.
　　　As we delight a the Manchus what fellate their newbies
　Or the Berbers what launch sticky loogies a their bambinae
What bof kinks pale a the mothers a Seres
　　　What gnaw the raw bloodsack
　　What us wee ubus abdicate.
What Hindi hang a their flesh
　　　What same hooks be a meat in a market
　　What fettered and helpless be a power endowed.
And d'un dis have the faint ring a the dog?
　　Or dem blue men a Brittania in their skinnies
What fashion a effigy a wicker bound about
　　　Some hapless guinea munifex
　　　What be born below Fortuna's rank
What she be moanin and clawin' the buttocks a King Servius
　　　What build a shrine a her anonymous incarnations.
What when Seres ambassador find foul Caracalla's baths
　As much the emperor detect the nuncio's need a one.
And wars be fought a alien stinks and smells.
　The Punic what be fought over offense a Hannibal's cologne,
What upon his fall be the rage a Rome.
　　　Or ancient Troy what be fought upon what aroma
　Best suit beauty's twat
　　Ta what odorous beauty be in a hero's rot.
Or the Peloponnesus what long peace be
　Reft a Samos what embrace the stink of a alien satrap.
　　　And a times custom bring comfort and comfort bring war
And alien comfort become custom what bring conflict before.

Note: At this point in the text a rather long anonymous marginalia
reads: Much inquisition be made a the origins a this Velius Cesinus.
Pliny what writeth he be a the Isle Taprobane and that the
inhabitants be so much desirous a the hot chilis there, their red coats
burn ta the touch on account a the many peppers they consume. And
Seneca attributes the ludeness of Roman women ta the propensity a

nakedness and wantonness a this people though there be little evidence that this "hairy race" be about Rome in any great numbers nor be a particular promiscuity there what Rome already be a quite randy and bawdy cess. Herodotus who calls these, Pilosus Sapinus, claims their unusual long and muscular arms have allowed them to climb up roots at the outer edge of the world and work their way inland and that one day the Empire will be overrun with these curious, hairy men. Strabo however speaks of 'crassus cultus deo' and describes this very Velius Cesinus as a citizen a Seres and worshiper of an obese Bodai that dwells there. I believe they all speak of a type a red ape I saw at the fair in Cappuccini.

Velius valiantly battles Apicius's warrior chefs

But here in medias res we take up, dear friend,
    Ta witness our hirsute hero stave off a bloody end.
Though end doth be what doth provoke
      What our Bodai's belly be overcome
     By ten dozen half-digested roasted rats
       Stuffed ta the guts wif raw jellyfish off the Amalfi Coast
What by our hairy Bodai's antic joke
     What a his homeland be
       But humorous custom a these exotic blokes.
   For our monk Velius about the rafters swung
What Apicius's Battalion the Chefs wif sharp instruments stung.
    But as be famed Odysseus or Pantera
   Such be our Bodai hero wif much aplumb
Pluck the darts from his shaggy bum
    As the barbs be but a fey infest a plump chiggers or mites
     And at the guard their very own missiles flung,
   Slaughterin' hundreds a sous and sommeliers
      Ta our host's infinite dismay
And in the chaos Velius and me made our bloody getaway.
    And if this above bit be a bit sing/song
     It be ta mimic the high wire swing and sway and
Bear witness ta the fidelity a Velius's tosses
    What for fear a Buddha I dare not abase
     Nor repay wif curses our host for his losses.
As cunning Linguinus in his Transiens ad Fluvium Styx ascribe

The world be paupered and the cosmos allayed
When thought be forced frough Spartan rhyme
Gallantry led about by the broach a sounds in common
What be honk or sneeze or grunt whatever,
How now 'brown cow' or some thing far less clever
What follow the stink a whatever the last mouth fart sounds
Be what by habit and worn flux we misplay
What direct the orbits a the stars
Much less the private rebellions a our words.
And by such repute poesy be less than better wif thought
For by love and death, death favored
Wif naught but love by little else wrought,
What give the world back its hymen, its cherry sound
Though the vessel be corrupted
A the heart and soul a pus and bile
The villain's rhyme be like honey
What rank blood doth trickle down
So that seeming either the world or the verse be false,
Poesy be seen as naught but a pretty conceit or worse,
Weak and fey unto its subject's discourse,
Where the world swipe its nouns and vowels,
Its colon's and its commas
What rhyme naught accord but rank sentiment
Ta leaden hypocrisy and bloody traumas
As be this last sad stanza's lineament.

What Apicius's belly be his bastion
His cooks served as his armed retinue,
What by the Bodai's hand
All about the ravaged banquet hall lie dead
All stout chefs at arms scattered among the bits and parts
Of a goodly number of guests.
Total be there ten thousand in all.
Gutted, trimmed, beheaded, tripe hanging out,
Carnage not unlike the planks a food knocked about.
All manner a meat be tossed a this mortal stew
Fish, flesh and fowl and a fat sous chef or two.
And there be Cabezeus Principio kaput
What served no less poached crocodiles' croquets

Ta Gaius Caligula and his feckless retinue.
And what lay beside in a pool a blood a either swine or swain
Such mingled be this corporeal goo
Be the sommelier, Micturio Fetinus,
Ferried home be he a Charon's happy crew.
And Caseus Perdomai, the same what Cicero dub
'Scent of a Nation'
And furious Crusti Calidius, what be called Hot Stone
By us local boffs, their flesh trimmed ta the bone.
And so Plano Superfecius, Coquis Epichysus, Cochleari Magnini,
Nuxi Buccelli, Testiculi Ulsus, Pedesi Scissos,
Ventrui Effercio, Sapidui Bulbi, and Maxillus Pingui.
And young Scullerius, and stout Quisquilinus.
And what in deaf still clean a spirit be Socci Mundi,
What lyric be a Fastididos' fame,
And our pup Brevio Braca what life be cut short as his trousers.
And the grind stones a Humero Porcino
What be our Sisyphus a the cutlets and filets,
Such be the bolden appetite's a his betters
What in the Empire's vomitoriums spew
What it be beyond Creation ta renew.
Farciminius Chorda a Domus a Chorda Intestini
What doubtless dutiful pinch and tied his mark,
What by dictum must issue a bit shy a Nero's schvantz
For what our emperors prove desultory a the arts
But for what art be stone and what stone be
But a mug a slow grimace blank wif the Lethe
Floating upon a drowsy omniscience.
So art what foster life be attenuate in war
Though words be but tools or promissories,
Donkeys conveying multiple meanings
Where pure but one be present before
And warriors' absolution diluted
What the cook kettles leach defrutum
Wif lead what hex Bacchus's wine wif madness
And art be confound a wealth and war
And his thyrsus wound about in ivy
And dripping sweet honey what the equestrian arts be money
And money Ovidian what shift Telos if not form,

24

Power what by oligarchs be well-served.
And Minerva though she be born a the crown a Zeus
    A shield and spear what a trade and war
    Though emblazoned wif the Gorgon,
        Her art be but a camp follower and wisdom, a pack mule,
For even the gods cannot forestall a war profiteer.
So what be I what sole be quarantined
    Be I a such value abandoned on a beach
Safe from the Consuls, Senatus and their Plutonic reach
    Ta preserve some custom, some hidden value
What by Rome's disease be lost.
    Be I ta catalogue, scribe here in solitude at little cost
Not spend a god's fortune in sacrifice
    But a copper's chance at dross.
They be desperate me a the mind say
        Wif growing hunger a this desole plot.
Comic what a kitchen be an arena
    What wif a helmet and strap be a handle and pot.
        And pugios be a butcher's knife,
And breastplate what be the goose's oven.
    What slaughter a 1000 beasts
        What a thousand smoky stalls
    About the thundering stadium's walls
What serve up the meat a some exotic brute.
        Or parts fetched of a Christian or two
    Be served up on the tailgate a some wagon's stew?
        What fat be a some slave or eunuch
Or gristle be a sinew a some Syriacan Jew
        What die or conscript ta be a gladiator;
What masque the step what affront in the arena.
        What it be ta be a warrior,
Weary, cold, fever, maggots a the meal and far from home.
    But what life and deaf some fit circus mug be
        A Janus Hoax. But the Carmentae's gratuity.

Canis Ictus the Cynic

So's sure I vent spleen and rash prate the stage.
    What be I Varus wif a capon's head?

Arrogant simpleton what neck be rung at Teutoburg
And our sons dead among the fens and swamps.
    What be I but ta nash and rail at such folly
        What alert me meaning pan me before their jingos
What be owned by circuses, baths and bread.
        This be me quarantine, and me exile.
    Me faif like the Vestales be unbreached even as the terror
        A their mocked and mocking gods be a no relief,
For mock what god does not honor sacrifice
    And sacrifice be not belief as it be mocked
What those wif eyes call fickle, fickle ta fancy
        What ta place fate upon a pyre
And look day ta day as a torch
    What be a premise a false desire
        And dangers what by the number arts
Prove misery cannot be prayed away.
    This be as a clear pool ta me and clean ta drink
What me betters render and foul and noxious stink
        And cast me out upon this load a dirt what I be saved
A what forbodes Rome a tidal wave what sweeps all aside
        And the Seven Hills be but watery keeps
A some Hebrew flood of a purer god
    Rome's crimes doth aggrieve.

    And mock they do wif me mere comfits a war.
        And true me condiments be poor.
Stage lights for campfires, standards scribbled on paper,
        Swords forged a pine.
    Combat what be but wrangling Dis for scraps a words
And like clown Bodai Velius the mob hurl they's turds
    And what shout "Bugger your wit.
            You be not blood, you be not in 'the shit'
What be our abashment, our rout, our discomfit
        Wif rage tear down your stage,
What turn our eye's angel ta foul Dis,
        And mortify our more worvy comfit."
What know yet take once the barbarian's blow
        And twice the states what for cold affection they doth go.

26

Or wars simple stratagems be much a ambush
    Like some jilted paramour what her hands taketh light
What a the dark wood whisper 'guess who'
    And by glint a steel and moonlight level the score.
What so mocked need panic I.
    What be me cautions a those what covert intention be ta die
And inverse what be but a me a learned warnin'
    More thrust themselves toward Avernus
As by death they prove me wrong and life
    Theirs' be but an isle wif a branded Siren's song.
What ask for little be accorded less.
    And a curious island I be,
What walked Rome's insulae,
    Beaten, perhaps beaten past sense, as me solicitor claim,
    By the hoppers what reign blows upon me hovel
Same what be me brevren a bloody thrashin's
    From our charitable, lovin' municipality.
What be these ta malign them yardies,
    Elysium's hods what our Senatus raise up
    An addled emperor as a god.
    What from their agents be urge ta malign me.
Oh, I not see the scrubbed hand raised out the tunic
    And by the bolt a clavi I know whence the blow.
Me dear Agregius say "Be somethin' in the water.
    An element what cause in 'uni sum'
    What make plebes act that way."

The people's blow be a weaned and tutored sting
    A them what knows ta play poverty ta folly.
Be it not Sabinus's granaries what abide me abuse from same
    What be but chaff what squabble over his empty sacks.
What be instruct but contempt for the likes a me
    A what very phantom chains be I helpless ta set them free
As they see freedom ascribe ta beat and ignore the likes a me.
    And Sabinus curate this brute artifice
    What pop and bang among the populace
And cook and fix what rush frough the veins a their brevren.
Be what me be but ta not exist
    Or so do as a jape, as but a bit a popular artifice

Some Juvenal malcontent whose cultural capital's spent
On the snark and smarm of an overweaning wit.
        But naught be worse than a Cicero or Cato
What be a jingo for his betters or class.
      What me pes be neither a Cossuti or Statili,
        But a me own sole what urge me pass.

Canis Ictus realizes that his new home is an insula comprised entirely of bleached bones

Now the crickets be me carping mob
     What fill wif fledgling chirp the silent din
No louder than me heart's loathing.
        And this ash a camp fires and corvis bones.
Be this Philoctetes remnant as I rub and coze the dust.
     But what as I drowse appear more bones,
       Millions thrust up from this insula
Til sense see this not bespeak a Strabo or Ptolemy
      Nor rich forage as be Polyphemus' Sicilia
      Nor the thick pine forests a Creta,
    But a Gordian pile a death, infinite in anatomy,
Some elk, some deer, some horse, some cow,
     Some ape, some man, some fish, some fowl.
A jumble what send great Alexander into a fit
      More than what done our Sinope's wit.
Anonymous bones as what be ta compare
       Ta brave Philoctetes what took ten years repast there.
    What extort Agamemnon's enterprise whole
Much aggrieved a his exile but possess Heracles quiver and bow
      What wifout, Helenus prophecy a Greek defeat.

But what be a Philoctetes wound that it be so rank
     What his comrades put a great sea between
      Their noses and his canker's stank?
Be it a snake bite festers what be by Hera loosed
    For Philoctetes' pa Poeas put torch ta Herakles' pyre
Or the tellin' he school his boy do the same for
     History be a whose annals you care ta name.
Or Philoctetes be by profane Greeks to plant his foot

Upon the ground a which Heracles ash be bound
Where the sore upon his heel did moor.
    Or what fable be afoot Achilles murder King Tenes,
Apollo's son, whereupon the Achaeans
        Set about the altar's sacrifice for wrongs done
    When from the fiery expiation a viper roused a his cool seam
And by myth's import stung hapless Philoctetes,
        What by men's ballads and books
        Has far more wounds than heels.
For again as go a tale Philoctetes
        Peep Apollo's nymph Chryse air her orchid
What merit the Greek another viper upon his marrow
    What bloodless moderns credit a mere graze
        From a poison arrow.

Could I be moored upon Chryse near echo bound a Lemnos
    Where the sequestered household
    A our ripe anchorite be found?
For he be not upon these anonymous bones
    But for the verse a brilliant Sophocles be owned
A version whereupon our brave Achaean dies.
        No god as be his risen benefactor, Herakles,
What various 'came ta the company a gods'
    'Wif a cloud what buoyed him and
Thunder what brought him up ta heaven',
        What these feathery Neo-Platons
        Do a dilute Odysseus,
    Whereas Theocritus say it from Tiresias
'The Thracian pyre hold all mortal nature a her son
        Whereas Herakles be a chosen one'.
What mutant Odysseus lack what ten years under sail
        To win his pots and spindle back.
Be I ta succumb but a bone upon bones.
        What Herakles foster a cure for Philoctetes
    Among Asclepius's sons, Machaon and Podalirius
What be beseech there be more truf in dual physicians
    Even one likely dead by Europylus' hand
Than in all of Odysseus reason and rhymes.
    What more ta attest our superior times.

Ta the Stoics Odysseus be virtue;
　　Ta the Epicureans pleasure;
　　　　Ta the Academics one what does not judge.
Simply all they might be a themselves,
　　　　But be not.
For in wif Odyssean omerta,
　　　　Them's what spout such preachment
　　Be those what intend it naught.
Such his fortitude be. And his courage. And his honor.
　　What be his, not be in doubt.
　　　　But his fortune made evil
　　　　　　By the world he no doubt bore.
For what be he ta Philoctetes, or blameless Polyxena,
　　　　And Hecuba not spared a mother's pain
By this frigid mouthpiece of raison d'Etat
　　　　What time delivers from superstition
What he once mugged as the insane wagging
　　A the caudal a reason.
What may be shades and fancies in Homeris and Socrates
　　　　Be confound a this Achaean breed
What become a most populace vermin;
　　　　What pay oblique homage
　　A our archetype a the cunnin' swill bucket rat.
Cunning animus what valorizes any quantum a denouement
　　As quality itself, what harks back
Knowing nothing a the mark upon which it harks,
　　　　Balked a its only timely measure.
There be but two creatures a the night.
　　Them's what can see in the dark.
　　　　And them's what see the dark.
And Odysseus be but the former
　　And the former forfeit all but its own.
And the latter be as Cassandra
　　　　And thus for me what me victory bow and darts
　　Be what be scored across me back.
What portend a man's future other than his heart?
　　And in this many proved heartless be.
This quality what Sophocles tol' that

Odysseus be not worthy ta snack
      The maggots from Philoctetes' canker.
Slave be oracle a his master's mind
      As Theophrastus gaze full upon a periwinkle.
Such me Achaeans bring no reprieve and
      Me arrows loosed upon them
        Fall short into poetry.

Canis Ictus despairs of being rescued

No Odysseus seek me
      As be no sense a me seeking
   An Odysseus among these what persecute me.
Philoctetes be a patriot and warrior as be his mates,
      As certain I be but a banty rage ta me betters.
        Me what be not a will or want tutored in war.
But them what chains me ta this far insula
      Be a some far more cunning race
          Than swat the Achaeans or mine.
What be a lip service what first wage war
      Upon the citizen's mind
      What be contrived ta spud in the eagle
And splash about in foreign blood.
      So ta me peace be ta be ignored.
      What one assuredly less than naught
Ta flick a speck a dust
      But me left in place rather than carry me off.
What be me Ovidian moment here amongst these bones
      What the glyphs they form mock me exile a print,
For what about either enterprise be understood?
        My words no more than snow on tile roofs a Firenze.
     For naught but bleats and squeaks I be impaled here
If not me small frictions ta heat the grease
      A the mercantile engine a mother lingua
        Much loved by our doctores and their patrones
What be their performance but a séance a mumbles and drones,
      An Orphic burial desiccate as this insula's bones.

But that the Achaean be most renowned for his lies.

Who trust a randy, goat-footed, back water Bacchus name Silenus
What accuse our famed Odysseus
A pinchin' Polyphemus's larder.
And some say what be his stories but these
Base grift chiseled in relief upon monuments
What make heroes a some Sicilian truck
What profit in spices and slaves,
Such that a sober truf be snuffed out
Under the urge of a drunken one.
And such be our poets and singers and their great gullets
What be deep six in the maelstrom,
Resurrect a pishta legend ere the storm pass
And rosy fingered dawn wash away the wellyboots and the snatters
In a heave a second comin' a lager and bile.
And thus be us all, such it be
We tele our Iliad and our Odyssey.
Shall I flip and float me tub, bone for oar,
Me staff for mast, me cloak for sail
Upon the sea what tide and winds to me home be?
Be it home? And be I tried a me journey like the Achaean
By me very earf, and water and its monsters
What I sudden as a squall be borne as some stranger
Ta some strange land as land and sea and earf and air
At once a this account be uncommon to us all?
What be these Greeks what lose their way in Telos' puzzles
What straight away once be their nature's flourish?
Set adrift all for a few serials and cliffhangers seasonal
As Demeter fucked in a furrow by our Iasus.
What be more than bored satiety ta set tales astray
And a specie's evil be lauded for sallyin' forf
And cuttin' down a forest ta pine
Upon a wooden gallows about the trees.
And what hero be so us cynics
For what crooner drone Homer in the thoroughfare
And not suppose frough fame and glory expose
Odysseus's prick in Penelope, a lust what be but equal
A honest Crates for his Hipparchia
What he ta part her thighs right there in this dust.
And besides be Hipparchia ta wisdom

What Penelope be ta wool.
What attest Crates chose well,
    And Odysseus be but a fool.

The Death of Peregrinus Proteus

What be Lucian ta mock our Proteus
    Wif true witness a false aspect.
      Do not his eyes see what his heart confounds?
What Lucian's puffery claim, us cynics
    Be as Actaeon's dogs upon his person
What he mock our master's blazing pyre.
    We what forsake in god's name.
      For what man deliver himself sentient
        To his funereal pyre.
    Be it such an easy thing as the smarm a Lucian's report
What ta his distress what make fables a Cynic violence
    As our smug, lyin', Assyriac hypocrite require
      Though there be not bite or scratch
Nor any aspect or gauge a our ire
    As we upon Peregrinus' fate
With Theagenes all our senses concentrate.
    Yet Lucian by his vile standards
Hope by feck and foil ta diminish in death
    What he ab exemplo diminish in life
    Ta project upon the good all evil what in him thrives.
What Peregrinus rise in esteem among the Christians
    And even a Lucian say, "How else could it be"
And when thus banished it be
    As Lucian out of jealousy
As Proteus Peregrinus birth this new cult of
    But one certain man hanged in Galilee.
Even as Lucian writes that the crowd say he be
    "The one and only rival a Crates and Diogenes."
Rival? What rival be a Peregrinus a Diogenes or Crates
    Or nay man but by in cloudy cess a Lucian's petty ambiguity.
And what martyr be not schooled a prison's middle passage.
    And what philosopher's fortune's turned.
Vespasian double-clutched Musonius' exile be he so revered.

And if the revered be fled what for speech fly
Ere both be dead. And if Peregrinus be but novel
    And a high degree what fail him his ingenuity
Or the failure be Lucian's
            What faithless his epistle be fully present.
Herakles burnin' wif Hydra's poison
        Sought relief upon the pyre.
What Lucian contra Zeus call no great thing
            What ta emblazon his words more than fire's sting.
What folly! Who craves fame but Lucian?
        And what golden idols beset a our Cynics
            What idols scorned be their scorning
What he ere as this Syriac Jesus foreswore.
        What appurtenance attend Lucian's imagination
            "Fearing [he] be crushed in such a throng."
Be his ta envy what find but himself worthy ta adore
        What care and canned laugh at Peregrinus' filfy shirt
            Be of Lucian in his despair?
Lucian altogether suspect
        What echo through his feigned laughter
As Proteus, oracle, burns
        And so too Rome soon after.

Diogenes of Sinope

What heir Proteus be a Diogenes
        What he be buried face down,
What sure and soon and wrong and ta what end
        Be he ta eat the dust he so well loved.
    Yet the grizzled visage a the world still be up.
    What dog make the magistrate's quake
Or he a Xeniades, his owner, by wisdom his servant make,
    For what folly beget a rally a those deluded
A the last first and first last and
        Where among the stupid gods no such agent be
And but a stick draw off most masihs ta chase
            As dogs be wont ta fetch.
        And what be he not so be skull crushed
            A the same cudgel.

And all this talk a the Sinope pissin'
    And shittin' and fornicatin' in the thoroughfare.
What be a loogie what it strike a man's sandal
      As no more than a sandal
Be ta block the spittle's rightful descent.
    Be it ta walk or clear one's throat
What the one that does be a better yew
    Cause only one task be bested a two.
    Or a the Sinope's brown strudel
      What render all Athens more nimble
    And spur trade wif Indus for grinded glass.
Diogenes scorn be a such extreme
    That some medium might find audience in between.
But in the interim all must be abandoned
    As early he be exiled for debasin' the coin
What he be ta conform it ta its users what abuse
      Be perforce brought ta it by their desires.
But he na more such accord a civitas
    What seem it in the manners and customs,
      Bills of particulars and ordnances,
        Restraints and whips, but incivility.
Men be free as long as
    They be free ta eat, drink and die
That be the pact a the citizenry.
    'Circuses and bread' go the covenant
While Crassus and Claudius and the Kochus frats
    Tally money well spent.
When Crixus boasted a the Pythian games
    He vanquished men, Diogenes say,
      'Nay, I defeat men, you defeat slaves.'
And a demos what take up threat wif arms
    What quarrel the wealfy goad and abide.
What Homer be ta ridicule a slaughter a nations
      For a sorry piece a ass.
And on and on the gore the heroes fuck no more
    Where once love's consent
Many a dalliance spent.
      And what be utile a our scant and rustic style
But pure, unleavened discourse amongst the dogs.

What dry cracker and bowl for home be affirmed
        When Epicurus's atoms
Be but a misplaced desire of omniscience
        For the 11 fold universe of a sheep's labia.
What wif rebellions in Egypt, Libya, Mauretania
        And Palestine treasure be lost
On swarming mosquitos what collide
        In the dank shadows a Hadrian's Wall.
        And automata what be a singular self-loathing
                Of Daedalus and Archytas
Or the Antikythera gears from Rhodes where
        Automatae stand
        Adornin' every street
        What seem ta breathe in stone.
        Or shift their marble feet
                There be a twitterin' boar
                There a growlin' parakeet
                Watch the door mouse roar
                And feel the lion's bleat.
        And there, there a sow doth hiss,
        While twined vipers kiss.
        And hot grease gums the metallic teeth
        A the block and tackle beneath.
What be unique a our philosophiam and scientia
                Be common by its impulse.
What this be our nature
        Be contra a what nature be.
What the man beat, the dog be circumspect.
        And the man be keen that the dog do bite.

The Last Man on Earth

For what be the last man a earf ta speak his tongue
        Be a fortune wif the first
For blows befriend a misunderstandin'
        And anger a words what defy query.
And this be cynic and Syriac Christian
        Last and first, for men a breed be short a congenial
                What threats their sense

36

And torture and torment follow as ta
                    What be the bloke's meanin'
        Be found in his screams and howls.
What brute he bellows or screech, thereof be his nature.
        Thus a me the dog will do.
Coulda let me wick burn out for all that suss me.
        But what be a me certain be a all men
But puzzled as a Nature, a god or goddess
            What tongue be cut out a me
What foretell nuffin' a me tormenters.

Dog Bite excoriates Clodius

Thems. Thems Epicures what be the patrones a polis
        What fancy they be Hesiods
But a many days and little work.
        Be seen a bit a alien fancy what not treat 'em
As though one must pierce a heel what them expire
            So much gold they wield
And wield men by gold collar
        As we a our city be a breed a dog,
        Servile and fanged at that.
And what pittance pay some plebe ta carry his standard
        A some campaign ta rob Cyrene a their silphium,
Or plunder Rumanian copper,
            Or rub eyeballs wif Parthia.
        Fuckin' blue blood bastards a humanity.
A these I run afoul as they be such.
        For what be ta come upon a rotting corpse in the road
And not have thy nose contest it.
        These what give themselves away
            What send yardies ta conquer naught but me,
        What fall a very few blows and curses assure.
And d'un I be accursed sure what so untimely
        A me civil desires and naked trufs me times be.
Wealf dress proxy in armor and purchase an epic
        A deeds unknown ta the gods
            What the heteroclite wombs of men conceive
Lies a the flesh what mock a god's indulgence

And deform truf for prided fancy.
Could they not have halted me siege by
    Beatin' til Thanatos eclipse me eyes?
Here. Here on this insula ta speak me last is ta breathe it.
    What requires communion ask not it be not false
    As this be much as not the god's afford,
But only that falsehood be the single coinage,
    That raised up lies be advantage ta every circle.
That the surgeon maim and the poet bore
    Ta as many laurels as there be breezes ta bough.
Let Clodius fuck his sisters
    What there be a ring of Augustus about it.
Let him confirm he be Fonteius's bastard and a plebe
    And thicken the broth a the Falcidia Lex.
Let him doodle the Aenead
    In his own shite a the Cloaca Maxima
    What attribute ta one Publius Clodius Pulcher
    In his noblest patrician scrawl
What it be the mere cowl of a plebeian prick.
    Did not our dear Clodius slip on a skirt
    Ta bear witness ta us cuckolds a Lesbia a the Bona Dea?
And, for good measure, did he not pound Pompeia from behind
    What before hinted but the sweaty siege
    A Caesar's short sword upon such a grand citadel.
    Is not Clodius favored by the people
    Though only by craft and circus and writ he be thereof?
Hail Clodius and his Leges if it bring Cicero to an insula's fate
    Or least what lack Pella's cushions and victuals thereabout.
Hail Clodius! For what be a vaccine a our litters,
    For what be a Clodius but a pox upon a pox.

**Canis Ictus discourses on begging and the bad name Empire
has given buggery**

And Augustus what many be worvy a his prick.
    But precious few his prick AND his name.
    Be not the requisite lie what stir concourse
What the whole a civility now be but a pack a lies and
    Cutthroat code what fill the courts

And markets wif "I be fucked by Caelinus, me solicitor" and
      What's more "I be fucked in me ass
         By me landlord, Quintus,"
      What words divert desire ta unholy things.
   And Trebonius wif a thousand slaves ta work his vineyards,
And a thousand more a Seleucia and Illyria what toil
      His fields a Cilician sorghum and wheat.
This Trebonius, what holds a 50 year note a Carthage
      And copper mines a Britannia, and gold a Gaul.
  And contract ta mend bofe the Segovian and Hadrian aqueducts.
      But not a denari ta games or bread
  For his service, it be a war debt
      By the state ta him
    What affords he buy a consul's ear
As it be naught but a mealy crustulam.
      And what Caesar reward his partisans
Trebonius be one a 60 what takes a late shank a the king.
      And thus Empire give buggery a bad name
As certain as drunkenness ta drink
      Or a mop ta blood.
      What hereupon sober I wake wifout the market's curse
A me ears as what I lay about among the commerce
      Appealin' a crumb from me dusty vantage
Wif a most spare gesture and concise plea.
      No evil's course for what sin be here a this insula.
    There be no buggery in a beggary a bones.
And no prospect as ta rely upon me self
      Be ta lie ta meself about me prospect
   And thus neither rub be ta self-congratulate me desires
Among dreams a pockets and gloves and purses and
      Cod pieces, mellons, and ovver tender scabbards.
    The nightingale be not false, nor the sparrow.
But me whereabouts show little fortune
      Unless starvation be such and so linked
Such as doth the starling sing
   "There be the prospect he starve."
      Certain as I the Dog need little
But sure me corpse need naught.
      What the city fathers can't urge, me belly can.

What be Lucan or Virgil here
Or even Hesiod's didact in this matter?
What be I ta find Diana pool side wif soapy frof,
Her bow and quiver reclined upon the bank,
Fresh from the hunt, nymphs attendin'
What appear a the season's celestial ritual
Be of our more immediate cosmos,
A boar cranked upon a spit.
What sooner I be Actaeon
Consumed by ravenous dogs.
Me what seek to be as they.
What those who reign, Crassus and Augustus,
Take great pains ta impel me servile,
A mere cur straining at their reins.
Yet I remain that stag what a torrent of Ovidian hounds
Rain upon me exile,
What be by celestial name
Archbrow, Bubblyjock, Curmutt, Topturd, Hoof'nmuff,
Nag, Pokejam, All the While, Malamutt,
Buggytoe, Beaverburn, Splayfoot, Pigpug, Scumnippers,
Praise the Hunt, Impertinax, Congestus, Stink Out,
Funky Harrow, Scoff Badger, Mincemeat, Prick'npuss,
Swine Harrow, Porklap, Dick'nmepud, Eagle Foot,
Fox Bite, Smutty Paw, Cat Mullet, Shitty Shank, Thumb Nose,
Stink Up, Bear Bait, Damp Flank, Torley Twat, and Hare Foot,
And Sedulus, Carnie Barker, Duck Lips, Zwoosh and
Cerberus, Harpalus, Credulus and Creampie.
The whole bloody celestial kennel.
What the Jew Elijah be a service and wield a me many arms
Ta flail and/or feed the godly mutts
As he done wif loaves and fishes
And what be sparrows about the market
That be peckish ta clean a purse or two.
Or some Hindi goddess wif dem many arms like scythes.
Or da many legs what be birf a Minos spooge'
Ta sate a worthy mongrel's deliverance a me
Ta me proper phylum or stay their hunger
Lest I crawl in a hole or voided stump ta tarry and abide.
For upon these nights a stump routs the stars

40

In its purpose
For what abode be cranking celestial lights
    What back home I blot wif a tub
        Such be them ta me.
And certain about be berries and mussels on the rocks
    And what the sea cast up wif fire as soon as
        Zeus come lookin' for me.
    In this, Nature be as any rich shite
What I beg on the street they provide not a glance,
        Not even gob upon me bare feet.
Thus be this isle what hath no use for beggars
    But what a beggar's labors can make a it
And what like ta make a beggar in perpetuity.
    Work? That I be in prefect quarantine a Antium
And no need a transport for such leisure
        As a hill a bones provide
What some do catch rain water and be a goblet thus,
    And what one day me skull spill a some wayfarer's cold brof.
What be they what do me this way.
    By shear lack be I bare a crime
Though me do fornicate in the road and shit in the hedges
    Or suppose ta shit in the road and bone in da bushes.
            But it not be envy what goad me curse me betters
But what they crown themselves thus wifout labor a virtue,
        For what be virtue a slaughter and virtue a greed.
What thus all meaning be worf not a shite in the hedges
        And all virtue be buggered in the road
    What be Ulpian's via publica be by ius publicandi,
A good road be certain a guinea stamp a equites,
        The highway and the my way a gold's fraternity,
    What by dispossess what good road beds make fleet
        What not sleep in theirs but under antique Krios
    What be cast a rustic by Caesars and Ptolemies
Ta the grief a the flight a them's
        What be blown about by dirty Senatus' wealf,
            Exiled if you will.
What be Empire's appetite but dominion,
    Ta bugger the world wif order.
What all stink be Roman stink.

A wood mowed a hay for the Classis.
Mountains sullied a copper and tin.
    And thus Empire doth give buggery a bad name
As what common bloke be fucked upon that weal.

Canis Ictus recounts his banishment upon this isle

Be I here at the end of the world because Apicius
        Has naught his silphium what ta season his cod
            Or Phineas lions enough for the circus.
Or Gaius Verres what bemoan his post ta Sicily
            What oak and pine be lost
So triremes be built to plunder Sardinia and Corsica
        What be but mill and plank ta Norf Africa.
From Hispania ta Syriaca there be are no leafy abode,
        No littoral left upon these sylvan shores,
From whence the Dryads have been chased,
        And much booze and leisure and congenial talk
Upon the coze a softer hills and softer women.
        But Gaius cries "There be not a main-mast
            In all of Nebrodi.'
What the chaste Naiads giggle.
    Were this but Ikaria and I at Asclepius's table
Savoring the Socratic rooster
        Simmering in a fine Balisca wine
    Sweetened by agency a the lead pot.
For here I be girthed about by the wisdoms
        A these ageless islanders, and our Athenian sage.
And the great healer and earth in a grape
        And Calumella's culinary instruct
For tender foul what be so brutal about the barnyard.
    No! No poison goblet for Canis Ictus!
No such truf. But a toad. You be ill, Canis. Here upon this
        Bone yard, this public dump, repose.
Here beyond ear shot you be free ta wax evangelical
        So get well, Canis. Cisterces will see to sacrifice
As be all morsels fancied by the gods be forsaken here.
        But there be mussels and pine cones, frogs.
But mind the yellow toads or the fate a Socrates

42

Be sure as secured a your own hand
As hungry as be such. And the vipers what meat be
        Delight but be deft a rock or stick ta dodge the bite.
No. No poison. Aye? But venomous laughter
        All fangs what free a me ta be stung
Not by goblet and flowery speech
        But thumb press upon the business end of a prickly meat.
    For what pansy be I ta survive
This barren osseous insula. Drowse what be next ta death
    And here verily among the stems and stalks
A dead things. Ovidius what writes a callow munifex
    What share a pot a adders seasoned wif garlic and garum.
And what I flattered wif lies worthy a Odysseus from young lips,
        And offered repast and wine
            And then but struck about me head and
        Lashed ta a mizzen mast, drunken guffaws
For siren song. What a day's journey, I be cast here upon
    What a discount Odysseus ta ignoble Philoctetes
A metamorphy neither Ovidius nor Sophocles oblige.
    What be cynic but a poor man's Epicure,
What moderation be but aspiration denied
        For what evils be between attaining a couch
            And stuffing oneself upon it.
    The triclinium's provision no more a stasis
A Epicurean comity as three to a klina
        Wrestling over a a pig's liver while discoursin' Aristotle
For what compat be appetite's and the mind.
    And these Epicures proscribed by Licinius Crassus
What his pleasure be rapine and fire
            And purchase a scorched fields for but a farthing
Such that if me tub be worthy a the pleasure a proscription
    So be I as its meat, a rank, stringy terrapin
And in any soup the brof be but ta offend.
    But it be Crassus' slave Hilarus sure
What mock me ta evangel the waves disperse
        And the shore rocks like smoke roil
For all be the import a me vagrant mind.
    "I be slave a Crassus and what scars be sure
But you be a slave ta poverty and your scar

Run deep and advance your fate,"
Say this lickspit, slog, Hilarus
    What Crassus for humor or wager discharge
As he be naught but a nit or flea.
And thus be the insolence a this
    Crassus what by decimation prove he be
Most dangerous a me enemies.
    But I be spared and freighted
Pierced but by Hilarus' Parthian Shot
      And left on this beach, king a the crabs, ta rot.
Mulling what great expense Crassus goes
    Ta disperse a fart.

Canis Ictus and Hilarus enter into dialogue

Ictus: "Dear Hilarus dost thou wish to contend
    In word and thought what idle claims
Many a sword has sour sung, its charms
    Bearing that of a rutting pig pushin' up filth
For a morsel a cob? Be you one by war
    This that be such and so,
Dyin' comrades last breaf on the field
    What be his last hack and wheeze in the jakes,
His dreams what err merit a life
    And his regrets what err merit his grief?
A lie told him what become his truf,
    And when a lie be truf best a that be scorched
Err this fool, this soldier, this slave be before me
    A shackled concubine to but a man."

Hilarus: "I'd bloody thee meself, me dimune Ictus,
    You what wait a dog's fate.
    But me master fancy I lay you here
But what perhaps I with a wink say I missed the 'S'.
    And if thus I heard 'slay',
Will he laugh and invite me drink?"

Ictus: "Or will he disembowel you
    And limp leave thee in thy stink.

For such easement he have upon you
  As whim he have upon me."

Hilarus: "And what call this exile paradise.
  What be a Crassus's hand and his alone."

Ictus: "He has and what I ta know
    As any damsel be fated to a satyr.
For Crassus cares me little but me words a lot.
    Or holds me care not at all
But a me words it be another everything.
    So that he care a me me silence
So that such care not extend ta me mouf
    And thus I starve a this odd hill.
What Crixus brag what at the Pythian games
    He slew men, Diogenes say,
"'Nay, I defeat men, you defeat slaves.'"
    And if this be quarantine where be thee rag
    That me fetor not topple thee?"

Hilarus: "Hardly but your mouf want ta speak
    And ta speak, bite. And what foul disease
    Attend thy froth. What bafflin' brew
Of occult As and Zs, trackless as mountain snow,
    And cold ta what life brings."
Ictus: "And what? Doth not life bring you the wit
    Thus are chattel ta another man,
Whether that man's abuse be just or as indeed many
    His rebuke be counterfeit.
Who does not know Crassus? His moods,
    His cruelties, his bunkos and frauds.
Buying the freehold a condemned men.
    His tempests brought on by wine
    In sweet sinks a lead and honey,
What you be beat full measure
    As one what next be prodded upon the gallows.
    You and me be but the same
When measure a our proxim ta power
    And what Crassus be. By temper or such conceal

45

Still you must obey whereas I must disabuse Crassus
     A his power over me like the Sinope done Alexander,
And by thus bring a glint a what thy freedom might be.
       Fright a this banishment? Bloody certain.
Regret it? Cold and hunger not yet have full play.
     But you be the cur what be on a leash.
What beat an old man for his feral emeute."

Hilarus: "Fool! For what I be but a lord
    What this very night sup upon savored lamb
And lie me face between the aromatic thighs
    A Abelia and Xanthe, so sated,
I roar a Herakles in me sleep.
     And if me master, Crassus, choose
By whim or guile a Jove's pretext or his simple soothsay
    Ta have me slay, I go upon waves
A wine and tides a Eros wifout Epicurean ration,
     Pure in me pleasure.
But I be a value. Slave account sure.
       But Crassus preserve me when be none ovver.
      I struggle certain. But thus I be.
    Doth no less Achilles say,
"O glitterin' Odysseus, never try a homily a me dyin'.
     What I rather follow the plow as a sharecropper's thrall
      Than be king over all the wretched dead."
   And me lord, Crassus, be utmost from such a fall.
Ictus, whilst thee rub thy chiggers and
    Fuck thy hobo mistress in the thoroughfare
      Even now less a those deprived
    As it consist in thee design.
Here I take leave before I be overcome wif envy
     A me own dinner
And swoon a me intimate prospects.
    And wif report of a job well-done
Disposin' a one a Rome's most famous vagrants anon
    One of a sect what coarse dispose most please.
What Plato accord a crude copy a Diogenes
    Whilst thou chiggers congress
      Ere thee starve or whilst thou freeze."

Brutus, Hilarus' Lieutenant:
"Hilarus, we must turn to our oars
      For what thy speech relate still here
    There be less a day
And certain no more a man
      What this Ictus declare his own fate
And the hour is growing late
      And we must harbor some leagues hence."

Ictus: "Yes, Hilarus, thy master awaits thy return
    Wif praises or some rumor a what you and
Master's concubine hath done.
    Sure you not know whence death doth come
Jealous rage a false calumny. A harlot's knife. Old age."

Hilarus: "Your risk be plied, not mine.
    You what taunt Crassus outside his walls
What ape your burlesque a me master's wealf
    And conquests as he be ta campaign
Against Parthia what country be blessed
      Ta not know your name
Much less your dispose a life and deaf
    Maybe upon Crassus's return he see fit
To fetch a you what remains and if it still can howl
    Like a bitch, put it on a spit.
Here. Take this kick as me farewell.
    No better leave off lest I snag your smell."

Ictus: "Push off to your master, slave,
    As I wave you back to Hell.
What I know a that darkness you inhabit
    Be what inform me bile.
Men condemned in Crassus' courts
    Such purchase their freehold upon dispatch.
Or you his slave what torch an insula,
    And then 5000 in Crassus' shackles
    Form up a fire brigade
And chuck charred chunks a children

Two the maws a your master's mastiffs."

Hilarus: "Compose an elegy, what you who be comic
    And small in all things.
Perhaps that skull there at thy feet be Spartacus,
    A slave what be a your likenin',
Unburdened a what the arena nor Crassus no longer task.
    Not even parched flesh about the bone
    Ta weigh up an earthly countenance.
It be your praises a the rebel what win you this desert trophy.
    And certain as days thy new acquaintance be this skull
What he and you may converse a me aberrant prick
    And hairy wine sack, and tsk tsk a me indulgence,
You ripe little fruit.
    Here, here. Take up this skull.
      Yo, yo. Do you be Spartacus?
Your poet darlin' be here,
    The same shite what taunt his betters
      And won him place at this table and court.
Let's see a flout. From thy moulderin' labors disport.
    Slave's lineage surpass the Palatine.
Surely among these be an asses jawbone
    And what say they be not a Son a Israel
In need of a good myth wif a side a redemption
    As Crassus hold much of Syriaca
And be about ta move on Parthia.
    What be thy freedom to forsake such ranks.
What say you Ictus? Speak.
    Lest I award thy magpies tongue ta Spartacus."

Ictus: "Slay me, chattel. Chop me about
    And carry me head off ta Crassus as be all me care.
Here toss Spartacus skull makin' surety what not,
    Such that he speak through me."

Hilarus: "Here vessel. Grasp thy guardian's bony pate."

Ictus: "Gladly vassal ta a feckless master."

Hilarus: "Most silent be thee. Thy head so down disposed.
And what be thy mute wif folly?"

Ictus: "Nay! Nay! Fuck nay! Spartacus be a them
      What need not dispute wif bootlickers,
Livin' or dead. For what would threat a hapless, baldin',
      Unarmed philosophe but such be surnamed a cur
Even as his object and trusted task be so named.
      For do I not communicate frough this dog, Ictus,
To bear witness ta your servile task.
      Mercy warden. Walk the mutt til he shites
Then back to his gutter in the Lupine hills
      Where he flourish as thy hero
Be a campaigns a terra speculatio
      And thee be but a pyro what pour oil
And pitch a torch a wretched insulae,
      What ghettos Crassus raze
      What the rents be raised in turn.
What be slave Spartacus ta such indulgent god, our Crassus?
      Ditissimus homo in Mundum.
What pack be descent a wolves?

And who but Ictus be ta wash lettuce
      But fear a good bath?
Who but Ictus be drunk on hunger
      But tender a phrase what incite Crassus' wrath?
Who but Ictus holding a filfy skull ta his ear
      Would wager ta make his warden laugh?
Be I garrulous before the garrote
      As on me knees thy shadow blots me,
And I diminished a me master be
      What by me name, Dog Bite, ended he.
So here fair Hilarus I lift me skirts ta thee
      That ye may gaze upon Vulcan's spindle crack
A what speed or patience be, taint ta back,
      Me smile be cast erect upon thee
      As any what a rectus be.
What mean this smile there be much mental contest
      For Graechus Flavius it be a strike a Hephaestus axe.

The same bundle a kindlin' what be
        Rapped in sticks what by 3 degrees
            Cleave a revered fasces from me stinkin' feces.
        Crispus Crus what see any aromatic hollow
But a receptacle for a rigor cock beat by the elements
        Until it be satiate and ta feckless pulp return.
As Socrates so might say
        Zeus loved Ganymede for his mind.
But Plato, a thorough swot a catamites a Crete,
        What tender Ganymede impart
            An enlightened god be from behind.
And swart Herodotus report on the Melopoeian shore
        The arse crease across as doth an horizon
            But ta tender a smile or frown
By way the end the crease be turned up or down
        What a mouf do and bold Pausanias bear
Ta visit a people what bof eat and excrete
            Norf and souf, from both bum and mouf
And their mouf be sheer as their bum be slit
            Be as the sun doth dawn and set
        Upon the drawn bow of the horizon."

Brutus: "And does not the sun so threat ta banish the day,
        Hilarus, be we off and be done a this dog's chatter.
What amuse be such whimpering
        That be he correct and be but a dog.
And a faithless one at that what bites the hand
        What feeds it.
But what be on all fours and beg thy not deny his nibbles."

NOTE: At this point in the text 14 leaves are missing from Father
Giuseppe Rastus's original transcription of Ictus's text. In 1204CE a
monk, Friar Piccolo Balsaccio quartered for the winter at the
Monastery at Subiaco. He was was given the task of collating some
30 texts in the abbey's library in exchange for bread and board.
During this process, it was discovered that 14 of the vellum leaves of
Canis Ictus's homily were missing at the present point in the text.
This omission remained a mystery until 1873CE when the renowned
Ecumenical scholar, Ubatzo Putzilini, working in the Vatican Library

under the Papal seal, discovered that in 819CE a monk, one Brother Azbesto Grasso, was assigned to clean the library chambers. While at his task Brother Azbesto received the call of Nature and since the library sits atop a tower at the end of a narrow, winding staircase our dear Brother had neither the will nor, as it is written in Galen, the musculus contractionem to properly attend the jakes which lay outside the abbey walls. Instead, Brother Grasso retreated to a convenient oriel at the top of the tower, and dropping his britches hung his bung over the casement and casting doubt upon the notion of God's image and likeness, shat like St. Paul's mule. Then upon relieving himself, which was no mean task having eaten dozens of ripe figs and much mutton stew, he proceeded to employ the leaves of Ictus's text to thoroughly absterget asinum, tossing the newly soiled manuscript into the fire. A record of a monastic hearing of early 820CE reveals that Brother Azbesto was punished with 60 rosaries, 100 lashes from six strong birch branches, his bung violated by a flaming votive candle every Tuesday during Lent, and he was ordered to dig a new latrine for the Abbot's Quarters and another for the convent. He also was ordered to abjure figs and mutton for two years. This crucial mystery so eloquently resolved through the art of scholarship, we may now move on.

Ictus: "This Isle be made Sirenum scopuli
      By me grunts and hoots
    What curious attract the sailor
For what be took for pig's meat
      Just a spear and tinder away.
What unwashed a Jason or Odysseus follow me stink
      And these fictions take a mercantile and sober turn,
What by scrawn and scab I be not worth a pig ta eat
      But yet put these sea scholars ta jest
    And set their empty stomachs to churn.
And tack aflamed rags ta monkeys' tails ta
      Roust their fleets ablaze.
For here there be no jagged rocks but quiet portage
      And much dry hemp and mazy forest.
So lift me cloak, Hilarus, and urge Aeolus
      Waft me ballocks up thy hero's nose."

Hilarus: "Enough Ictus. Brutus smite this thing what
     Can't speak but ta bitch his bread."

Ictus: "Me corpse be a sweeter perfume
     What those like you what be employed a it.
Those what be gobs a death below decks.
       Death what be so common
     Be thee now not its creator
       And all mortal stone for thy creation?
Smite me! Smite me.
       See if I not prove an indifferent idolatry?
     Shall I parry thee Brutus wif this dead mackerel,
What wash ashore about me time a deliverance
     And what die not so taken by me preachment
As lingering Hilarus."

Hilarus: "Hours now our sword we waste upon thee.
Be we off dear Brutus lest wif your blood, Ictus,
     We scorn thee."

Ictus: "Go. Go then. Eschew me siren's song
Proof more I be the last what abide this tongue.
    Its true portage be a barren seas
Far from your stripling comraderies.
     You sail ta land as I land ta sail.
I curse thy affair as thee indifferent curse me
    And like dogs follow naught but Crassus' orders,
But not it what be between your master and me
     What we doth come to loggers.
What be your master beyond his coin
    As I see you turn away?
And push off at tide and strike the oars
     What pangs I feel so loud,
So much louder they slap the sea,
    But not so hard, no, not so hard
As their debark hath smote me.
    For what all I say when the sayin' amount ta sand,
Ta addle what be a beggar's bread anyway
     As be me speech, and be me actions,

But vagabond upon me fellows' ears.
　　　Be thee not even fellows a what they hear
Yet their mind's pass and impasse be well made in me
　　　　　And limits scorned what like children be
Naught ta act beyond a child or dog's capacity.
　　　How live I so alone what know but scoldin' and beggin',
Beggin' and scoldin' and mind
　　　But a cozy hole when it gets cold
As desires but it double for a grave.
　　　What I bank a flame wif me steel and flint
And cook me jousting mackerel
　　　　　Ere it bruise the face a Brutus
Its mortal stink so profound
　　　　　It fend off mortal combat.
Stink do it like me dear Loquatia's cunt
　　　But me recall there be a bit a herring
　　　　　About her nether airs.
Some maidies what be bred a goat's milk and veal,
　　　So say Epicurus, be a mild snatch
What be sweet and composed. And Omnigedes
　　　　　Claim ta mate a hundred breed a pisces
What cognate wif the very stinks a Athenian pussy.
　　　And sage Socrates swore
There be aroma a cuttle between Diotoma's thighs,
　　　Where Cicero find Clodia rank as a carp.
And where dwell Plotinus but among Gemina's hedge
　　　Find conch be there composed,
　　　　　What there he speak of be his nose.
　　　While Epictetus rendered naught upon lovely twat
While Plato, odd, find snatch so mild a temper ta be cod.
　　　And myriad philosophes
What accord be there amorous lot
　　　Find muff sweet as a scallop or but Piscean rot.
　　　And so I muse whilst me tongue doth dance
　　　　　Between these spiky mackerel bones
A me Lady Loquatia's tender button
　　　And ta whose septum find her stink his home.
For a slave best win a queen with daunt olfaction
　　　And tongue what be root naught for words

But parries like a sword."

Hilarus: "Brutus leave four skins a port
        Ta cloud this wretche's fate.
For I think he be but bark and would stay us company
        Even me knife jig about his neck."

You don't have to be drunk to be an asshole:
Two schools a thought

Four skins, Hilarus! Four skins stave me confine but a few days.
            We Dog's drink moderate,
But that be drink in the gutters a Rome.
            But here naught be temperate
                On this hump a sand and bone?
        No 'port' be among these rocks
            So too soon me mind be clear
                That spite 4 bags a port death be near.
There be two schools a thought:
            One say excess. And one say naught.
Where Pittacus hisself be labored hard
            Upon me words and actions
                Ta double fines
What be fungible but a few hours
        And sustain but a few days,
What Hippocrates commend a terebinth tree
        And what as tree's foliage self-hanged I be.

Even if I drink four sacks all in a solitary Bacchanal
        And deem two ta fresh water
And usin' the round red berries what flourish hereabout
        Occupy two sacks what affirm future ferment straightaway
Lest I stumble 'pon a terebinth tree today
        And I do stumble more than most
For want a wine I smash me head upon this stony coast.

Words, mere words, and man's love a them
        Be excess's accelerant and in haste be error.
And error abide brazen content.

And what coarse but appeal ta the senses
And blot ta dreary mind what drag the cart
        Ta some lofty peak
And few attend what aught we speak
            And haute trade fame for art.
But the booze find many companions
        And companions find publishers
            What a sure their heads not bear eggs.
So better quell skill and sapient urges
            What mistake be coined cynics
What with mere bowl and stars
        Much reflect and outlast all in our simplicity.
But time strip temperance and make sweet liquor
        But dice for salad or soak for fish.
Such that I imbibe me first sack upon the thought
        There be a rank quality among the Equestrians
What let denarii some blotted bloke be his war surrogate.
        What not appeal ta me outlaw sense, be statute sure.
But as sentience doth comport with being
            And being be sole right and just
What need not make any appeal to law
        Yet wealth be by statute supposed,...
Here let me drink to edge me thought,...
(He drinks)
            And, and statute be supposed a wealth
        But laws wif sagacity be not riddles
            Ah, here's me engine,
As what be a chicken or an egg arose
        But surely a capon in Equestrian robes
And a feeble army a feeble bred.
        So fuck you Pittacus. Grave laws be broke by light a day
            By sober men made drunk wif wealf
A mean cowardice liquid courage would abate
        And put him piteous wif Achilles at the Trojan gates.

All business a Empire shall be conducted while drunk

Else parties a the first part see the perfidy
      A the second part and daggers be drawn,
          Or vice versa what lead ta curses and blood
      Or worse solicitors,
Where perfidy be a comely word for lies
      And boost be a oaken word for steal.
These be common compost a law.
(Takes a swig)
          Alexander's mum, Olympias, be a souce true
      And her boy be a rude drunk
What stand in Diogenes light and straightaway
      Does not our Dog, plum eloquent,
          Stripe the noble punk.
Same Alexander what conquered the world
      Though it be but another giddy binge.
Or Zeno what many a drunk he offend wif syllogism
      What a drunk can't seal or secrete when
The heat come knockabout and quiz 'em.
      What paradox what Zeno be so blind
          At tollin' as Polyphemus what tallies his goats
Or city state what stay Alexander's wraf wif wine
          By o'er-filling its moats.

Cato frowns upon drinkin' games, du'n he now.
      While crapulous Pausanias need 'the hair a the dog'
          To converse the mind a the gods.
      But I repeat it be the Crassus' a the world
          What drive a cynic ta the sack and jar.
Broke down, what accommodate one palsy
      There be but another attack
And rents and liens, their be more beggars in the road
      Than honest philosophes.
Philistines what not seek out poverty but that it find them
      What sort hunger and shelter a some rookie amalgam.
   And many be a trough a Hilarus stripe.
          Slave sure baptized in other's blood,
      And bull's blood be sure, at Crassus' behest.

What encumbered Spartacus what day
Fell upon me as all evil blot good
As the vulgus mark the moon blotted sun
Be an omen of Romulus, what superstition bond.
What Alexander's soothsay use ignorance to rally victory
And Pompey from Spain straightaway
Trash Crassus what claim C.
But knob a bit a knavery.
At once I be free ta wail in the streets.
Stride naked and bereft
What profit that these not be free
And here I be free born too be bereft
And the fuckin' thing not even be about me.
Where's that wine sack me pinwheel cosmos?
Where's hooved Komos among these knaves?

For Komos be a pretty beast
And comely be his wanton feast
Til every ember and every piss rod cease.
What be Komos temptation but he have the lady?
What chase be they he have her not?
For there be many ladies ta sport,
And many woodland spots ta shade a bed.
The forest, the fen, the burial plot.
So be there a lady randy for sport
The merchant's road ply much slutty cultae and perfume
Yet upon the body there remain
And many spots ta decor what it may room.
The lips, the nips, the twat, the pits.
The bum, the ear, the flower, the clit
Behind the knee and the toes,
O the toes and their funky bits.
Here they be as here she sit.
Ere stultified the Indus make a coil
Or clenched serpent a it.
But so time and neglect speaks ta acceptance.
But ta accept what here I cannot have
Speaks hollow virtue and mental vice
Here a cunt be second fiddle

Ta a half sack a wine and a thimble a rice.

Does drink be a despair? For here I swear
    Much Dionysius be in me what pain us
As we be but clumps a Promethean favor.
    What Sinope find a Pandora consequent his bed
As but consent ta fuck and left unfed?
        One bag a Dionysius down.
If the crabs retreat this beach
        Me be compelled ta boil this skin.
What same hunger be the tellin'a truths.
    Truth be I be drunk and pity quite suit solitude.
O'er chance be it the wine or circumstance
    What make me doubt the tale
        A Master Dog and Magnus A,
    Its gawky happenin'.
Be it this sad dark sea lappin' at me feet
    These waves kneelin' before me
        Leave, leave, leave
    Nothin' but desperate verities, unrestrained
As they be leashed ta Neptune ere a god's gravitas
        Over the slavering kiss a the tide.
Hear this dog howl at the moon
        What be me fettered ta me exile.
Dire. There be no bathos a this isle
    Just yawnin' surround a dark twice o'er the dark drink
What cast me off ta Hypnos
    Til betwixt the juniper again Apollo wink.

End of Part I.

Part II. The Insula

The Dream or What Drunkenness Imparts Be Not All Fancy
Or Canis Ictus Awakens from a Nightmare

What this be a sea a wine
    What I be lashed a lines flush wif grapes
What bunch be a bubbles
        What be but bursting heads a men
           Their bloody bulbs what impart the dark
    As I nailed against a torrent wall
Ship's hull, brick bound and seamed
        What cracklin' sound clash 'bout me ear
Like the song a cacklin' sirens
        Whetted amidst Jove's reports.
What pounded ferment scourge me firmament
      And pound me fundament a figment
        A me mind's base breech
Was what be fucked a merry condiment
        Wif a jar we jolly jam on our bread.
For be it folly I be inwit a half full sack a port
          Spyin' through the birf canal at
The howlin' cantilever a me heart
But struck me pose that be not twat
    A me dear Loquatia for I sense a far off breeze
What squeeze the brass fittings a me nose
      And close as would a noose.
        And me mouf be a salt
As I be a fortnight a Edie's poon
    And beyond the wall be desert
        And somethin' Parthian what come soon
What through the long end a the glass portend a tomb.
        Spilled winesacks and slain sheep about the ground
      What for blood and concourse arise Tiresias

Wif Odysseus and Achilles what be two hounds.
Sniffin' rude Philoctetes ere his wound doth stank,
    "Me smell be a carrion as thy do well ta note,
For it be a timber rot ere Charon's boat
    What port thee ta this very isle
      What be less a earth and more a Hell."
    And hound dog Achilles speak
      But all be howls as be his heel
    As Philotectes punished by a poison arrow.
So Odysseus "See here and hear me as dogs don't lie.
      So this me first truf as a dog be I.
And certain I No Man in this pelt.
    And most wise no man may comprehend me whelp.
So who you be dog when we be thus.
      We may but bark but thee not speak for us.
So dogs be dogs and men be men.
    And don't dream me ta tell ya again."
      And I shudder and loose me bowels
    As his teef grow sharper and keen wif his howls.
And relief he vanish behind the heroines a the Palatine,
    Tyra what fucked Poseidon at the water's edge.
And Antiope what queued up ta be at Zeus's prick.
    And Epikaste who fucked her baby boy
      Ere she knew her blood.
    And Cloris what be Neleus' trophy wife
And Leda and Iphimedeia and Ariadne
    What me head be nog, and nog grog,
      But du'n custom parse heroine from whore
    What tug and tittle an emperor's golden sack.
And nip me flesh doth these heroine harlots do
    And probed me parts and precipice
And tippy toe up me thigh and breast
    And pry at the mounds a me arse
And pluck the lobe a me ear.

And pleasure me anon til I awake
Wif a start what be debauched
            By a thousand crabs at me nads,
      What Okypodinus name 'ghost,'
And what myf proper call maenads
            What Orpheus disembowel,
Now nip a me nether parts
            And be vice upon me toes,
      And be at the jelly a me eyes
            If one not ta shear the tip a me prick
What like a Semite I be circumcise,
            As at where all I cry,
"What Morpheus take such base shapes
            Upon these rocks
      What would in sweet dream off mine.
Certain our gods not be as comely as a crab
      Barter be better than whelm and stab."
But I be not Caesar or other desserts.
      And me exile sure not be ta Cilicia
Where he be a bit player ta crush Spartacus
      And the siege a Mytilene
But our Crassus make me ragged bait
            On some cosmos' sandy shore.

So's me drop tunic and make straight for the sea
      Shakin' the bloody bitin' nippers offa me.
And then back crush a bushel wif a rock
      And wif me flint catch a fire
And so me tormentors in their own juices cook.
            And respite take a the second sack a wine
What Hilarus saw fit ta leave behind.
      What it be his mercy or me wit.
And gaze out at what null point be Rome
      What me I ken if Crassus build a bridge ta me here

I burn it down ravver than clamor home.
    What be home if hearth be kept a desert dung
        Or drowned wif a plummet a Jovean piss.
And what wif the women a munifex mingle jizz
      As about the cook fire they mingle gods
When brood and days be far flung
      A this bloody damned ruin Romulun kingdom.

Rome think its vassals be a Remus kingdom come.
    Dead by bloods hand such that others gods and vices
What be not wholly undone, and offer as gift
      The insult a citizen. What digest a Rome be Sabines.
Its sons set upon the world wif flagrum at their backs
    More than this toad Hilarus alack.
What be a slave or freeman but a cold indulgence.
      Whim a the maintenance a wealf and kingdom.
What shut me up for the right ta wed
    Or build a tannery or set up shop.
This not be worvy a Jove anymore a Ictus.

And Hilaris Fuscus. He be a Germania, be he not.
    So he be as much a Roman as I be a quarantine.
And slave and traitor what be more his stylin'
      For me ingenii et verum prove out me exile.
So what be they what in chains deny their ancestors
      For franchise. Be they slaves to futility
And the Roman yoke. Or Spartacus
    What throw off such yoke
Ta be slave ta futility a arms.
    Bondage be death at its moment
What seek life on this side or that.

Where be that skull? And I be need a stout stick.
    Ah, here be the toothless bugger.

What be I call ye? Be I call ye Oraculum.
　　　　A seer ya say a bloody Brittannia
How ye be this way? I mean
　　Tides and leagues wise. Not
What motte bear your bones
　　　　For that be but result a such a breach.
What? You be ward a Tuathal. Ya don't say.
　　　　　What our dear Tacitus
　　Claim be a exiled Prince a Ire riven from his home
What that Agricola use his throne as pretext
　　　A the conquering armies a Rome.
I mean, every Julian some soulless plutocrat
　　　Pinch an empire?
And thee be a nameless cog a Tuey's retinue.
　　Certain you have no Latin and
　　　　What good be no common tongue
What be ta converse.
　　No offense, but be you leave this bony pate,
　　　　As l call upon that insurrect, Spartacus.
What we plot til me hide rots away.
　　　I not want ta sit in silent stare
Or tutelage a some heathen tongue,
　　This exile be not sanctuary, more a boar in a pen
What mill about in his own filf at Crassus's whim.
　　And be all I know Crassus purchase this island
Wif the blood a what few here inhabit.
　　　Such a fortune erase a race a giants
As quick as the science a Archimedes or Democritus dispose,
　　For what be immortal be nature exposed
What the gods be stunts and blind volition
　　　　And Crassus bilk from a credulous rube
Or better yet bet his man Hilarus
　　Render by arms the island monster free
Wif a half dozen mutilate and rot corpses a gargantua

Stabbed and plucked from the sea
Or bears wif dead gladiator's faces jigged in
What hexed his insula be what no incarnation
Be he man or god or demi-god but Crassus protect
Not even Herakles' or Alexander's
Wif their tragic defect
What be hot fury not calm bunko as be Crassus' combat.
Not ta say Crassus' not gird Hermes belt wifout a sword.

Canis Ictus discourses wif the Spirit a Spartacus

Ictus: "So Spartacus, what say you. We be bofe men a folly.
I aggrieved a me tongue, you a your life.
What life there be but for servitude."

Spartacus: "Hold Ictus what compare thee ta me.
What be slave a thee what Hilarus say
But chained ta your consign drivel?
What you be free here ta spout
Where none be afflict a your infect.
If it be audience thy want
The Roman arena awaits,
For it be struggle what be a thy nature,
But not thy implement or device.
What be a rebel what cower at the blade?
For if it be blade versus debate and venomous verbs
There be no second chance ta be afraid.
And did'n I crucify a munifex, not a poet. And
Though a thousand sycophants
Sing the praise a Licinius Crassus,
What out a ear shot or in defeat or good wine
Soon as sing the praises a me.
And Crassus hang 6000 along the Appian Way
Ta warrant all who pass be slaves

What liberty be but ta be ta enslave ourselves.
And much prized this manumission ta embrace cares and woes
    And the cares and woes a thousands
That be mere death's enslavement
    What point lesser men abide without hope a necessity.
I be slave ta killin' til I kill what enslave me.
    You. You be a slave lest thou kill what be you.
Crassus what ported thee here be your master, be he not.
    What he not even feel the burden of a single wave
        To toss thee here.
I know not whence or what
        By speech or temperament thy be a slave
Or what intemperate heat like Hero's turbine
        Sizzles from your hole what spin a tiny globe
    To name it but ta be one's own.
    But if here not slave you be but a rock
What waves dash ta rouse thy fury.
        What forge be ta make a Vulcan toy?
    Here you may cry fathoms ta Rome's shores
Or hurry thy addle what declare thee the emperor a crabs.
        This be as much a threat a thy purpose
    Even as you steam and gobble your bold citizenry.
Thousands cast off their chains and slit throats
        Ta follow me
    While you and your cell of mopey dissolute
Think parryin' wif your prick on the Palatine
    Or announcin' up be down or right left
        Be such revolt.
    Or babble confound a Crassus
        Ta topple what be gained by blood.
Ah, poet. Thou be but a poet.
    What be called when all else fails."

Canis: "What I be but ta amuse the patriarchy,

What be Crassus assign his best slave
    Ta traffic me here?
Be not such wisdom as tell Crassus 'Go Fuck Himself'
      Writ in shit upon his atrium wall
        What set fire in thy breast?
What not me spit upon his drapery
        Embolden thee perched next his divan or litter,
    What I'll wager me words pried thy hand
From thy festerin' crotch to scratch thy pate?
  Be me and mine the root a rebellion
What steal fruit from the field
    And plant seed a me own hard ground.
First it be in the head. Then it be in the arm. This liberty.
    As you say, what man know he naught
Be a slave til a glimmer a change come at the lash.
    And then extreme me visage, naked, rank,
As the arena dirt be baked on thee.
  Wif Hilarus appetite blind him what it is ta be free.
What Cynics foil not appetite but its attendant luxury.
  Base in all things, all things that be base."

Spartacus: "You speak a me servitude
    But naught a insurrection.
What be you rebel but what wipes his arse
    Upon Artemis' drapes and piss on passersby.
And pick on slow Plato
    What converse be ground ta dust in your mind
Wif his ten twinks and they's rich daddies
    And the sweet, faint aroma a rectum at symposia,
    What thy few catamites prove what study
  Be firm what be thy take a hygiene.
No slave seek thee out for one not seek
    The Nothin' he already knows."

Ictus: "Slave knows a little a me as I be a him.
    For as such I be disport a what I choose
What bed I lie. What temple portico I dream under.
        What be imbibe a the gods what nature be
Not restrained by simple logic and Pythagorean confine.
    If I be strapped like Hilarus or Crassus
        Could we here speak frank?"

Spartacus: "What frank to hear but this skull
    Wif what you propose me.
        Dare say you, you be the lesser man
What doth not take up arms?
    No. You be the lesser slave
What wants all ta be slave in you.
    Slave wif what appears no fetters
    What eat, drink, fuck and shit
        But ta quibble wif his betters.
What be a lady's finery ta you?
    What be Crassus's treasure?
You, Ictus, lose every bout,
    Blade sheathed or wif out."

Ictus: "Should this be ghost talk
    What be a no substance ta furtherize his cause.
Crassus's does not bear upon a discrete cosmos.
    His very city, Rome, be replete wif his blood cause.
Better be shackled by our better nature
    Than contend wif our worse."

Spartacus: "What say thee a bonds
    What must be broken
Before a slave entertain some betta nature
    What be true a you as it be me.
Thy assess be flawed

For many in me death see life.
For it's me betta nature
What break off these chains?"

Ictus: "Is what be now as thee be but in death.
And what be thee as Empedocles be chucked a Aetna,
What by deed thee be immortal
What the crowd mob the amphitheaters
And Lucian be consiliare to one's soul
What exurgo launch Empedocles up to the dewy moon
What be back hand for the fool be burnt.
These be what deem these what thee be.
What prate the stage ta adorn or mock.
What be scented grey and scrubbed Epicure
What moves among the divans
Piquant a any dainty and scoff a any good,
What beset his quiesce be buoyed upon other's labor
As his bon mots be acquitted by Vergilius.
For here thy bones attest
What man as we dwell here live on dew?
False and immortal what Aetna belch back thy shoe.
Where's me wine sack?
For bickerin' over franchise upon this prospect dries me out.
Slave be I never. Neither taken nor taken in.
Shackles and bond be not affair a mine,
For who would bond me what has so little need
And speaks none a puttin' butter
And honey upon the table.
A swig a wine ta beat back these heroes.
(takes swig and a long belch).
Ah, there be me clarion call.
Hail! Me little sandy devils.
Stay thy claws til thy hear me poem.
Lucian out done enough ta be hopeful a Peregrinus.

These stars stab me as thee done Herakles.
But stage our god, Lucian, what make a Crassus a demi-god
And Spartacus a goat. And what say in a generation
There be but falsehoods.
What be better guide than these furbelows?
What be but belletristic shades a bestiality?
What an empire starin' down a Roman nose
Be led down a garden paf
Wif some greater myf in the hedges.
Hah! Bless be Hilarus what leave me sack
So's a mine me feels a bit a heft.
What little sage be left.
This Lucian Samasote what mock Peregrinus
And be not direct and concise about our dear Diogenes.
Still d'un he beat thrice his Alexander wif a Parthian Shot.
What make out the Paphlagonian
Ta be a babblin' busker and two bit oracle.
What be a mix a this Jesu fella
What at same the Paphlagonain despise
And report of a client's son back from India
Wif preachment a past lives
What unfailin' be royal and peerless.
And a snake, Glycon, what be a fearful purport
What be a little more than a hand puppet,
Always in shadow as truf be in time.
And Jesu's proxy a the second comin'
As be this Simon Magus what retool Christus
And after purchase a some Philip's bag a tricks
Storms the empire wif his sorcery.
Christian this Simon, I say, what Magus despise
And Magus be austere Christus but to veil his franchise
Such clear evil what ta question callow intent
Be as forgivin' these cults
What be well-meaning but ignorant.

69

And Spartacus fall silent as he be a the dead.
What be me silence
As these dead but be in me head.
And so Charon and master Pluto.
The whole Pantheon be in me skull
Wif its stone dome be there ta gull.
It too be empty wifout wit.
And claws gather what sleep doth feed
What me spent ta deny such need,
But ta smash and feast ta supply me own.
Watch them scurry about the surf
What me rocks and fire prove their worf.
Me fire lit. Me quarry scorched.
Will thy not eat, Spartacus? No.
Drink? Fine claret Hilarus leave by.
Bring out thy gout and leaden thy eye.
(Phlegmy laugh) The cosmic joke be on us tanight.
What Lucian rakes the bones from the dust
What fancy he cert character ta fate
Ta right the temper a the universe.
But any toss be circumscribed a Jove.
Hesiod say 'Very far off dwell virtue.'
While you and I say 'Very far off dwell Rome',
And fuck Nature it be damned
As I be at eat these crabs
What me shite be funked a million corpses,
What all me days me praise the bottom feeder.
The underdog what
Consider me more the victual than the eater.
But Rome be a bit more distant for you,
For you be but boxed
A some macabre bounty
And not make much a it
Likely be you too dead ta light out

Or hope or yearn
Or what poets wif theys backs ta the dark
   Mistake a cracklin' flame for a rebel heart."

Canis Ictus Is overwhelmed wif Self-Pity

But if this be quarantine what some phantom pox
   Or infect a me preachment
Be more ta follow unless Crassus
   Will me enisled a more bitter pill.
Even lepers fair have mates ta
   Share what mystery afflict and doty pain
What relief be in it echoed in mutual howl.
   What Hippocrates name the Phoenician Scourge
What be maritime ta me a what agent
   Carry such cruel consequence upon merchant seas
The same what be about our luxuries.
   As Plutarch and Herodotus mark pig's milk lepra's source
      And swine rut a the moon's wane,
   What sow wise Leviticus,
      The Semites condemn unclean
And the Egypt's imbibe but once a Julian
   What sacrifice a pig ta the moon
But be it not this concourse between nations
   What barter this foul disease
Where before none exist.
      Did not the cynic, Onesicritus, companion
Alexander ta Indus and Taprobane
      What his brain become mealy wif lies.
   And some say cholera be a me nature
      What wif me bein' a the filfy sort
So's none invite me ta vesperna much less cena
   For fear a what me sunken eyes not exhibit
      But thirst for sorcery and magic contrive.

Or that I be mad what preach and spread such
As me scat about the garden what consider like me mind
          Quite nourish the soul a Ceres.
     The vote be as the divans be empty when I arrive.
Yet I possess not a leper's cankers.
          Nor express outward sheath a sores.
          The Rome what billeted me here,
Such as we circle this provocation each ta other
     Claiming which be ill and close tenders death.
Thus the dance a death be no absolute a pustules,
     The clamoring a fevers and hack of rheums,
And biles and phlegms upon the bed sheets.
          But be beaten iron cunning and sharp still hot
Upon this rind, this husk what malevolent natures reprove
          As we do the god's work mistaken in our station
And nothing spared of this insolence caste down in turn
          Ta clench and hiss in Vulcan's constant forge.

Canis Ictus names Cynics the Guard Dogs a the Gods

Be it here I am deprived of me contempt
          A what counterfeit Rome be aglow.
Here in the darkness where but the boar's grunt rebukes
     And the crickets chatter a their marketplace
And assignate in the salty marsh.
               As little as I be a their kind it be a dog
What world ease me passin' here?
          More than a skull on a stick I dare say.
Or whereabouts on this insula be a wolf
     What I steal a pup what be weaned
And make it crazy wif care
          Such that it know not its nature
Ta subserve mine. But why be we dogs?
          For what turnspit breed seek deprivation

What find a master's hearth and
     Ward off all what would approach
What be more Hilarus than Ictus
    Whose slander be feral as his bite and bespeak infect
     And rupture and wivvered limbs.
Be me not more wolf what be a breed
    What raise up this very Rome
And remnant a some course a fealty ta Mars
    So's us Cynics be guard dogs a the gods
And hunt our prey wif deeds and words.
     What he fancy toy wif Ovid,
Our Sinope jape he be Melitan when rapacious
    But Molossian when sated
    What not pegged breed or gaze.
     And don't this portend favor a the gods,
    At least what be wit's assurance.
But sure slave what Hilarus be chained by day
     As be Cato's dictum,
    Ta be keen ta protect Crassus wealf at night.
     And what Hilarus hunt the likes a me
    It be at bid a Crassus.
     And what be Varro's idyll?
Hilarus be perfect wif a bulbous head
    What sustain a boulder's blow,
Sturdy teef in a ruddy jowel wif a well spring a drool,
    And droopsy ears wif mange and ticks,
Thick shoulders wif a melium about its neck,
     Wide damp paws,
     And a thick tail, wif a deep, rheumy bark and
    White ta discern from thief or prey in the dark.
Does this not describe Hilarus
    As a momma ferret smell out her brood?
Hilarus what hunts not for himself but his master.
    Crassus what crucify 6000 rebels along the Appian Way.

And me left here ta account the day
      What I regret he not crucify me.
    Soon me wine runs out and
Crabs and cockles leave me belly off ta bloat and churn,
      Wif me spare cynicism draggin' out the sentence.
For be not Crassus or Hipparchus already take up Ira's mask,
      Whirlin' in moonlight at water's edge
Keenin' shards a Livius and Seneca.

Canis Ictus recalls how the Roman Cynic, Foetipedus, Is credited wif the discovery of Pecorino Romano

What our dear Foetipedus rescue several chickens
      From the fate of another's belly.
This be from a poor village a Apulia
      What over patrone Blandus Balbus preside,
And where before him Foetipedus be brought.
    But a the moment Balbus be about his Cicero
For his speech be spew of a sputtering pot
      And this be all ta say a its charm.
    But far from what our carus Ciceronis present
For toadies and prophets be
      But perfect in what be their presentiment
        Concealin' imperfection in their true intent
Lest their heads be shed a their body whole.
    So Baldus order "La-la-lo-lock this
Foetipe-pe-pe-d-d-dus fellow among the sheep
      Until me dispatch quin-quin-quin-que
Canno-no-no-nonicus wifout shame
      Be set before Ci-ci-ci-cicero
        And Demo-mo-mo-mo-thenes."
And thus Foetipedus be cast among the sheep
      What stable take on the stink
        What jam our dear cynic harbor

Tween the toes a his feet
        And under the roof a his limp arbor.
And here languish our dear cynic
        Refreshed a hot milk right way from the tit
But soon a foul sour curdle be imbue a it
        What colonies a muck what engage upon
Foetis feet and scrote be soaked up
        A bofe milk and meat.
        And stored in such a pungent state
The flesh grow funk and the milk thick and rank,
        What take on the stank a Foetis' feet's auric crust.
And for a fee farmers brought their bland cheese,
        For a fortnight our cynic's feet upon it take their ease
        And like water ta wine
        Or Simon Magus what serve all Rome
        A fine cheese a thin air,
        Foetipedus dallied many a year upon his back
        And thought namore of philosophy - alack, alack, alack.
For what not only by upending did he please the palate
        But the patron Baldus be not estranged a Cicero
And his factitious doxy na more
        For what cure our Foeti provide
        Baldus have his cavern frescoed in the cynic's jam
And thus have cache a pecorino what
        Come down ta this day and much please us,
        What sauce and pasta much abide,
And what filf again be once ta the cynics shame
        Now be tribute of assurance and fame.

Canis Ictus comes upon the Graveyard of Shipwrecks

What be a this? Sandy beach and southy peak?
        What be the paces a me insula?
Shall I be eat by a bear or by a boar be gored?

Is there a cool repast and spring?
Or fiery lip upon the summit
           What likewise invite Empedocles?
    Thoughts what occupy a cynic's walk
'Til he come upon a boneyard a Minoan merchants,
    Stone cypress piled in heaps by Santorini's wrath
Wif skeletons wove as please this isle.
    And in the distance the prow of a trireme
        Nods toward a spit
A human bones picked clean by Neptune's yardies.
    And six stadi hence the Semite's ship,
      The keel 300 cubits bakin' in the sun,
   Wif scattered vittles ne'r time nor crabs undone,
Driven aground in the Great Flood and truf be told
     All lost and not a fawn or cub survive;
An Arawat be this tombstone a animal bone
     What rival any carnage a Apicius' table.
   Too late for this flesh but what fed from it be about.
What be the world's menagerie be reduced
    A these what scuttle about
     Bones chastened wif arcadian piety.
Piled like Vulcan's broom across Etna's floor
    And heaped upon this insula's shore.
   Elephants wif teeth struck from their jowels,
Like me dear Hipparchia, and bones
    Weaned a their flesh, half in tide,
  As here at the Pillars of Herakles
    They perish as though at Hannibal's labors
      And not folly a flood a some Semite god.
   And bones a dragons and giants
    What be as trunks a trees
  Or columns six times the size the beasts
 Hannibal marched across the Pyrenees.
Skulls a lions, leopard and cameleopard and bears entwined

Wif the wildebeest, lambs, zebras and serpents a all kinds,
    What sundry the earf be a revelation ta mankind
And a fine minced tartar or cold soup for the oofy few
    What be masters what take dominion and make a stew.
And camel's bones what got its dugs hoist on its back.
    And dogs and cats what Roman households not lack.
    Hyenas, jackals, panthers and wolves.
    Jaguars, stags, bears and boars
    Piled against the waves pummeling the shore.
A more melancholic scape no Sophocles out keen,
    Where be this Noah scattered as others there
As me fancy Spartacus' be an alien skull
    What ta sharpen me wit lest by disuse
    It and me become as it were, dull.
Thus I play out this course
    A eruption, flood, transmogrified Jew
    Lest farce be niggled and bound a me and you.

And there be the shipwreck a the Achaeans
    What from hunger defy the gods
What form the man and fate the hardship
    Like a worm what squirm half under a boot.
For what be Helios' beef for these lost sailors
    For ta starve be ta thwart fear
    For but a stew what be made more savory
In a land replete a leeks and turnips, lentils, peas
    And a sinewy shank a Zeus's steer.
    For what vengeful god forsake such legumes
    Among a gravy a kidney and tripe
And pursue cunnin' Odysseus's no less his ignoble crew.
    For half the men lay dead at the bottom a the sea
    But for splash a pepper and garum
    And the citement thereof.
And these what be weary a Odysseus' folly wif stars

For naught less a Calypso say keep the Bear ta thy left
Whilst watchin' the Pleaides.
          But these be as Odysseus
               Tappin' his head and rubbin' his abs,
All the fornicator bring ta bear
      Droozy a Calypso's bed what that cunt suck
The very marrow a your bones.
     A mem what upon this insula
        And bearin' shipwreck be right ta home.
What Homer say, Odysseus be wif Pyfias at his side
     And still bring his fleet naught from the lot.
What ten years ta go but
         A few paces from Troy ta Ithaca?
Admitted the gods do fuck wif the sticky shite
   And weary the plot, liar what conclude mal content
Wif his last lothario breaf what be far from home
      Lest he pitch his tent upon the sea.
And that be the last we hear a the bloody liar
      But for the burblin' a poets what be little worf
And such say Aristoteles be cast out from this earf
     For such accounts a the Achaean's lies urge
Men on ta greater canards, monumental wrongs
     And hideous purge.

At this juncture a note appears in the margin of Ictus's text which
reads "'Rodrigo Borgia has had glory holes drilled in the
confessionals so the fine ladies of Subiaco may more diligently offer
up their penance.' - Da dietro a Gesù Cristo, 1492"

And Atrahasis a Akkadian Fame
      What no blame be placed by gods upon mankind
For such chapter like the world be flushed away.
  And this Gilgamesh revive what every beast alive
    Be consigned wifin a 120 cubits

Where the circus a Rome stay a hundred times
    Brutes in cages and pens what hold not a fraction,
Not a myriadum a the world's catabuli.
    What the wise cynic by ratio suss out lies
And leave off such bruits and canards.
      And as content such hazards be on-dit,
Men what die a commerce
      Market myth ta cut their losses.
And as our hero Ictus ponder this
    As Empedocles might the edge a his best abyss
He spied a skull and what ta speak
      Cupped it by the jaw
But ta have the phantoms bones arise entire.
      And up gli umidi another upon another
And this collegium followed him
      And crowd about his small campfire.
And each held a short sword
      And a dragon's tooth about his neck
For these be the Spartoi spawned
    A Cadmus what wif them seed the earf.
"Does Agenor's boy know you're about?
      Does Ovidius?
    Does your serpent here creep
  For here he be but meat?
No lark a you lot what be spawn
    But set upon one anovver.
Not no Jovian curse a ancestors
    Or illicit Thrinacian barbie here.
      Not no fuck a some pale goddess
What blush her guilt ta her celestial spouse
    Or confess it outright and hurl a golden comb.
No winsome Io what an immortal might envy
    And out of pique plunge thee upon one another.
No demand a Agenor, father ta proxy son,

Ta rescue a runaway daughter from no less than Jove.
You wif no patrimony at all, no father or mother.
From the muck half-formed like worms and toads
What brood a earth
And call man back to his mortal state.
Deprived of every pleasure but slaughter
And yet turned one upon another in that
Like feral dogs on a scrap
For the purses a poets
And what keep the hoi polio trump wif whit and jot
Cozen such exotica as you be."

At this juncture a note appears in the lower margin of Ictus's text, which reads, "Rodrigo Borgia has had grilles placed in the jakes whereby the clergy may confess their sins whilst the aroma of their morning ablutions reminds them of their mortality. - Da dietro a Gesù Cristo, 1492"

Canis Ictus addresses the Spartoi

I, poor Ictus before you be,
But a retiari a the arena what parry wif me trident
And cast me net
Ta press the arrant wages a the sycophants and hypocrites,
Posers and frauds,
All but ta be cast out for me wit and virtue,
Spared but that me death be slow ignominy
Upon this insula a bones.
And thus a Rome I have an axe ta grind
And attend its use upon skulls not trees.
I be not fierce a stature but among these crabs
Me veins be right sauced wif venom
And me jowels hard grip sinewed a much incessant speech,
More terse and blunt what cause me homeland's breach

80

And ta stifle got me cast upon this beach.

What say I be your general, your Arminius, me friends,
             And you be me horde
All skull and bone, armored outward
             Like me crabs,
Hung wif short sword and trident.
         And back we sail ta assail Rome
It's transgress upon our goodly natures.
         Much as you be the livin' dead
Much abused by the poets.
         And me likes, makes Crassus' see red.
And be I the drift if not the cast a general?
             Have not I the bandy legs of an equestrian
         If but ta mount me queen Loquatia?
And thunderous roar a me nether parts
             What attest Jove's favor a our campaigns.
         And I be spared a saddle
As you spare a pack train a stores
         What you bein' but bone
             And but me remain a skin and guts alone.
         And as I be bareback into battle
Thee sans prick as need not a caravan a whores.
         Nor cooks and scullery, be I not aright.
And as I s'pose your lot,
             No tabernaculum of games and wine
         Though such pleasures risk mutiny
             If left behind.

And marked forward one Spartoi who knelt.
         Be this homage a arms what be what I felt?
But wif his claws he dug amongst the sand
         And dislodge a toad
             What croaked a such rude dismay

81

Til our Spartoi impale it upon a spoke
A the bony cage in what pass for his froat
    And by shift and breaf,
And simple play a the neck,
    Tuned liked a filthy cithara the bufo
What from bestial croak til a passable Latin
    In this manner bespoke.

I be Ekhion and thee be daft
    What forgone between Rome and this shore
Be a great moat between you and your fellows
    See as we, Rome be uroburos a the sea
And we be dragon teef dislodged
    And scattered a the Aegeaum Mare
    Shards a what pitiable men call Limnos, Lesbos and Chios,
Andros, Naxos and Ikaria.
    Our home be Asiana, the head a what be this guinea empire
    Its upper jaw flush wif rocky shoreline
And the lower a teeming shoal,
    And Greece be its cold embrace and
Italia a rear leg and gripping claw
    What be all tail ta Gaul.
    Thus Rome be Uroboros of the Mare Nostrum.
A dragon what head and upper jaw
    Be a hard shore a Pergamum and Ephesus.
What cast thy here in this delirium
    Ta desire ta take up arms 'gainst this imperium.

What I be Ictus and be I be mad if I say
    These crabs be our phalanx
What be armored by Neptune.
    Dost thou need roads or doth thee scud the ground
A grace a some filial god what take pity
    A all joy lost ta you.

Ekhion: None dare call it madness
　　　For none before be so struck.
A new age a folly be upon us
　　　What baffle our physic.
Not even crazed Cleomenes crowned king
　　What from pique drove bruvver Dorieus
　　　From Sparta's shore
Be so mad as to take on Darius at Miletus behest.
　　Even he what be exiled as you be
　　　And what on some desert isle cut out his woe
And spilled it ta the crabs.
　　Nor be this lunacy a yours be a the Muses
For you by your smell and manner be bereft a poesy
　　What be preserve of perfumed dandies
If I takes me Petronius and Juvenal aright.
　　Nor by thy stink Dionysius
And his drunken revelers
　　What ask their vomit be result a drink
Not ta share a sack wif one
　　Whose breaf is foul, covered in sores,
Wif his tunic hoist in his crack.
　　Nor so addled a plan belie prophecy
What not envision thy own bloodied body
　　In a butchered heap certain
As many a reluctant confederate not but see
　　　But seek it so.

Ictus: Ah, an educated death mask.
　　What empty skulls do polly.
It be true, courage come not from bones
　　For there be no heart in thy cage
　　Nor nerves ta pluck.
Nor what be called guts or balls
　　Where none upon you clot or hang

And such be these what see naught pecker or puss
     And be reluctant a your sad state.
Though I s'pose backbone doth speak ta valor
    And spirit address pneuma
      Though ye be wifout bellows
Likes us livin', breavin' fellas.
    A man a arms, no I be naught
But ta boot pikeys what mull me blanket
     Or mice what peck me millet,
Though I aright some success thereof.
    Show which end a the sword and we tally
So much I be affronted by Rome.

Ekhion: Ah! Take Rome for pique?
Then what about Elysium a Thursday?
    Or be that reserved for Avernus
What by proxim a Cumae
    We might tell what bits a us be scattered where.
Oh, Ekhion, thy shin bone be a the shadow
    A the volcanoes foot next the head a this Canis,
What it ever possess one be bereft of a brain.
   What be we? Some dire cult?
What can yours know a
    What it be ta be spring from a fang
What nurture be but a brief nuzzle a Gaia?
    What be Rome's stores ta us?
And what's more what they be ta you
   What philosophy seem born a fury
What in all things Diogenes and Crates
    And Agregius be spare.
  As not bear what thee harbor?

Pelorus: Wait. For sure he be mad.
What not bear olfactory cause

Still be racked a his smell,
As filth cling to cloak and beard
And empty wineskins about,
What he be besot and mad as old Herakles
Wif stains a where his prick and asshole be.
And such be Sterquilinus what our dimune cynic
Be fertile a chiggers and mites
And what all manner a flies be about
As though he be but a pikey road apple
What sprout legs.
And certain be Cloacina what carry away
All Rome's shite what surpass
All but Hades in stink. Hades, soul rank, what Orpheus
Barnstorm before Pluto and Persephone
Ta best plush Eurydice's escape.
What Horace say Pluto be obdurate
What not a tear shed a any smell
Even the malodor a verse.
But Claudian claim the Emperor a Hell
With iron cloak wipes his tears
The better employ be ta wipe his arse.
Such a bitter fruit doth Orpheus release
It sparkle a common man's nether hairs
Wif shards of funky, fetid airs.
And doth not Ovidius cite rank odor
A Zeus's ballocks as he ape in shape of a bull
What fuck Io whilst stamping
About a his own stool
What Io be cow find solace
What make such a rank god tolerable.
And goose be funky so doubt a bit a swan.
Certain these gods be petty and whimsy
As be mankind, so stink be sure ta follow
For Tiberius be he not reluctant god

What for his blistered skin and runny cankers
    Be dishonored wif those what stole
A rag about their nose and not distinguish between
   Slave or kin for what offends did them in.
Thus as Tibi stench drive one ta believe
   He be a god by an uncanny sense's prerogative.

Yet hath he not power to bring us forth?
    And does not madness spring a divinity?
This be divine as divine be inscrutable ta us
   As it be ta what outward be his kind.

Ekhion: You mean he be what Socrates call a poet?
If he be poet I slay the thing right here
   And scoop his marrow ta the crabs.
For if this be divine, Jove be ta pack up heaven
   And grab an oar ta wander in time
As thus we be fated.

Ictus: Poet? What be I
   Orpheus wif crabs for Maenads.
    Or Argos' destiny
As me song be a mewling cunt
   What buskin' 'bout the Appian
Account herself a siren.
   Listen:
'I will count meself blest by fate
When all Rome calls Caesar great.
And wif many spoils you from Parthia return
A goat and a chicken to Jove I'll burn.'

Ekhion: Nay. He be no poet. But what ta Achilles
Agamemnon confide "Zeus rob me a me wits."
   Not what precise a what Socrates say be divine.

But what thee say be prudent, Pelorus,
    For his poem be martial
And little a the poet be a the martial mind.
    And in kind a little mind be like ta be martial.
But be that poet's face divine?

Pelorus: Did not Dionigi,
        What the Minyades tell ta bugger off
Warp inta a bull, a lion, and a panther in turn
        What fright the sisters?
And Jupiter be a bull what rape Io
        And a swan what same upon Leda,
And sent a golden shower upon Danae
        What from Vernacchio ta Terence
Doth Rome's fearless comics ape ad nauseam
        And happily spray upon a witting audience
Even as our Ictus stink
        A many such cloudy yellow bursts
From the nozzle a his wrinkled purse.

Ekhion: Well said. But a bull or swan by nature
    Reflect beauty what be a its kind.
But this Ictus, he be a misshapen bit
    What be not a favorable compare
What all in nature be contradict.
            Mad sure. But
Be this stick a twisted driftwood, divine?
        Cast out a Rome bein' a lumbago ta contentment,
Ta roam in rags this jagged coast,
    A hearth wif stars for eave and
What boast but the hiss a crabs and mussels
    And what be a brace a winded wine sacks
Be orphaned Orpheus a brew a bitter sea grass.
        This be a demi-god's temple?

Rocks, bone and sand?
  And no Siren song a this Ictus,
Me sword drawn lest he sing again.
  Be this Ictus a spawn a Zeus
And a his own palaver be he not a the arts
  And wine like mos' but ta drink it,
What be common among less than gods
   What savor ambrosia and
What ichor flood their veins.
  What he be ol' Ira's pot and pan
His plot be but frenzy and rage
  And he be by cynics wage, 'Dog Bite',
As what be the Greek's Lyssa,
  Daughter a the Night's Sky, Nyx and Ouranos,
   What in mini-skirt wore a cur's head
  What outlook be the actor Vernacchio
What don a carcass of a Papillon
  What dear, dark, pocky Tiberius revere.
And an emperor's death writ
  Hound the actor's scent
What would play wif Ira's mantel
   His stench traced among the Semites
More so a his hot and fearful flight.
  For does a daimona stink like our Ictus?
Or what dolt believe Tibi be a god
  Much less our Canis?
Gods bear no odor a flesh unless
  In such mantle they doth dress.

Pelorus: But does not Neptune reek a fish
What wif them he doth abide?

Ekhion: No, asshole. This be an idle wish
For Neptune doth constant bathe.

Pelorus: Then Hephaistos what in perpetuity
     Be muckin' 'bout his forge.
Or again Hades for are not the dead rank,
     What be other teloi but custom
What hold spices and herbs fend the stank.
     Or Doth not Ictus bung perfect mimic
A Mephitis what gas rise above a swamp?
     Not so much Mena's cunnie
What want the caked rot a Pales' dung
     About the flanks a his sheep.
There be many which ways Ictus
     Doth stink like a god.

Ictus: Enough! What god lean its divinity upon smell?
Doth not Aristoteles name sight and sound,
     Touch and taste as well.

Pelorus: Shall we then lick thee Ictus,
     Or bite thee?
For we be 'bout the sight and sound a ye
    And ye be as heavy ta the touch as mordant ta smell.
And thus we be imbue a thee by watch thy feature
     And that be thy stink.

Ekhion: And so even as a hound track vermin in the dark
     But naught but wet nose ta the ground
Ictus, we not be a your escapade ta Rome
      For no matter how brusk thy aroma be
  You be passed sense.
     You what brandish a sword like a stick
Wif a toggle a sizzlin' goat gristle
     And offal secured ta it
Wif fragrant smoke but ta favor thy belly,

Sore, as no god favor thee.

Udaeus, another Spartoi: Pelorus, Ekhion
   Glance east upon the sea. Beyond the hump
A the homunculus with the sun at his back,
     Two ships appear
  Light a load as they ride high.
Best we scatter among these bones
   'Til this Ictus suss out who they be.

And the Spartoi shed their shape
    And wif a clatter fell ta ground in heaps
As though so many augur bones tossed a Cumae cooze
  And blend as they be wif the dead.
For certain two liburnae approach
   And me wif the settin' sun straight in me mincers
    And what lollygag about its goin' down.
'Til not three actae be between me and the two scows
   What I see Hilarus and his customary retinue
     A Crassus cutthroats. But lo, bare above the rail be
The ruddy scalp and quick eyes a me dear Loquatia,
   Her wif what coil like cobras
     A many a gutter, hedge and thorougfare wif yours truly.
And fore upon the ovver skiff be
   Me mates Captius Hectorus and Factitius Bilius
    Wif his mistress Bodacia
What be runner-up a Julia's appetites
   In the great butt bangin' tournaments a Cloacina
Where the sewers be host the Eleusian mysteries
   As part and parcel be shit to fecundity.
And our dear Bodacia be queen what make Julia blush
   And a Tiberian office what in high honor
     Lead pilgrims ta Eleusis
   Where even Cicero find the fertile measure a fuckin'

If not the pleasure. And our good emissary
        Stay limber 'bout the year
What she weigh not a libra
        And what that be half pud
What abide prick like a quiver doth arrows.

Canis Ictus and Loquatia make the Beast wif Two Backs

Me heart leapt at such,
        At least about what be its confinement,
            And me prick be unfettered agent a me joy
When the prow a Hilarus fleet
        Breach the lonesome sand a the beach
And me and me dear Loquatia
        Fucked a clear day and night in the sand
Where crabs nibble and tides wash
    While our passion dispose
        Beyond all Pythagorean ration
And salt crust our padlocked lips.
    What so long I be tuggin' me slug
What straight away ta exhaustion
        Me and Loquatia spooge on the beach.
Conjure Morpheus when Hilarus wakes us.
        "While you two fucked and slept
Bodacia service the entire crew
        Thrice over though the cabin boy be but six
            And the first mate a leper
        Wif but a wee bump for a pecker.
It's time we disembark
        And leave you to your rituals and appetites."

Note: Here in the margins and for some pages Gentilli O. Nelli and
other members of the Umbrian school have scrawled many
renderings with the figure of Bodacia being sodomized with various

devices, implements of war and implements of ecclesiastical benediction by various emperors, kings, merchants, saints and popes, etc. including St. Benedict. In a number of illustrations the likeness of Benedict's sister, St. Scholastica, is placed upon the naked body of the Roman diva, Bodacia. The meaning of such blasphemy is left to the reader. But it must be recalled that the monks of Subiaco attempted to poison Benedict due to the harshness of his rule. Elsewhere in the monastery compound, the frescoes on either side of the west window depict Florentius's Attempt to Poison St. Benedict. On the left, a woman dressed in pink delivers a poisoned loaf of bread to St. Benedict in a cave. On the right, Benedict directs his raven to carry the poisoned loaf away where it can do only harm to the innocent creatures of the wood.

Bodacia be a Roman fame what inspire
    Many a epic verse what shame sage Vergil
Or certain be no worse. For ta the kittim
    She be Gaia incarnate
        A cooch like the Gates a Cumae
    Or the grotto at Praeneste.
        A legationi what Crassus bank
    What feign belief lest he confound the masses.
And to by pomp and coin right
        What Vergil amend a this Aeneas chap
    When Rome be found a Romulus and Remus
        Suckled at Lupa's pap.
And she be a Pompeius Trogus' account,
    The tale a the late King Claudico
        What Bodacia be his queen
When from lack a heat under her ol' pot 'n' pan
She take a shepherd's farcimini into her roaring oven
        What these a this rude employ be fit for lovin'
As wif their staff in tow they frolic 'mongst their flock
    And she be a right fit bird

What be left ta truck wif her king,
That ol' dry turd.
        But Claudico menace Bodacia, havin' none a it.
    And a spite his puckered pizzle test her might
What she alterate him ta a fly
    What ply the walls about their bed
Where every shepherd, farrier and hod
        A her fecund and supple cunt she be wed.
And what a shear chance a new empire be born
    What o'er shadow Rome in all but scorn
        And tarry out its thousand years.
And she be inspire a Nimius Monoesius' Catalog Mulerium
    A geneaology a rapes by gladiators and emperors
        What by their own decree be the incarnate a gods
What be wry remark
        For many stand and stink likes a you 'n' me.
    And as Previus Varius plucked from Tacitus,
        Princess Boudica, the warrior queen a Britannia,
Our Bodacia prate the stage what wif sex and sword
    And lay bare wif fond and vengeful verse
        What whatever come a empire at end come worse.

Or Atrabilus in his Concordia what noble Odysseus
    Fagged a Ithaca and sick for the sea
Spread Bodacia's bodice for sail and her hairpin as rudder
        What immortal lines be pickled
    What our poets put their heroes in such,
        And what our Odysseus be clearly in much brine
    Whist his shriveled prick stalk the Mare Nostrum.
'And lo, Bodacia what see the Ithacan's plight
        Drain the cock a Neptune
What leave the godly reprobate quite contrite
    And the sea lull as his pizzle entire be spent
And to the oars and upon the backs

A the Ithacan's yardies
The sleepy waters be circumvent.'
But in verses 4002 ta 5009 yet yawns a chasm like a drain
Shape a fearsome maelstrom and a sovereign thing
What suck many a warship
As such in the heaven's Nigri Formeni
Vigilant seek stars aflame
What gather worlds about them
As gyrate waters do the same.

And Livius Andronicus be known a his Odusia
What confirm by such verse what Greek guile
Not be apportioned by the gods entire.
But a little renown be his Tragodeia Bodatiae;
A fabula palliata what the heroine sails her fleet
Beyond the Pillars of Herakles
And all but outdo Odyssi in amours, blood and lies.
Or though slight a build and firm
She what test Apicius's table in a caustic farce
Worvy a Archestratus as recipes be diced about
From Homeric hexameter's epical redoubt.
Thus a clot a curds and milk be compare
A concourse wif the divine
Or slabs a bacon and grease wif Circe's swine.
And mackerel be got on the third day
Took wif bread and wine
Before the brine beset the flesh and stay.
Or finely ground flour be as Ithacan youth
Dashed upon the rocks
Or what be poached amongst Polyphemi's flocks.
But Dionisi Jackleg paste a folly what Archestratus
"Be but ignorant of mos' fings and tell us nuffin'."
What our 'eroes be but a barley muffin?
This Archie-stratus chap not be worvy a Homer

94

Wif his baked boarfish, mushrooms, asparagus
And Parmesan toppin',
What do speak ta hunger but as verse be rubbish
Fit fodder but for the bowel's concoction.
And what by Ennius many a Greek dysfunction
Be sung frough the veil a Bodacia.
What a lad shag his mum and such,
And rash done up his dad.
What so Plautus, many a royal be done in by bad help
What very employ me mum had
When I be but a whelp.
For who but the gods know such things
What by Paris, Achillles' heel the fatal arrow stings.
Paris, what his Trojan boner burst his tunic
Ta rival the wars we kittim calls Punic.
Yet, Paris what his pap, King Priam, once again
Be done in by the help,
The shepherd, Agelaus, what the king employ
Ta drown or stab or strangle the boy,
What leave him ta starve upon Mount Ida
What the infant be suckled beside a bear
The lad live ta be the undoin' a the Trojan Imperium,
Felled by Philoctetes' arrow who like Achilles too
Suffer a wound ta the foot
What appear, dear reader, the gods
Supply these Greeks with but a dearth a plot,
Couple a arrow wounds, two at the ankle
What one be left to weep and rot
And as yours truly personal attests
The plot a Ajax be exile and barbs
And abandonment upon some alien plot
Not native as our Hebrews wif their tale a Moses
What wif the good sense be of a happier end
If not for old Moses for Moses kin.

What I not be bitter
   What need not a bear ta suckle nor a shewolf,
  Nor be a ward a Rome.
What I certain be closer ta myf
   More I be abandoned a home.
And here among these rocks and bones
   Found a kingdom wif me wife Loquatia
  What naught a Clytemnestra
For we have no daughter, nor I mistress
  Much less a young one
What wif prophecy distress us and the polis.
   And Hilarus's skiff breach the last wave ashore,
And a scow second wif our two cynics
   And our two daughters a Rome not far behind.
And Hilarus bound ashore wif two swart Mollosian's
  On a leash a either hand,
And swagger atop a berm a bones
   Followed by his cutthroat band
Whilst Loquatia and Bodacia, and Hectoris and Bilius
  What latter by their dimmer lights
In a shady spot keep a certain Sinopean cynic in view
   But of not such fashion for there be but a few.

The Spartoi slay Hilarus' retinue

And as all deboard and stand upon the sandy shore
   From the heaps a bones the Spartoi erupt
And forfright Ekhion distance one a Crassus' mercs
  From his head.
      The Spartoi broch no strategem
And a legion a 10,000, so sewn be the Dragon Teeth
   What wif the speed a Hermes
      If not for Hilarus
His entire crew be dead. Hilarus what sally forth

And rally his force and against all odds
Dismantled a 1000 Spartoi
   Before Pelorus and 100 spiny mates take him down,
      Slice his gullet what evince that bubblin' sound
What presage death and the after life,
   And the Spartoi Udaeus take the slave's mullet
      Wif his knife.
   And Hilarus be on his way ta the River Styx
Far from any home he ever knew
      While all his bloody mates be slew. Hilarus
   Wifout so much as a denari under his tongue
What like his master, wifout coin, Charon cast
   Souls out as they be but dung.
Hilarus not pass the Three Headed Dog
   And feel their hot tongues upon his cheek.
Nor give account what he be but Crassus' slave
   What as his master he be a cruel and vile knave.
         A this me wholly attest.
      So not likely be his fate what Persephone or Dis
Place a kiss upon his mouth and such breaf
   Restore him ta this life.

But me woe be deep for I doth glimpse,
   Lo among the carnage dear sweet Loquatia
And Bodacia and the two cynics laid low.
      Me dear, dear wife and Rome's great diva,
   And Captius Hectorus, in the fray
      All receive a fatal blow.
While Bilius writhe wif a mortal wound
   He be all a me love and friendship what survive.
And I cradle his stove in skull
   As he choke up blood
What soak me ragged mantle and cloak
   And such words spoke:

97

"This isle portend me death for it be compost
    A Cyclop bones, monsters
        What feed on any meat well their own
    And wif such strength
Chuck the leavin's a hundred leagues.
            I know you Ictus.
    But if you believe not in omens,
You believe not in me.
        For this be foretold ta be by a Cumae Sybil."

"Far be it from me ta call the words of a dyin' bloke drivel,
    Special what one what preach the Dog.
    But your gash be not trivial and
        What be utile a your thought mind your survival."
At what Bilius but spout more prophecy,
    Between gouts a blood,
    What, though futile, he say he prefer,
        And conclude in me arms,
    As ta me those what choose the Sybil
As certain dead upon arrival
        What comin' inta the light, we call birf.

And true, be this insula the bony leavin's a Polyphemus?
    And the brothers Brontes, Steropes and Arges
What Hesiod attest, be born a Gaia and Uranus?
    And Homer' sons a Poseidon,
        What all these be ta want much meat
Wif the force to litter a shoal leagues hence
    What I now stand 'mongst the bloody consequence.
All 50 a Hilarus retinue
    The Spartoi in an instant slew
And scatterd Roman limbs
        What this be a supernatural Teuteburg.
And now quiet, quiet but for the lop, lop, lop

A the blood red sea.
What a sudden eyes poke above the hull
A the Roman scow in tow
And certain a stout and much pocked man
What I know be name a Scabiopilus
What Volcatius Sedigitus heap enormous praise
For this Scabiopilus much raise up
The Palliata Comoedia,
And ta the tabloids delight
Be a tumultuous paramour a Bodacia.
And held up at the shit bucket
As many a work a Plautus gain ear
What exploit the infamy a the nose.
And not pose ashore among those
What Hilarus at behest a Crassus come ta exile.
And while The Spartoi gather the kittim
And heap them upon a pyre
Pilus weeps a his mistress and me wife
What sear me heart and flush ta wrath,
What I turn ta Ekhion and shout
"Burn not these. These slaves ta Crassus'.
Deny not the crabs
What have nourished me
Ta strip their flesh and leave their bones
As clean as thee.
There in Rome sits Crassus fully robed
In the living mantle of live flesh upon bone.
O! What joy it be ta alter that state."

"Then ta Rome!" Cries Ekhion
And ten thousand Spartoi shew their arms,
A roar a such din one sense
Upon distant shores it raise alarums.
What cynics heart be such

Not avenge Loquatia's murder.
And what Neptune has fated this Spartoi force
   Ta challenge Crassus larder,
And all the thieved wealf a Rome.
     "Fuck Rome then," I hail.
"Such in me hate for me regionem swell.
    We, me comrades, need not drive them ta hell.
Hades imbibe in all upon they conquer and dwell.
    So rank be the Imperium
Even what be the edge a the world
       The dogs a Cerberus scent the smell
    And strain at their chains."
But "Whoa" say Pelorus,
   "It's one thing ta call upon the gods.
But false ta contrive their answer
    Ta suit thy selfsame rancor. Hot hate
      What has now o'er taken thy soul
    What raise anchor nay steady the keel that
Your hand employ your sword right or left?
   What I suspect so little sword play a ya,
     Of me interrogative yo'r answer be bereft,
But for the same what ya scratch yo'r pate,
    Cuff yo'r carrot or wipe yo'r ass.
What talent be no matter ta the blade
    When all the killin' be but 'said'."

"What Pelorus? Doth thou too much fear Rome?" says I,
   "Upon thee be naught skin such as you risk but bone.
And this your fate be but a connive a the gods,
    What whim Rome's oracles float upon
   And in quick turn angle an offerin'.
Be not thee seed a Ares?
   And so be but suited for war
What have eternal life, be it in the raiment death."

"Well, if thy heat, Ictus, conduct
        Us back ta Rome," say Pelorus
    Whilst thou hide behind our leafless boughs?
Be thou not a cynic what decry war?"

Ictus: "Nay, what that war be not a dog's concern
    But ta nosh upon the jiblets a the fallen."

Pelorus: "Be thee a cannibal thus?
        As thou imbibe crabs
            What feast upon Roman flesh."

Ictus: "What dogs be, be I.
        Pelorus. What be supposed a the gods,
        Be the fancy a man.
And be I man what thou be but ghoul."

What upon Scabiopilus interject.
        "Pelorus, take not Ictus at his word
For he out a anger be a reckless surmise
        And thus rattle thy cage
    What indeed thy ribs be so imagined
        As ta comport a dove or two.
Our dear cynic be apprized a the Sinope
    What cheek he be ta warlike Alexander,
'Stand out a me light and such'.
        A wound what by words lodge so deep a sting
By shock be no attendant blow
    A king or king's retinue arise."
Pelorus: "What have we here?
    Plautus and Naevius under one blade?"

Here a note appears in the margin "Patricio has stolen a suckling pig from the Priory and will receive forty lashes on St. Michaelmas." The maginalia seems to bear no connection to the text.

"I be Squire Scabiopilus as you be want a flesh."

Pelorus: "Well, squire. Shall we ta Rome?"

Scabiopilus: "Sir, much spur me ta Rome return
      As I doth prize goose flesh and figs.
But thee, I think not. For thy comport
    Has none the ports and harbors
What wine and meat make whole.
     Beginnin' wif the teef and tongue
One ta chew as you doth of some possess
      But to pleasure the other
Of which you be bereft.
    Nor the belly what dalliance full
      Be most heaven sent.
Nor the anus what gentle coax the feel a it's linin'
    What be as a liken a lictor fillin' a ripe young bung.
Vengeance prod Ictus. As me belly me.
    What be it a thee ta transverse the sea
And fall upon the Romans."

Pelorus: "Thou valor shaped by a chop or a goose liver
     Seem but numinous ta me.
Ta starve not, yes, as your kind do,
    A mob'll stand a bear up in a pen if its meat.
But do not these comforts feature in exile?"

Scabiopilus: "Ictus joust wif Cicero what contest
     Be a doppel a Diogenes and Plato.
And the Epicures their mean
      Be at the keen spur of a whip.

We cynics be wifout sinecure.
    Sure the world see our shard a Rome be pure."

Ictus: "Certain. What transgress if it be not treason
            What Cicero done.
What retire ta Thessalonika
    And its splendors be put forth before him.
What I never power or splendor seek
        And thus be obscure and weak
    Be set upon this boneyard grim.
Me couch a rocks
            What Cicero's be a bed a down
    And exile be but ta succor him."

Pelorus: "But doth not Antony have him slain?"

Ictus: "Why 'Bones'. You be well informed.
Yes, and slain right proper as be his behest.
    And his hands and head be scythed and tacked
        Ta the Rostrum a the Forum,
A right pretty sight for all
        What not be buggered by his charm.
    His nog and donnies what it be a heathen wreath
        Not warm ta brood
But cold a winter harvest as they be so eaved."

Ekhion: "But yo. Be we ta Rome?
    For many a trireme we need ta crew
Wif you two fine fightin' cynics in our retinue."

Ictus: "Go on, Ekhion. Mock me skills a war.
    But fancy some a the mugs
What be generals a Roman Legions
    And sense my wit,

What like a Caesar I be a runty shit
   But I learn stratagem night and day
      In the streets and alleys
   Of a city so brutish
As Astraeus conclude a dusk it not allay
      Great Jove contemplate
     Hisself or likes a you Spartoi proxy
   And make but a gory smear of it all,
What our average citizen be but
     A race a petty, ignorant, graspin' Icarae.
   And Ekhion, lest I be but ta howl at the moon.
What this General Varus be but a Pantaloon
   What prize Arminius's ass above his ear
And 20,000 boys lay dead at Teutoburg
   Twice the gaggle a Spartoi what rally here."

Osteos, another Spartoi:
   "Sir Ictus, what on many shores
     Thy kind be known by kittim
Which be not a name of a people
     Or what theys' subjects think
   So much as what a race a people think a Rome
      What be the blind end of a ox,
Their talks bein' what Rome administer
   Its steam and stink ta the world.
Why be we ta Rome
     What wif but bony stalks
   Be spared it's wreak, the dowse a lilies
What bear but blood upon the blossoms?
     Or what be Apicius' tables ta us
What hath no viscera ta partake a such fare
   Nor nerves ta feel or eyes ta see
For it's beyond sense we air our being
     As you err us as being kin ta your lusts.

So what be it ta us, your race
Whose desires are driven by wealf?
Where we Spartoi hang neither piffle or purse
Nor brace a baculum.

Ictus: Baculum!" What the Semites say
Be the source a Eve.

Osteos: "So little thy kitts know thy subjects' patrimony
Whevver it be a rod or rib what be at stake.
What the Hebrew there be 'ahat'
What convey 'one of'
What you imply this Semite Adam possess many puds.
Maybe the bloke be so
What be a ballocks a hydra
But not be a Semite bloke what possess such now;
What would a long ago been paraded
In your Circus ta be eaten by lion's
Labeled by your worthless oracles a bad omen or such
For janglin' a gaggle of Dandy Doolies
Like they be a ring a keys ere his crotch."

Ictus: "Osteos, as thee be ignorant
A the greatness a Rome
What aqueducts water field and home
And by grace a Cloacina flush our filth
Away from us.
And many roads for conquest and trade
And dredge and foundation of ports be made.
And triremes ta dock.
What shopkeeps doth stock."
Osteos: "What schoolboy pride from likes a thee.
Next be the cynic salute the Signum.
So little us phantoms carry any a it.

If Ekhion so commands it's on ta Rome
Ta lay waste our Dog Bite's ancestral home.
    Doth thou vengeance over Loquatia flow so hot,
More me satisfaction as I think not."

Ekhion: "All to in our state stripped a flesh,
  Or not what hairy crust we never possess.
'On ta Rome' be we
    Ta unseat the godly founders
A such a loose and carnal shuffle a Democritus
    As be this Roman citizenry."

End of Part II.

PART III: Gathering Force

Building the Fleet

And what our Spartoi need neither drink nor meat
      Nor warmth, nor fuck, shit, nor sleep
All ten thousand the bony lads set 'bout concoctin' a fleet
      A smart triremes wif hull and masts a bones
And pitch a guano, seaweed and loam
      All wif nails so cunnin' they rive not brittle bone.
And arm wif missiles tipped wif iron
      And a ballista aft a every ship
A such power Archimedes' lithobolos not be fit.
    What they be master smithies a the forgin' arts
      The bellows wheeze and farts a Hephaistos officina
Same what wif the Cyclops they cast Ares armor
    And not but those as a sudden apparition
      A me dear, dead Loquatia
    Not yet upon a pyre what saw
Two bulls what Jason sew the dragon's teef
      What forf a brood a Spartoi grew
    And at Jason's ploy one another slew.
The Argonauts plot of a worthless stone's throw
      A stratagem so low it sure be common ta Rome.
    But wif this fleet and these 10,000
We need not defeat for mere gods' sortin' out
      The Spartoi fall victim ta demiurges and men
But wif me counsel, what I not like Cadmus recoil
      A their violent airs, and as I be
      Poison ta Odysseus what
    Their betrayal wif me word not occur again.
What speak a Spartacus not glint a arms
      And what slaves rose to him so

A queer turn when such army by chance be set before thee
     Ta avenge what Rome doth misaprize.

What be it cunnin' or sentiment's blowback,
          Or Rome's good offices or bad,
     What bring me luv, Loquatia to dis spot.
Much less the troop a cynics, Hectoris and Bilius
          And, Bodacia queen a the broad Appian Way.
Loquatia I but glimpse and she me, but ta tear me heart
     Ere she die upon this prison isle.
But what a the other three, innocent a all crime
     Lest crime be ta entertain and edify,
And occasional poach a scrap or beg a tithe.
          And Scabiopilus, what acts in all them palliatas, survives
               What be the sunny side a Fortuna
          For all the nights he be in a drunken swoon
On the bank a Trastevere
          And dream below Fortuna's Porticos,
What one be Servius Tullius
          What it goes gossip ta history, he fuckt the goddess,
Til such things not favor the common mind.
     ·   And the other, Ancus Marcius
Built a stone altar ta credit her favors.
          And every snore of our Scabiopilus be a offerin'
               Ta that goddess and
A those great minds and men a deeds what surpass him,
     Where Hypnos lead him ta long meditation
               And Arai ta pray.
What the Greeks season our lesser wits,
     Plautus and Caecilius,
               Terence and Naevius and all
     What we pilfer a the Hellenes.
What our nature be as common as our gags

What such sense possess
What clear the gods mortify us wifout redress
        For our concern a empire as not for art
        Such as it is, I confess.

Industry be a this Spartoi race
            What neither a tire nor hunger complain
        But fashion me navy apace
What collect great hollow bones
        What some be bowed
Ta suit the huge ribbings of a ship,
        What no doubt a some great bird
            Be strong and light,
Or be the pinions of a dragon's flight
        What huge be snug a bow a bark
        And easy buoy a crew, arms and freight.
And hemp for riggin' and sail
            What provide a vantage great.
        And Scabiopilus smoke but a trifle
What exclaim "I be but one vessel.
        And these before us be many."
    Such be this Spartoi naval acumen
            And taste for war
What but a fortnight we be fit ta sail
        And off ta Rome, navigatin'
By what be Polyphemus's refuse,
    What from his isle, Sicilia, he hurl ta this spot
The bones what their tendon and marrow rot.
        And by this we aproxim ta land in Ostia, me home,
What be a mere 70 leagues from shore ta shore
        And what leave but a short march ta Rome.

Scabiopilus's Vision

After riggin' and hull be corked
   Our dear Scabiopilus imbibe much hemp,
A the damp flashin' what be about the camp.
    And once so seized
      Don' he be crazed and whirl about
    Flickin' his tongue in and out like a mountain asp,
  And tears cascade a his cheeks
      He call "See thee not his throne.
  What a rainbow doth crown."
And slappin' his face wif his beefy palms
    Abjure a sense and a blight ta alms.
And hurl hisself ta the ground
    What many a Spartoi gather round
And ghastly laugh as Scabby churn his legs in the mud
    Wif a shoulder dug as a rudder be jammed
Into the froffy ooze like a pinwheel on a rood.
     Then jump up and kiss
    The pates of our boney Spartoi
What his antics brake their employ.
    "Look Ictus! Here be seven lamps and four beasts
Wif a mantel a eyes what their vigil never cease
    Doth thou not see, Ictus?
     Have thee not but one eye?
The Antikytherae gears a the cosmos shine before me;
    What the stars churn.
  Wheels within wheels, the heavens burn.
    And what be these angels what block me way
    What I be ta god's visage this very day?"
"Scabby, these be not angels but our Spartoi band."
    At what Ekhion and his lot drew their swords
Upon the portly guinea what be as a demon possessed

But one possessed a little consequence.
"If this be the first heaven I be ta despair,
    I abandon all hope and set me cakes down here."
And as this be his desire what short a bane or loon he be,
    Scabie plop down in the muck and mire.
And from the Calcaneus scraps a this insula
    What not Pliny or Photius conceive,
        What Scabby fasten bone ta bone monsters
    What remains be no kith or kin,
        What be scattered in the filfy loam.
Our daft Scabby be certain not aware
    The skull be a lion and paw be a bear
        Wif wing and tail of a dragon
    A chimera most intemperate fashioned there.
Or what be the ten leopard heads
    And ten horns arrayed like a sunburst or a spiny pig.
        And again mount upon the feet of a bear
    As about the cess many paws be strewn about
And also again wif a dragon, for
        We be confound a the parts' whiches and wheres
What reckon chimeras and monsters and such be there
        And these be choice and rare, a revelation,
A what be cast aside a Polyphemus' pot.
    And Scabie babble on "What encumbered
        The beasts be be numbered four.
But heaven be a seven
    What the beasts times two be eight;
So eight be meat and d'un meat before light be more
    As be as darkness what firelight be for,
        Wedded ta the belly lest the belly ache?"
Shout me guinea mate, "Behold a new empire."
    "What be this but us," ta judgment rush, Pelorus.
"Yea, me bony mate. Us. Me likes the sound a that."

But I say, "Nay, no prophet he.
But by smoke, as prophecies go up in such,
     False, too, me fop he be.
Behold? Behold what Scabie? What thou
       Empire rise in a waft a burnin' weed
  What burn a barn as work doth breed contempt,
Or a pedant unleash a good story
   As any madman be worf a pint ta tell his sample.
Me mate best be
     The first disciple a Polycephalus,
  A god what be a mere anomaly,
What be as rare as his circumstance;
     And from not entire above board.
   For what as Hesiod or Crassus or Symmachus,
The latter, what ferry the very monsters
     From beyond Juba, attest,
   What be a two headed calf or a three headed dog
    Much less the bloomin' rest,
  But ta pry a copper from the plebs,
What watch some mailed and manacled Gaul
   Bleed the brute out upon the hot arena floor
And some greasy stall, a tuppance,
    Barbie its kidney beyond the wall."

And Scabie: "Ictus there be more than exotic beasts
   What spring out of me lixor'd breach.
There be a god in here what broach not thy folly."

Ictus: "My friend thou is burnished in shit
   All signs declare thee lolly."

Scabie: "Ictus, tell me people…"

Ictus: "Friend, thou hast no people.
      And few what break sweat ta revile thee."

At this Scabie bite down upon a length a hemp
      Soaked wif what be datura mix a rue
And careen ta darker visions ere his stew.
      What his bone beasts shake off their rank and rot
And Scabie naked, covered in dung
      His two dingles and dangle clutched ere some
And the Spartoi laugh but ta abet his state.
      What Scabie cry out:
"I saw an angel what come down from heaven,
      What have the key a the bottomless pit
And great chain in his hand.
      And he laid hold of a dragon,…"

"What dragon, Scabie? Where be this dragon
      But from thy tongue?
What piddle a words thy scatter
      But ta floresce the dung."

"See you not before us in animate bone
      A new empire what supplant Rome.
      Ta lay waste the city
What at lyre and wine blotto
      What stir songs a home
      Wif grievous portends and monsters on our flanks
And stithied swords what chafe our shanks.
      And quakes and plagues abreast
What we our enemies sorely test.
      Do you not believe, you cynic cur?
Sure for Ictus I not mistook you.
      You but the very beast what coils its chains.

I fell you, snake. And feast upon your flesh."
     What he rushed upon me but fell
And merciful passed out where he quell
     What for a time we let him
         In peace tend ta his fancied hell.
     What a roar come of a fearsome snore
What empires rise behind one's eyes
     What he wager neither blood nor gore
As may it be a turnip attack a mule
     What sense this day we coax a this guinea fool.

And as Scabie lay face down in the muck
     The eager Spartoi erect our fleet
Wif what be 'bout ta press Rome ta defeat.
     And thus I reflect upon Scabie and his visions
For in entire our guinea be not wrong
     Whevver hunger induced or herb or bile
     What augur but a muddy abstract
What oft be worse than timorous concision
     What augur be ta stun a vagary
Whence our backs be turned and buttocks bare.
     So best be what lay outside the eye observe
Than what be a tale plucked out the ocular nerve
     For as sight follow gracious contours
     It predicts a favored outcome
     What tell a tale what defy the annals.
     And what annals too bear mistrust
     For but be service a scraps ta us.
     History be replete a what be bias, counterfeit
     But foremost incomplete
And who trust a god when we be daily wif our eyes
     Bear their very error and illusion.
And the muck a our intent ta right a beastly past,

What privy our sense ta assail consequence
We can but leaven with sense and risk all.
    But worse be gods in numbers
What our philosophes flaunt
    What be an arc more tragic than Aristoteles' poetry
For as the bow be bent
    The bend a arrow in flight
For that motley grip what be as well finite
    What even if it's ordnance be sunlight.
      It be such as ta bow ta Gaia
Ta display its neck ta the goddess.
    And what rise and come down in some divined place,
    Be a disservice a omen's many arrows,
What appear a cordial prophetic space
    And what be gift a our bloody race
What in time be but Gaia's due.

And marvel ta see these ships rise
    A bone, hemp and pitch a kelp.
Worvy a the sea as the sea be the worvy
    Abode a Poseidon and Amphitrite.
And Scabie prepare a sacrifice
    A the god's way we transit.
    An altar, a pyre and a bloody screechin' gull.
But hatred a the gods be the Spartoi lot
    What be more abused a them as not.
What the altar stone they hurl inta the sea
    What Scabie a terror moan.
And what be ta waste his stack a sticks,
    I light the wood a the pyre
    And a the gutted gull make a tasty fricassee.

And as one the Spartoi set the isle ablaze

Such heat what make the sea boil.
Flames blunted like nails upon the ceil a the earth.
    Scabie and me driven into the roiling swell
What in mossy caves escape the heat.
    Then the utter Spartoi retinue gather
What whip a fierce cold
            For deaf be kin their natural state
    Such that Aeolus be trapped between the two.
Hot and cold, so constrained the air's fury grew,
        A wind what Odysseus and his yardies never knew.
    And burst forf, and though the 200 ships had
But phantom sails they burst their moorings
    And the Spartoi followed suit what man the crafts,
Ekhion bearing both Scabie and I aboard.
    And thus we race wif these wretched hoard
            Ta lay waste a wayward Rome
As by wind and sea me insula a exile
        Was scattered ta the gods.

Canis Ictus revels at being under sail

There be nuffin' like bein' upon the sea
        The wind like salty spittle upon me pate.
    Scabio yacking his repast aft wif the gulls
Like hatchlin's clamorin' for a muvva's sodden, sour taste.
    Me mates and the rhythm of a thousand oar thrusts,
            Not a scrap a flesh upon 'em
        Nor the tender failings a such.
And me mood turn, thinkin' upon me dirty dear Loquatia
    Her bony, glistenin' thighs
            What like two gutters what led the way ta Cumae.
And though spindle, she be no cooch a stone
    What be that happy portico a flesh and bone.

So hard in revery he doth keep
    When a beast what conjure his distress
        Transpire from the deep.
And this monster stay abreast the bow
    And much ta Ictus' fear mix wif delight
        This ballaena speak.
But not ear ta ear nor wif its maw
    But a image what hover behind the eyes
        What he affirm wif his awefull gaze.
"What me son it be ta bear these tears?
        Thou be richly rewarded by these guinea gods.
What forfwif tire a its Roman creation
    As gods after folly be wont ta do.
And look about and behold thy lance,
        What gods oft flood the earf
    What this very sea be remnant of."
And I what be me near ta stupefy,
        "What god here me amaze."
    And she, "Not god though Poseidon bear me
        Of a Titan's trollope
I once upon the land circumscribe
    But forced by tooth and fang back ta the sea.
Though giant, I be a gentle nature
    And speech be me heart's felicity."

Why don't we do it in the road?

Not Herodotus, nor Fimopiscius
    A such wondrous creature speak.
  What words what transit air be not her lot.
But what be more a light
    And much digress a time
As it not want matter.

And thus we be a immanent converse.
"Ictus, Loquatia be not far
As much a her purchase a thy present space
What you be purchase a this deck.
And thus you mingle and this touch found
What be unsuspect thou call loss.
Thus loss abide a presence.
And be thee two fused anon ere
Thee two be concord a thy tears."
"But when," sought I.
"Seek not in time nor place.
But in thy fond heart what escew thy hunger's haste.
For Odysseus forego constant Penelope
For many a good and godly fuck.
Whilst his trouble and strife
Fend many a noble home wrecker
Wif her canard a tapestry
What put hold upon those princes
What strut and flout their peckers.
What stint proport a king's cod
Be ta a goddess's poon.
What a mere wife be but a cast a the divine
Where a divinity err but a her own kind.
But as lowly as thee
Time be ta coax a cock ta any sow's behind.
So wait not for Loquatia and not by Venus
Either set the stars.
Thou whilst in some form meet."
"Doth thou hint she be a visage of a sheep.
Or cow. Or bear. A lion or a mouse.
A duck or chicken. Or the afore mention sow.
For all sort beg a store
A organs, fancies, and natures

And their rich employ. Some a mud be fond
  What too be haven a me dear Loquatia.
Some shite a the thoroughfare as dost me love.
  Some beat and kick against their stall.
And others peck and dither
   A the shade a the garden wall.
  How tell me dearest?
   Such me sweet L. thus do all."

"Ictus, Loquatia be not a Ovid,
   A mere wench what fell
  By some jealous god's spell.
Be certain an arrow pierced her neck
   As she crouched upon the deck
A one a Crassus's wretched scows.
 And be I not mistaken but Circe for lust
A cocky Odysseus turn his crew ta bacon
  What drunken ere now
   Their species wallow as sows.
And Jove be a studious beast
  For swans be a rare peckered foul
What us mortals not nullify a 'how' wif 'why'?
  A fuckin' god lift Leda's gown, and flap
And straddle upon the stunned missy's lap
 Or Juno's wife's downy charges
What alert the Roman a the besiegin' Gauls
 Ere Manlius repel them
   From stormin' the Capitol's walls."

"My ye be a learned ballaeno.
  What tutors have ye thus?"

"Aye. Several seafarin' scholars mentor me

What in their broad travels
    Shame Plutarch, Pausanias and Herodotus
What be Galenus, Marinus and Nemo by name.
    What by urgent study
        And much beginnin' and begoins'
Be famed for recordin' the abundant epochs a calm,
    Where there be no war nor strife.
Many states and fiefs what be no record
    Among you warmongering kitts
What by imperial greed think not the possible a it.
        What sure a pleasant life
    Be seen as bad for commerce, armies and invention,
        What be for sages what discount greed
    For be it in our hearts and custom
        What stirs our need.
But rare be it chronicled what mos'
        Pass life in contentment and peace
    Between bitter anecdotal spasms a war
Or near ta what borin' monotony doth transverse
    And make valor a pity and love
And what would bathe a calm waters
    Forget and abandon full bellies
        For what be far worse."

"For what peace be but the common state
    What freaks and farce a war be most oft writ
A what chronicle a brute spasm a battle
        Be a snug fit
    Ta wring the dog or jackal from
        What in truth not abide a it
Even as lo his wife and toddles it doth slay
        And straight way bring sorrows and tears
And revenge what make no promise a peace.

But what say ta those
      What flout they's pugios
And though quivering won't be loathe
      Ta shut their bloody traps about it.
What they flout their colors, gorge they's wine,
      Yack they's terrors,
And beat the missus wif leather kisses,
      And consequent a darkness
          Ta beat back night's panics
      Cuff they's carrots
          Lest one offended apply the garotte.
   And ta allay discomfit
Scribe such tales a what such be a clannish charm,
      What by kick and punch abort a child
          Or by grip break another's arm.
   But be left in wonderment
      A what not fare well but be judged foul.
          Or loosed ta violence
In the simplest mode a discourse
      So petty, mad Lyssa deny infect,
That it be neither heaven nor hell
      Sift a shard a profit from it."

"Such be Rome," says I,
      "Where Crassus, Pompey and Caesar prate.
And many crushed under the heel of this Triumvirate.
      Crassus, as say Plutarch, profit 'by fire and rapine,
      Make his advantage of public calamities'.
          And slaves, silver and covetin' the earth
And not the valor a Spartacus strike
      This demon as virtue and worth."
And as I fix me mind upon the image a me hate,
      The ballaeno still unnamed make her escape

For she see me amity
      But arise from sour pity.

And from the helm Ictus doth contemplate
      The wine-dark sea and gaze upon his fleet.
Hundreds strong led by fearless Ekhion.
      But be it bravery what breast be wifout heart?
      Be it courage what lack birf and deaf?

      What burden an immortal carry
            If it be not breaf?
And as though Ekhion sense - but be it sense
      What smell might do but I be upwind?
I discern me mouf make no cry
      Nor me hands clap. Or me feet stomp.
No sudden jig or spasm move at all.
      Yet Ehkion wif his perpetuate grizzly grin
Upon his face or what be stripped below any man's flesh.
      That grin. And no eyes. No muscle,
No meat a any kind. Doth this be sense, Aristoteles,
      What turn ta me all visage in spray
And shout straightaway,
      "There be a vessel a league out.
Very large and heavy populate a kind of barge
      What like a bloke in his cups uneasy on the waves."
What souls be washed away at every toss
      Yet appear no loss a this great watery metropolis.
And as we approach wif regard the whole bloody populace
      What list toward us, carryin' tiny mirrors a burnished tin
And commence ta recite wif the most unctuous looks
      What text their bellyachin' cast before 'em.
Such a din what not be heard but a Dis
      What release from the abyss a hell some unrequite soul

What wif her paramour ta embrace sweet reconcile.
        Or the legion a nestin' gulls
            What spyin' a kestril
        Squawk about Heracles precipice.
Epics about the loss of a tooth.
            Anecdotes what plumb the deepest truth.
Pets and patriarchs be summed in elegies.
        And a mistress so pious she abides upon her knees.
    And don't these pilgrims all the while
Scream and wail as a boozy bloke struck about the head
            Might awake a drowsing constable.
What Homer declaim Odysseus find pleasure
        In the siren's song.
But all the same may and wif due respect
            May our bloody hero be wrong
    For this drone and posturin' throng before us
Poison the brain and rot the ears,
        What not be drowned by desire
    But the sea's mute and constant otic
    What while the buzzin' prove out ta Morpheus
And the Spartoi take ta sleep and snore
        And neglect their riggin', charts and oars.
What drowsy pain emit a this source,
        And threat our whole fleet be humdrummed off course.

    And wif rope secure ta our ship
Wif brass and sun we
        Bid our helmsmen move on.
    What a groan arose from the mob
        As all hope a rescue certain be gone.
And above the moans and sobs ask I
        Who be you what be in such a wretched state.
But all rush forward muttering their texts

What none rise above an incessant murmur
Somewhere between the grunts and growls of Eleusis
   And the chant of a Semite what dispatch a goose.
What sudden Scabiopilus from a drunken stupor rise
   And tug me robe "I know these abandoned layabouts.
They be by their folly a dangerous lot
     Like a course a beached jellyfish underfoot,
      Cankers in the mouf or worms in the meal.
 And their tale a woe
    What from they's own vanity they begot.
And the ol' sot mount the dragon's head a our lead keel
   From what Scabie salt spittle in his beard
     Make his appeal.
"Among you lot what by thy own image spy
    The world. What brings you by and by?"
And upon his confederates as he clamor a pile a dung,
    A single voice like a thunderclap rung
"I be Imago what speak. And, I swear, this be a tale a woe.
   But ne'er I tell it lest upon your poop deck I go.
And a square and hot brof a foul or beef.
    And oil and a reed ta brush me teef."
And Scabio laughed, "First thy tale
    Must be in good order and tolerable true.
Before we set oil and strigel upon the likes a you."
   "Would thou deny me meat and sink thy fleet?
By the quatrain your lot grows worse.
   We put the dead ta sleep wif our verse."
And indeed even the Spartoi what sert neither bread
    Nor wine grow somnolent
  At the waves a they's mutterin' mots and monodies.
At what forfwif brave Ekhion leap and reduce this Imago
    From the neck up wif one fell stroke
And his nog bob about the waves

What be the end a the cheeky bloke.
And what our Spartoi scent Roman blood
And swarm about like wasps upon the corpse.
And the multitude rush back what cast they's barge
Against the swell.
But desperate reverse their retreat
What one Primus offer their plight
What upon oaf ta not extort wine or meat
Though be but two what thereupon imbibe
Among our salubrious fleet.
And this Primus begin,
"We hail a Andes near Mantua a Cisalpine Gaul,
Homeland a Vergilius Maro,
What renowned in verse rise above all.
And Augustus stay the Aenead's burnin'
What ta Vergil's intent be but a poem for the gods
And what we a Andes spit in this wound
What wif a modest purse, a laurel and our verse
We contest our city's best,
What anger Apollo what witness a jest.
But many a bit a laurel seek
And claim fortune what not be made a Delphic Book
But the shallow shoals a Nemesis.
And resting a sprig upon their cheek
Claim a ration a every household,
And demand a couch a every table
What a bare cynic starve and
Epicure's sound sense be tried.
What like a tin shingle in the wind
Wifout regard a harm
They lodge themselves where able,
And drain amphoras a wine
But ta prime their tongues

125

And tutor the city's pampered
Wif the sentiment a fatuous song,
      And abate the purse a such a simple throng.
   What by this our Pietole Vecchia
            Put very Vergil, Hesiod and Homer at risk.
What Socrates pollute the Athenian youth
      And be impious a the gods;
   What wif their self-mollycoddle a the truf
These plague a poets be far worse
      What wrench and force
         Their commonplace inta verse
What every layabout sing but what they know
      And what they know be nuffin'
A lyre plucked by a rag a bones and soggy stuffin'."
   As sudden bound forward
      Like Actaeon what been bleeped a stag
         Pursued by hounds,
A poet, Gluccia climbed upon the backs
      As some blue bugger might ascend Hadrian's Wall,
   Rappel a mountain a her fellows, them aforesaid hacks
Ta plead her fate wif lines a verse
      What if there be a goddess for oblivion
A disciple could do no worse.
         "Quid dabo tibi equum non possum."
   Such be her plaintiff cry
When Tergus a furtive Spartoi on the sly
      Caught her by the nape.
"What say thou, dear lady," said he "Be a horse
      What free me a thee?
It certain for want a fat and gristle
      What his pizzle blast me culo bloody.
   Now, I'll be done a that such be grist for poesy.
Blimey if what a that don't me show a knack.

What ol' soppy So-crates be slipped a mickey in his wine
I be nice dun I, slittin' froats and partin' ways from behind."
    And Ekhion wif a Homeric laugh,
        "What know thee a bung or cunny
What bones a anime be but thy design."
    And another poet like the devil's monkey sprung
And headlong commence waggin' his tongue;
        "Die faciunt me spendidi
        Iustus amo habilli…"
Forget the slack jawed, corruptible young.
        Such prats earn many a Socratic rope.
For one must be ill-taken wif thyself
            Before such shite claim thee for a dope,
    A poser what our dear Tergus straightway dispatch.
And thus this barge be squat arse ta arse
            Wif versifiers from the burgher class.
And though such this burg be Vergil's town
        Ne'er a piss or plug a the poet there be found
What for art not forestall fresh nappies and clear complect
            And be thus mirror bound.
    What there object love not reject
            What borne a the first line a each verse,
A virgin birf what the world bear not hope
        For such so blest can do but worse.
    Such be Ilinia Mylius mount her fellows a forge her cry
"Ego semper esurit & volentes futuo."
        But bold be but by and by what
        "Hoc verum est." Vain surety
    Ta sway the hearts a what have naught
For screaming gulls what hatch the Sapphic fracture.
            Or dispatch words a some paper mangonel
And other devices what the stylus stab
        Mere melting wax what melt a heart

But here hold no sway.
   Or so dear reader for your disposal
      What soon be meat for Tergus' knife.
One Danus Ioius what keep a beat as beats beat all
      But a mind what be but a knobby squall.
"Sciebas sponsum a collegio.
Quod amicus sponsi…"
      He muster upon his confreres' backs
"Miseriti pueros bellos,
et pulchri, et Apollo…"
       More pity mankind not suffer such slack
     And praise Tergus tempered and considered cuts
     A his sharp pugio ever keen
    Not wane in its troth ta silence such mutts.
For little of the poet there be left said
     What his supine body cannot gaze
   Across the deck at his head.
And this Tergus prepared a torch
    And fired the barge's bow
Yet still ventures another, a bloated hag,
   What be Lynia Hejinius,
    Upon the sodden pile,
"Scribo nunc in praeiudiciis conciliata
Qui sexus et funibas…"
   Upon what Ekhion declare, "None a these board
    What bear such bad omens.
If this be poetry, it be fit for no man
   Much less for us beings thus,
    What tender some undying fame,
Sure as we possess a bloodless immortality.
   Urge on the fleet, the flames rise,
    And soon this scourge be gone
But what these atomized echoes and cries

A tormented flesh no longer
Choke another passin' empire wif song."

And wail they did as the flames rose
And we set our course with the wind
As did once before their polis and kin
And left in our wake that soppy din,
'Til distance and death augur true reflect again.
But soon a fog outstrip our haste
And our fleet what be so vast we set aside the oars
Lest we scatter our barks
And be less our bite.
And what ambitions ta defeat the guineas
Be sewn to oblivion.
So's we furled our sails what be lash ta the mast,
Such the vapor be so thick and overcast
What upon Scabiopilus regale us wif a tale
A some sot what his sorry self set sail,
But lo be rash like me mate Velius
And wif an arrow shot a great white bird
What be near too stringy ta eat
What 3 days boiled wif onion, parsnip, potato and beet
And what's the Norsemen call albatross.
And what a this loss the Venti wifdrew and
A hunger and thirst a many days
And a crew a 200 be lost,
And Scabie what settle his bum aft in the bucket
A the ship's catapult.
"But the bloke what murder the bird show no cost
But like you Ictus a sourpuss what bereft a all communion,
And like you his refuge be what his comrades be dead.
And as it oft but not oft enough be said
What many a citizen, no harm no foul,

Rather die than a your shite be fed.
So you be willed but two scholars a Solus,
Encephaledes and Mendacius what praise thy thought
A poison what make the mind sour and overwrought
And certain to weaken the listener's resolve."
"Enough Scabie," said I. "Thee wander from thy tale.
What be some Roman merchant
              Trust thee wif a caravan a goods
What be trade for treasures a Tashkurgan.
What be a year out and threadbare.
              What eats whats ta be eat
                     And fuck whats ta be fucked.
Then ya confer wif the stars your wantin' contract?"
"Nay, Ictus. So bereft I steal the train
              And hide behind Parthia and scarce be heard again
But ta trade wif Rome's enemies
              And bring them guinea buggers ta their knees."
"Spoken like a true Greek and slave.
      Now, continue thy tale what I assume be a Gaul.
What denunciation be art ta denounce us all."

"Likes I says," Scabie again set sail upon his tale
              And upon his tail what course the muddy pond a his mind.
"Likes Ictus, boys, this man be bitter ugly about the face.
      Uglier than you Spartoi blokes or any ovver heathen race.
Now, what I be sole warden a our wine
              I not put much stock in ugly
      What a force be so bereft a beauty.
Why what Achilles have fair Patroclus to gaze and graze upon.
              And Calypso and Circe what be goddesses
      Shed' their gowns ta go down on Odysseus.
But what god, man or woman looks upon me?
      What, here be but one bitter cynic, ten thousand bony freaks

130

And this bloody endless sea."
And thus Tergus "And that be it. A god must be this bird?
    This albatroth. Be he at thy bum?"
   "No, Tergus, ya bristlin' turd.
It be but a bird. No Jovean swan."

  "But what magic doth god not direct?" sayeth Tergus.
What another Spartoi, Mendelas interject,
    "What I hear a this poofter Odysseus
What we drive from the earth
      But for the gods what hate us."
 And I, "Shite. Let me set the bar.
     I fear we have a seminar."
What enter a certain Gervasius,
     "What by Jove he be a white bull
Be mistake for Mifra. But this bird, this albatrough.
    Did not it quiet the seas
What seem he be a Jove a sort, dun' he?"
   "But he be dead. This bird."
What by way the Mendelas bloke fancy a joke,
   "Likes a Ictus kill a god,
    No doubt such god stay dead."
What these literal heartless Spartoi
    Guffaws what be hearty japes and jeers
What take aim a me human frails and fears."
    What in heat says I, "You bony cunts.
  What our mafematicians
By such logs and rhythms at a leagues pace
     Put a brick in thee nog,
   What our race fancy it bloody do ta thee."
And Ekhion, "Rash talk, Ictus, what we be a ways to Rome
    What ta dislodge that bloody race's hearf and home
      Seems thee hold some sentiment for creatures

What eat flesh and blood and such excrete
A brown cotechino and rank yellow mead,
    What stink and offend the nose by your very admit.
What incur bitter jokes and nasty japes
What you two find death and a stinkin' corpse
    More ta your likin' than us bloodless Spartoi
What wif mortal japes we upon Roman shores
    Our ambitions not disappoint."

What Scabie rise havin' shat the ballista's bucket.
    "Ah fuck it," pined Ekhion, "Ya filfy twat.
What missile abide this muck.
    Gervasius and Mendalas load the fool into the mangonel
And launch he and his fellow upon their way.
    And Scabie sat upon where he shat
And me upon his meager harpoon
    What, I swear, swell a me bum in his pantaloon.
"Mercy Ekhion. Mercy," Our two man chorus cried.
    The same what be tied toggled for the ride.
The taut rope groaned as the Spartoi jigged
    Or swarm about as hornets in trespassed nest
    Or better ta spectate climbed the rig.
"Ictus don't beggar me. Say you Mendalas be all aboard?"
    And the fiend grinned eager accord
And Ekhion raised his sword and its sharp blade
    Come down and like a midwife cut the cord
What here in a sauce a irony be ta end a life
    Hurled be we from our shite smeared car.

This obscure note suddenly appears scrawled in the margin
of the text: "Or this William what observe the knob a me
ball peen what meet the frons of me bruvver Tunny,
card cheats as they be a Lent a fish stew and rag water"

Eyes shut, what fright be ta bawl
           Or beg Clementia's mercy.
    What rush a air whelm the lung.
  Like a coiled serpent
           What mean ta make thy death.
Swept a arch what me nog tipped the moon,
    What a moment we be Aristoteles fire,
           Then pause upon the apex
           And next we return ta
What be our nature in accord a Vitruvius
               But a sodden clot a earf
           What plunge like Icarus to our certain doom.
  It appears what any man be eager ta fly like a bird
Must be contrite as a stone.
      Frough clouds and scores
           A bewildered gods and goddesses,
      Sipping ichor naked in repose,
Myriad birds and winged dragons
           And hail and snow
And topple back ta wrangle the myfs
      From what exhaust the eye.
From what unknown can arc back into the known
      What Zopyros wif the number arts prophecy
What his war engines and missiles draw nigh
      And fright the citizens a Milet and Cumae.
What me and Scabie be launch a many a league
      And our screams be ta fill the outer air
As though Helios drag his sister, Eos, by the hair.
      Kickin' and sceamin' we two back into this world
Prepare as best in panic ta receive our due.
      What behind Scabie still stream a rheumy poo.
What be kin this arc and prophecy
      What transpire a the empire's artillery?

133

What limit be ta rock or dart
    The soothsay's variable art?
We plunge where fortune dare
      All our future unaware.
Down, down, down fall us two
    Breaf forced back to our bowels,
What sea rushin' toward us
      When asudden arise two flukes
What shape a V wif all the gravis
      What speak a kinship wif the sea
The same ballaeno what prophecy
       Sweet Loquatia be reborn ta me.
And its maw a bristling Sargasso
     What tend its massive jaws,
Into what parlous fall Scabie and me
      Be caught as a catch a trigons
What say a Petronius a his Trilmachio.
     And we heave and pitch down the beasty gullet
And come ta rest in chamber a great arched bone.
  "Blimey! What worse
    Because a thy mouf this be our bloody home."
"How say, Scabiopilus," says I.
    "This from one what shat their ballista.
For fuck sakes what mistook a hurlin' basket for a jakes.
   Dost thou need a swami's hook
     What scrape the muck from thy eyes.
For I see not a future contract here
   As thee be unwise beyond thy years."
     And Scabie, "Did I not attend your Loquatia
      Here what I shield her from harm."
"O foul liar!," says I . "Crassus as soon be done a thee.
   And Loquatia lay dead no matter
     What this monster promise me."

Thus among the foul and half-digested settled we,
    As I pondered me studies of anatomy
And a this beast orifices ta escape. What Acron,
    Intestinus, Sputus, Pausanias and later Aristoteles
Analyze ass from mouf and proper ends a many creatures
        What me and Scabie root about for the bung
What I sudden recall as a tender catamite a me Pyro,
    A sabbatical a Egypts I took
What I look about the library a Alexandria
    One Cetaceous what talk a beasts what
Piss from they's skulls a jet a water
    What been formed by Jove a rocks a Thule
        The same what Pyfeas describe.
    Rocks what piss a mist what be hot likes
        A Caracalla's caldarium.
And dunn I reckon one these piss holes
        For that be what I calls 'em
What be somewhere 'bout dis brute's lid.
        And be me salvation.
        But Scabie what have a better grasp
A the tried and true route a the bowels ta the ass
        What he witness the fester and growl a his inner casing
            And the much oft breach a gas.
What like all nature and in recent temper
            As it be his bumcakes what first tumble ta earf
    What I cannot dispute for it stands ta reason
        Droppin' a toad be in fashion a any season,
What eels and serpents gli umidi crawl.
    So's if there be one what know his ass monkeys,
        It be Scabiopilus.

But what be this treacherous Bollaenus
        What swallow us whole.

135

And where about be me Loquatia when Lo!
Behold I her in the belly's dark
And doth we embrace, nay fall upon one another
Like the famished upon prey and
In that carnal arch what love aspire,
And there among the half-digest mire we squirm
And twist and upon one anovvers
Pud and prick clasp our lips.
O wrive we do like two serpents. O joy!
Every orifice we employ.
O feast as I be again upon thy bony thigh.
And suck thy taint wif a famished polypus grip.
Wouldst I have a hundred mouths ta troll thy hips
And engorge thy cunt.
We be a Orpheus and his Eurydice
Entangle in love divine, you be me honey
What stir in me wine.
Coil, meld, spasm, arch as one.
What sing 'Alleluia',
A prayer what a bloke praise wif his spills and spritzes.
Me soulmate what be bit by that snake Crassus,
And me, me own bard what spar wif Crassus guard
And put Orpheus ta shame
What love-sick companion but little heart
Attend his feckless name.

And here me fondest wish
Be observed in me soothsay, this very fish,
What a ovver time be a dish what swim in garum
What me and me Loquatia in passion swim in him.
O such a this beast, I, as Pyramus,
Suffer not Crassus and the lion's a Rome,
But faith keep me what dear Thisbe be rendered home

As Antony and Cleopatra be naught,
And flee back ta Egypt
    Or Paris what fair Helen bore
Ta render weepy gobs upon the Trojan shore.

And so much we grieve ta love
    A froth in the belly's beast arise
        And distend his walls and baze his eyes
And the gurgle of a thousand brooks
    Our lovely agita make his belly burst.
What our esteemed Pausanias and Adiposus teach
    What the breath the behemoth take
        Bears no cavern at the ventrem
    Ta provoke a gack or choke.
What be back stories a tragedies a sage Sophocles,
    Sniggulus a Tyana be but havin'a laugh
What his trifles play much bile but little craft
    What write all a Rome eat but ta heave its board,
A lie what ta slander as such be untoward.

Note: At this point in the text several lines have been excised in pig's blood. Text resumes:

But swear I did a such a foam arise a
    Me and Loqui's ravaged thighs
Burst we through the blowhole atop the pate
    What we be hurled skyward

Note: At this point in the text several lines have been excised in goat's blood. Text resumes:

    Scabiopilius be hurled upon this shore
Covered wif a foul malodorous gore

137

And a bony beak 'pon his head.

Note: At this point in the text several lines have been excised in the scribe's blood. Text resumes.

"I comes out the beast's asshole, didn' I now.
   What be all fecal brown and yellow slime
And 'pon me head I bore dis gryphon's beak
   What be misplaced 'pon this murky deep
What be stuck upon me pate. I say,
   Ictus come and pull this bony galea
      Away me nog.
It be bloody hot what beast or foul what stands it
   And certain scourged a gore by the maulin' sea
   A bloody crown it not be."

"What be our fishy host tuck in a gryphon or two
   A beast what naught in Tibi's zoo,
Nor for all its wondrous lore
   Be not bled out upon the arena's floor.
For such divine beast be not dealt a sand and gore
   Nor, so prove out his evil nay the beast
      Not set ta guard Crassus's ore."

But such thought I left behind
   For upon the shore me sweet jam pot, Loqui, I ne'er find,
Nor her smell, nor taste, nor bony buns or coital jelly
   Just the rank, salty offal of a fish's bloody belly.
And me heart sunk what Loqui be not nag
What I stole a second chance
   'Til fuckin' Hermes claimed me swag.

A good meal after the catapult ordeal

"You Ictus," say Scabie, "Be but froth in a acid dream
What as the sarpa salpa or siganspinus
Our behemof exude a its behemof spleen.
There be no Loquatia in the flesh."
What sudden creatures scurried like crabs
But wif togas worvy of Roman lord.
But porcine and short on six stout claws
All hung wif a patrician's sword.
And as Scabie approached and bore down
The dozen or so bowed their backs
And blew translucent bubbles from pellicle sacks
What arched out over their entire frame
And look upon them frough this gummy door
What squat bit a creation
'Peared larger by a factor a four upon four
And the glutenous canopy be adorned
Wif a fierce grimace and bared teef,
What Scabie say, "Boo," and
They scurry inta the reef.
And back out as the mist and air bring relief.
And as Scabie and I make for shore
Our new friends hiss and spit
And speak not ta us
As though our mouths be unfit for it.
"Queer," says I, "But what Scrotus and Bollox
and Pausanias knew,
What these very creatures be
What dart about the feet a you and me,
The offspring a Jove and crusted Cancer
The same what pinched the foot a Herakles
And upon this sand spread its seed

For this be a cove a this line a royals
Assigned by Juno, and as fat and toothsome
As they may look,
They bear not the pot
But upon a spit, Jove hisself declare,
May impart sweet and juicy comfit
For by Jovean lineage believin', they be the top.
They scavenge the ocean bottom
And feed upon slough and shit a their own kind
What gone ta reek and rot
What be immortal only in
What kin dine upon their noxious scraps
What only said inbred be predisposed
Ta digest such fetid crap.

"I be famished," sayeth Scabie, "Let's dig a pit
And wittle scewers ta make a spit.
We got no pot so fuck Juno's edict
What these buggers be not by mortal ett.
For bofe me clankin' balls
Whippin' the stank what mire me Stymphalic flanks,
The ol' royal fustylugs can suck me pandoodle,
Alls them bloody blue bloods done a me
And final leave me orphaned a this carnal sea."

"Spoken like a true poet," says I.
"And prompt ta give Jove a privy laugh
Lest too loud his trouble and strife here a guffaw
And she out a pique redouble his grief."
So we back up a ponce royal freak what some
Have scales like a martinet's epinards
What a briny slime hung down.
And a bulbous crimson shell what house its eyes

What behind, one suspect, be a bit a sense.
    But be its claws what like a lobsters
Bite the air what upon a myriad a tiny feet
    In soft slippers bearded wif fucus and brack,
Retreat our famished lunges and stabs.
    What I say these be a bit but not much more
        Sensate than crabs.
And when at final denoue rear they up
    And weep a mucous what encase their whole
Like a curd be sweated under a wooden bowl.
    But this shield be clear and of effect
That under the dome full erect
        They swell four times four their earthly size.
A ruse what be meant for birds and beast
    For Scabie breach bofe bubble and brain
        Wif the ease of an olive upon a wooden tine.
And out went its light and hunger hastened its guttin'
    What required strippin' cutenous growths upon its breast,
        Worthless shells a bright and various color
    Ta distract no doubt a this beast's scavenous odor.
And then unbuttoning twenty tiny knobs
    What held its offal in and
What still a cut run from scabby bollocks ta chin
    And loppin' off its head as mankind hungry for bread
Has been called to do and if by circumstance will do again.
    The creature, headless, furious run about some
A geyser a black bile bursting from its neck,
    And after a bit and Scabie and I have a good laugh,
    Fell bloodied upon its blighted bum.

What wif dry kelp and tinder we sally a fire
    And Scabie dress the milk white meat
        What ooze and hiss upon the spit

What he slow turn our fledgling feast
Whilst tell a tale a gods and goddesses.

King Stercus: Man a Stool

And the tale: "Before sage Homer and Hesiod the Plowboy;
Before Theseus and Achilles and Anchises;
Before Troy and certain before Odysseus and Ajax;
Before Priscus and Superbus;
Before the Aqua Marcio, the Anio Novus, Tepula,
Mariana, Claudio, Iulia and Felice; before Caesaria;
Before Rome and the Cloaca Maxima,
Before the Empress Julia.
Before there be a Sterquilinus and Saturn.
Before them all there be Fluminiba, goddess a rivers,
What be conceive a Zeus and Maia, daughter a Atlas,
What water be where cloud mates rock
And tumble ta the sea.
Below be the Kingdom a Bog and King Stercus
What crystal waters a the river Lethe
In all her eternal flushin' not relieve.
So arduous this King Stercus seek his bowel abet
He consult an ancient physick, Cardimonus,
What say the intestine be jigged and jogged
Wif a good run what be future called a marathon,
So's the king climb ta the clouds,
Whereby he come upon the nymph Maia
Pleasurin' herself as Zeus be about fuckin'
Some cow or goose or some such beast.
And the King what see the nymph in such a frenzied state
Waste not the moment and rape dear Maia.
What anger the goddess not ta mention Zeus
What be hisself so inspired ta greed and rapine

142

As Juvenal report whole races follow suit,
Whereby a lesser god, what the Hebrews call Mammon,
And we Ploutus, and such a our chroniclers,
Herodotus, Thucydides, Anaximenes, Polybius,
Et al ad nauseam
What be a urgent and grave necessity
Ta archive all a it,
Such it be a prized and wicked pursuit
What be fancied by our poets
What the moral feign a maxim
But the margin be the mayhem.
But here not fault the gods. Even Zeus
What cannot keep it in his pants
What be jealous of a like organ
What certain in plenty and a godlike origin be found
As said scribbler long lines be so endowed.
But Zeus submit a wild fury and curse King Stercus
What his relief become his bane
Wherefore his bowels much loosed
First ease his distress and pain in his guts
But soon anon our King's ass blast again
As though his guts be like a fine trebuchet
What hurl a plug a shite what dwarf the Seven Hills
Upon the Bog's woeful neighbors leagues away
What white flags be besmeared
By this ass ballista's apocalyptic skills.
And the King's bum become a constant refrain,
For forty days and forty nights
His shite be what pass for rain.
Such that one thought his chambers
And all about be the Augean stable
What be conscript for a new army a Herakles
What shovel shite and scrub upon their knees.

And the smell, O the smell!
Like an open compost a Gauls slew at Alesia
Or some say Polyphemus taint it be like.
    Or, for a laugh, the mangy ass a your Sinopean Dog
    What for all his bile be held in low regard.
Or the mud flaps a one a Caius's jennies.
    Or a what Pindar knew
            The unsavory shank in Tantalus' stew
Simmered a his son Pelops
        What the King a Sipylus, hisself, slew.
What only Demeter wif tears amock
        As her Persephone be stole away
Not the regard the stench a Pelops parts
        As me Loqui's feet embody
The Gallic cheesemaker's art .
        And what by many a siege
An army by trebuchet hurl its latrines
        Upon the city walls.
Only ta abide scaling such
            What the defenders counter wif feces
A their own makin', the stench a death,
        Such be the glories a war.

What King Stercus at one end take no meat
        What his bowels and bum be rife wif dung
Such that at first the fields be fertile
        Wif a glowing monarchical guano,
    But soon be smothered in a fick mantle a shite.
What his clan, his court, the merchants and tradesmen,
    And his slaves and the peasantry take their flight.
And he seated upon a mount, a throne a stool
        Curse Zeus and Maia and the gossipy poets too.
    And desperate a his fetid plight,

Implore Saturn and Sterquilinus
  What certain as Cloacina be ken a their shite.
   What a King and his gods can do
Ta, as lead ta gold, or god ta bull, take such a sink
  And turn ta advantage a royal's abject stink.
And by route a his populace Sterquilinus fancy;
  'What these fields be fit for Mars
   What he be a familiar a the scars a war,
  Takin' turf and town from every sop and nancy.
What better warrior and a god
   Ta weaponize me shite,
  Whevver wif threats a arms or
   Fatuous provocation despite."
But Mars what most be booked heavy
  In the matters a arms what his tribute
   And sacrifice be beyond accountin'.
Thus worn ta a nub merchandizin' ta the dogs a war,
  Mars be heard upon Aeropagu ta snore
   What the locals took for a lion's roar
Or the sea poundin' out mea culpas upon the shore.
  But Stercus' aroma waft upon the breeze,
Foul, so foul it bring even a god ta his knees.
  And wif funk tampin' his beak, Mars awoke,
What wif the smithy Hephaistos
  What built a bonfire a thick, black smoke
   Ta cloak the stink. But still
The stench cause all Olympus ta choke
   Wif some the godly ladies and gents spillin'
  Beyond and bereft a all but one sense
Their diced and simmered candies and meats.
  And mind ya, this Mars, this Ares, be a celestial bloke
What love the smell a ignis graeca
  Ere Aurora lift her cloak.

And sudden our meat began ta quiver upon the spit
    As alas what crude spirit abandon it.
And again it be at rest, well charred,
    If on this wretched isle pass all grace and reason,
    Wild, strange, our piece a meat be not proper seasoned.

Scabie renews his tale

Even Ares snort and bellow,
      "What misfortune source this smell.'
   But by fear a censure, exile, wound or worse
     Silence kept the frighted king
    For he had not yet reconiled his purse.
Say Ares, "Just as well.
    For I woke wif corpses in me nose
     What put killin' on me mind
As killin' be me the reason I be
     And prelude ta this smell
Though some say me cause
     And course bear not reason,
No more what winter betoken the other seasons."

What a desperate state
     Or what be spoke a greed
What when its blow be at hand,
     Override all ovver need.
Stercus come forf, a walking mound a shite,
   And ta much surprise as seein' said king
Wif his own immortal eyes, Ares beam delight.
   "What have we here bloody Stercus
What be well-suited for the circus a Tartarus.
   Stercus what piss up me uncles and aunts

And what ta mime King Zeus, can't keep it in his pants.
　　　But you ain't a god are you boy?
Oh you prate like a god and, certain as dawn, work us
　　Wif your constant sacrifice, billowing clouds and clots
A blood attestin' to your need."
　　"Sire, god," Stercus cry, "Hear me plea
For I think thee find me mind quite congenial ta thee nature."
　　So Ares says: "What wif this stench at least
　　　Thy thoughts better smell pleasant ta me
　　　As all ovver fronts be asses and cunts."
　　"Quite," Stercus reply, "I route me own subjects
And turn me enemies from me borders.
　　Ta consider me be so bold ta take the world
And what offering take but stench ta heaven,
　　Under thy tutelage, if thy give the order,
And me foe be routed such I say not 'Zeus',
　　　A this conquest be Ares order given.
And wif a god at me side, so me be but his tool
　　　　And at that shite besmeared and underhanded
　　Not even a Zeus stand forth
　　　What such be countermanded.
And wif favors I be worthy ta lift me curse
　　And for thee wifout censure
　　　　Or regard for your bent a slaughter,
Or protestation what this constant stench a war be worse,
　　What we say when this conquest be complete
It be praised the war what end all wars
　　And, Zeus be damned, the world be thy open purse."

Now, Ictus, sayeth Scabie, we scholars know a gods
　　　What tempt man, royal and the like.
But this King Stercus, utterly beshite
　　Be man what tempt god

What cunning out lie even foul Odysseus.
    Yes, said Ictus, these be great lies and liars indeed
What cover heaven and earth.
    What the Semites speak flood, thou speak shite
And shite speak more a the self o'er loved
    What waters be ta purify and renew.
But shite say DIE. Just bloody DIE!
    What the world be rid a you!

And Stercus? So Zeus be routed
    For all heaven and earth seek solace a this mire.
And Ares and Vulcan strap the beshat king down
        Upon a ponderous siege wagon
Surfeit a the War a the Peloponnesus,
    What wif flies and vermin roillin' all about
Aim his royal bum toward
        The neighborin' fiefdom a Forticum…

Done. Done. Our dinner is done
    I'll finish our kingly tale anon.
But now I be famished a this feast.
    Mmm. The meat be wan and sickly sweet
What upon corpses it be fed.
    What Zeus play a godly trick
What hungry pilgrims place
        Such demigods upon a spit
So famished and want a sauce they gobble it;
    What I do now and gladly
As Herakles kick its cousin to the stars
    And Scabie grunt and growl as he peel the shell
        A this fine mongrel a god and element.
From water what men's minds never stir.
        And satiate of our banty hosts

A wood full what could be abode a ghosts
　　Lurked unto us what by the grace
A our godly hosts we be spared.

Ictus discovers a shipwreck in a well

　　When upon me eyes befell
A deep earthen depression like unto a well
　　And wif torch in hand bofe Scabie and me
Make way a murky bottom where dwell
　　A hundred thousand bones a every
Creature be ta roam earth or ply the heavens.
　　All scattered about the rotted planks
A some huge ship a size none ovver
　　Than a Hebrew tale Noach's Ark be fit
And none spared a this grizzly hoard
　　And dear Noah's bones remain aboard
And what might be a wife and kin
　　And what a our kind a ship might a been.
Upon the scene Scabie squat and wept and
　　Rent his hair what a the gods and
Their brutal fancy be take these what
　　Some believe be the seed a life
So deceived and by such deception be led ta strife.

But I be not a such a melancholy nature,
　　And a practiced mind what holds ta truf
Such what Plato apprise light spurt from the eyes,
　　What Aristotle hold it be held in the efer,
　　And the brain be but bit ta soak
　　In the tub a bone 'bout our ears,
　Such that Plato and Alkmaeon be
　　Subject ta his airs what conflates or contradicts

I now hold in certitude as me earthly fellows does
      Spare a care and a such neglect
        Completely unawares.
What ovverwise naught be done at all,
      What better be done in error.
Lesson a Noah in this pit
    Can naught I think of a moral more fit.
 Fit as the joists ta his ship what now provide me
      Me strength, me salvation and me comfit.
But these planks be cut ta bear worlds.
    What Archimedes be among our feeble race
Ta raise these out this pitiless space.

Just then far above two heads, enormous, brute, one-eyed
    Peered a the abyss's edge, "What be thee about
Fair wanderers."
         "Lost and in want of a ship," said I.
    "Much a this store a planks and beams be sea worvy.
But beyond our strengf ta hoist and carry."
    "Worry not. Me name be Unoculus.
And this blind fellow be Polyphemus.
    We have a winch on loan a Hephaistos
What we employ ta move mountains.
    Your planks be but little fair.
Me mate Polyphemus will climb down
      While I fetch it here."

Polyphemus relates how he was blinded by that scoundrel, Odysseus

    What the bones a Lanuvium be made flesh here
A this Polyphemus chap. Wif one-eye thorough done out,
    What be fifteen feet tall wif a dense bony pate

And a sturdy asses jaw.
And thick necked, wif a breast bone
      Likened ta Hannibal's monumental brutes.
And muscled wif massive femurs
      Want ta support such weight.
The giant sat upon a rock, quiet, shy clutchin' his staff.
   "I be Ictus" says I, as ways a bein'polite,
     Seein's how our blind rustic
Be naught a cosmopolite. "May I be so bold
   Ta ask how come ye ta be blinded?
Such be ye a gentle, prudent soul."
    "It be at the hand a the Achaeans
What come upon our pastoral isle. And as I dozed
     Outside me abode of a sudden,
    They put out me eye what
Covet me wine, me cheese and me mutton;
    What these Greeks be intemperate in all things,
Gluttons for drink, and violence, and fuckin'.
    And their imperial Captain what lie
Ta the whole world his tale
     What me here voiceless wif me eye impale.
What be a world what believe such false
    What I be falsely accused what bear the cost.
  Didn' he weasel Herakles bow and quivver
    From noble sufferin' Philoctetes.
And have the daughter a Agamemnon slain.
   No doubt, that shite bear false witness a his favver
    On a whim or a whim wif an aim
And he a serial adulterer be
     Wif a catalogue a immortal doxy
What weary a his hearth and home
   Ta Sparta roam and nip up Helen a second time
   A thus cuckold Menelaus in a second Greek's rhyme.

I hear that Mycenean pikey Homer,
　　　The blind old sotted poet spit an epic
Ta his perfidious hero and his thievin', schemin' race.
　　　Homer, what be blind ta virtue,
　　　　　What to his Odysseus wif a pointed stick
　　　　　　　Open me eye.
Though much admired a the Roman world
　　　We hear this Achaean weasel be
　　　　　When his cunnin' go wanderlust
And mad ta disrupt and raise alarum
　　　　　What me just favver, Poseidon,
　　　　　　Fated the lyin' Greek be back in chains ta me."

"What? Odysseus here upon this isle?
　　　How this be what 6 centuries pass," says I,
"For no mortal man survive the while."

And Polyphemus laugh and slap me back
　　　What me fellowship felt abide the rack.
"Dear Ictus. All upon this isle immortal be.
　　　Thus me favvers tides ship this rank prize ta me.
There be this hirsute king, King Velius,
　　　　Orange from head to toe,
Wif more ta four arms than two legs…"

　　　"I know this Velius. Doth he not speak," says I,
"Silent but not be took for anchorite or aesthete."
　　　"Yes, that be him. Wee world
　　　　What some sages say all men be kin.
But Odysseus and this Prince Motherth
　　　Fancy Velius himself Bodhi
What be for our King a great miscalculate,
　　　For Velius want of the banquet's first course,

Visit his liege upon the stable
And press his cooks ta set the table
And served his guest his butchered horse."

"This and Velius I must see," say I.
"In good time," thus my good host, Polyphemus.
"Ah, here return Unoculus wif our winch and ropes."
What our two cyclops, for as such they come to be called,
Ease a rope down the sinkhole's perilous walls,
What wif great art and facility
They choose fit beams a this doomed Noach's Ark
And raise them and us ta the light above
What the air might impart it's rejuvenate force.
And soon we have enough plank
What ta build a swart ship
Wif blind Polyphemus and hail Unoculus
What aid us fit ta man it.
And soon we share repast a mutton and wine
As the sun go down.
"But before we sleep Unoculus and I have a gift,"
What the cyclops carry forth a rude gunny sack
And dropped it at our feet where it twitch and jerk.
"Be this a jibe," says Scabie. "Be there a serpent therein."
"Ah, once as there be riddles, what many call this thing.
But by the grace a the gods it be now defanged.
Though it remain a loathsome being."
And at that Unoculus untied the bag
And dumped a heapened mass upon the ground,
What our snouts recoiled at the stench
Which oozed upon the air from many its sores.
And matted hair and desert nomad eyes
What never cease though lame and weak
Ta plot into the dark its escape.

"This be our Odysseus," chimed Polyphemus.
    "What me favver resolve we not blind him
Lest some misguided god or goddess
        Seek some mischief a this end."

I saw such craft and guile be bled from the Achaean,
    What little more than his delusions be he;
        An oarless craft upon a boiling sea.
What our ascetic counsel care naught
        For whips and chains. Some survive
What see a prophet's former sins paid in irons
        For his fakes, frauds and false harlequins.
            But me old friend, Velius, what soothsay
        A Poseidon so be known a me plight
Have Unoculus drag Odysseus before me aright.
    And here the Greek pirate heap next ta me
        As tame as any Bodhi dog."

And I gaze deep about this being's rheumy eye,
    "Be you he as they say. The charmin' Greek
What twice sail away a your hearth and home
        Ta stir mayhem and mischief
            Whereever thou dost roam or be blown.
What disturb the peace a others and decry their customs.
        Burn their idols and temples and books such that
They learn when the hour arrives
        What aggrieve and suffer thee most, they destroy.
Be that you?
    I swear, out a deference ta your pitiable state
        I will not spit upon your filthy countenance."
At which he closed his eyes turnin' inward
        And rubbed his scabrous pate.
"Sir, I know thee not," says he. "Nor if thou be worthy

Of an answer such an ass be thee."
"Thank you sir. Such your futile lies be," says I.
   "What self-deluded fool but Odysseus
What dwell like a snake in a gunny sack
      Would answer so.
   What barbarous, backwater mind
  Cannot see conspicuous danger from another in kind?
Carry him wif us back ta Velius
  Or kill him here and now.
     The gods care not. Nor do I."
What by Polyphemus say,
    "We leave him in the care and feedin'
  A Custopecas what just abode down the way."
"No, P.," say Unoculus. "The prick be not
    Immortal but upon this isle.
And I swear we suffer his torments
    Beyond what our nature allow in kind.
Let us take the shite and suffer him a while ta straight away
  As these shores recede he wither up and die.
I for one be done playin' the cat toyin' wif the rat.
   His kind not suffer for sufferin' be for virtue lost.
What none he possess so there be in torment no cost.
  King Velius and your favver act in good intent
But this viper soon as be chopped ta pieces be whole again."

"It's not thy eye what this bastard took.
   But delight ta hear him ring his bell
     What he hang drowsy amidst me rafters
Wif vespertiliones and Arachne's sorores,
    Twistin' about in fitful spell.
   For as Morpheus decree
What go about in the mind's eye be cradled in dark.
   Make many cry out wif agonizin' screams

What unfeigned his dreams sour ta nightmares
    Where the truf what be outside his conscious mind
        Air its bloody tribunal upon his soul,
Such he not sleep but jabber til dawn
      Lest honest slumber seek an evil deed's recompense
      And exact its toll."

And soon the beams from below
    Are dried by the balm a the sun.
And tied wif rude vines,
    Three enormous sails woven a sheep's fleece
Rigged ta three great masts
    And trimmed wif bone and tusk.
Thus Polyphemus and Unoculus fashion a ship
    Worvy of a second flood,
      What Scabiopilus name Antidiluvium straightaway.
And by nightfall the vessel be rigged and wif sails trimmed,
    What soon find us borne upon the sea;
Borne upon the domain a our comrades favver, Poseidon.
  And at dawn Polyphemus fetch Odysseus
    Stuffed in his gunny sack
Down from the branch of an olive tree,
    And dangle the sack and contents from the mizzenmast
      And didn't our Ithacan hero wriggle and squeal
    As we harvest conchyli for our morning meal,
Morsels a soft, sweet sea bound flesh in armored shells
    What dwell among the jagged rocks.
    And by mid morn we set sail
      Fit and sure as if we push off Ostia's docks.

Scabio tells a Strange Tale

And sure as we be on our way,
    Scabie clear his froat and thus shred his lyre
    Tellin' a tale of a land bizarre.
"This land a exotic and tragic hue.
And all men a its race, no matter repute,
      Be at his begettin' ta beget its fate
    Such what Athens call democrat.
    They raise' their right hand
      What signify be a 'yea' from each.
All's well but though this place where
    All manner a men in common govern,
    As be our stubborn nature they be evil ta a man.
What wrong be but ta do as our kind,
    What tend our violence, greed and rapine.
    And they by privilege and good fortuned
    A the torch and sword,
    And not least the pride ta vote,
      Possess no conscience what wif ta hinder.
There be a King Monoesus a much murder and malice
    What rule this kingdom
    A bloody insurrection flared,
And seixed this lord be confined sans booty,
    Stark naked ta the burnt out remnants
    A the stables behind his palace.
What before the first cock's crow
    Be heard the agonies a civil war
  Far bloodier than before what in desperate truce
    What as proof the tyrant be,
      His mediation if not wisdom be sought.
What this one time ogre decree, out a mischief I know not,
    A proposition what stem

Of a surfeit a murder and mayhem.
The King propose what ever sir or sire violates anovver
Shall have his offendin' hand cut off.
And those what cast their faith in the ballot agreed
By raisin' the very appendage
What the Kings' propose their guilt accede.
But as evil attend what be a mere vote,
Vote equal ta remove a hand be a common sight
And in short order few hands be left ta note.
And a one handed man fall easy prey
What the bloke be left wif two.
So soon come a day the folk summon the King.
All the ovvers be wif but one wing.
And nary a one but the King possess the appendage ta vote.
Thus his powers by ballot, one ta zero, be born anew
And as certain as dirt, his evil deeds too.
Murder, rapine and greed fill his day.
And what be worse he field a one handed army
What met certain, constant and bloody defeat.
Such that King Monoesus be not judged above his decree,
And the citizenry lopped off both his hands straight away
And ta assure his wily head.
And rose up the women
What see such hunger and havoc all around
What weaning their toddlies
Watch their husbands lop the King's right hand,
And then his left,
And grant Fortune give him not three.
Such the two handed women seized the vote.
And his the King's Queen, Hepatiti, rule the court
But wif franchise the goodly wives
Come subject ta the laws
And dormant impulses be a their husbands same.

And soon womanly franchise too be right handed but in name.
   Havoc redoubled what left the populace vexed.
'Did we not give each man and woman equal say?
      Did we not provide this way?'
       What be heard in the churches, courts and taverns.
  Til one what be wise made such by his loss
     'What be we not consider.
 What a vote not strike.
       What be what we be at heart?
    What take on such a heady task.
  We err a ourselves what thought ta never ask.
 It be our baseness what makes us free.
   Some point ghost fingers at democracy.
  Some scoff what original the franchise make us whole.
Some speak ironical a history.
     Others condemn the Cult of Aeschines
       And blame it on the theater.
   But all agree hands or no
 The innocent children, 'our only hope',
    Must franchised be.
But when soon after, the children set the kingdom ablaze
    So inured wif bloody suffrage and the folk,
With the show of hands left with but their vengeful slaves,
      By weary consent stamped hoove, and flappin' wing.
   A moo, a quack, and a bleat,
     The livestock what be such raised up things.
And finally as this bowed and tested republic go,
    Here among the dullard cow and duck and goat,
     Final, there be true meaning and solace ere the vote.
And what transpire among the herds, and pens and flocks
   Be evil ta match
      What got ten thousand fingers so forlornly chopped.
Thus these false people a their template they do not waiver

Til they grant the franchise ere the trees and rocks."

Ictus proposes they dunk Odysseus in the sea

And silence but there be the call a gulls,
    And the restless seas. So's I say,
  Wif a bit a punt and play. D'un I?
"Ah Scabie, tales so delicate, subtle and sublime,
    The listener know not if he be edified
        Or just piss away his bloody time.
What be this right hand decide
    What don't know their right a their left.
What bent over wif the temple virtue
    After a busy fortnight a theft.
I have a better game what see us on our way.
  Polyphemus, if it be thy will,
    Unhook Odysseus's gunny sack
And fetch the devious fucker here.
    Beware. Be a care. But woven hemp stand
Between your charge and his fond escape.
    Aged he be but neither nature nor custom drive this man.
     What he be accustomed ta all perfidy and pinch.
   Nick and blag, what done up many a bloke, I'll wager.
    And stay his crew for some tart, Circe,
  What Circe, as Hesiod declare,
   Bore this wretched man three sons,
Though certain there be more.
    And I speak ta both bastards and affairs.
    What as be offense
All his flint be ta shock what all revere
    Not least a all, what below earth
  And sea lie, as this forge a love and honor be.
So as ta while away our time at sea

What we tie a rope about his sack
And put ta him some truf what he not tell
    And if a customary lie we detect,
        We dunk him like a bag a cats.
And after pause draw him back.
        Gauge whevver he be dead or not.
As, I suspect, none your shore line be about
        What puts him a the mercy a the wine dark sea
    And the kibosh on his immortality."

"A magnificent game," cried Scabie.
    But Polyphemus what be bedeviled wif doubts
About leavin' such a cunnin' fuck as Odysseus
    Out a sight even if it be
        But at the end a his rope in a sack
        Dragged aft a our splendid raft
            And bein' blinded by said fuck at that.
For this bloke have a nack a cheatin' deaf
    Even now what consider
            All his knavery, crimes and peccadillos
No god see fit ta turn him into a tree frog,
        A block a marble, a mocking crow, a wheel a cheese,
            Or like dear Io, a bloody milk cow.

"Be we ta let Scabie overboard what ta test the rope
        Before we test our Greek's veracity," says I.

"Nay! Nay, Ictus! Abandon me
        As me mum have ye abandon this whim.
For, as these sons a Poseidon attest,
        I cannot swim but sink ta the bottom
What ta some clan a crabs
        I be but a bit a tasty trim."

161

"Easy, Scabie. It be a joke. I be havin' a laugh.
	I not wish thee dead drowned."

"Well, then Sir Ictus.
	Keep thy laughter inside thy head.
After all manner a slander and vanity.
	What thy not be so blandished a Rome
That from thy orifice more need be said,
		For the age be drafty with thy sayin'
	That no more may be made a it.
And it may be the joker what find a laugh
	In pitchin' me from this moanin' raft,
		Though moored
What may offend one god too many
		And wind up dead."

"Oh fuck off, Scabie. Thy wind and mew
	Like a pup what lost a place
A your mama's tit. It be but a passin' jape. So shut it.
	Polyphemus, fetch the real sack now,
Wif our hero aboard. So thee may be free
	To meet again wif our Spartoi band
Ta sack Rome and then we see what drownin',
	Drownin' in blood mean ta thee."

"What a mean turn what be but a lark," say Polyphemus.
	"Let's cast off this rancor
		And dunk our charge such that we may twice laugh.
	Once a his gasps and second a his gaffs.
For truf be accident if not poison a the likes a him
	What spews his mortal air everywhere.
Unolocus, here test they back
	And bring our hero in his sack."

Athena and Poseidon argue over Odysseus' Fate

What straightway Polyphemus fasten
    The Odyssean sack ta a long rope
And cast the deceitful bloke over the side
      Inta the ceaseless vacillatin' swell and tide
What his one-eyed sons see
      Their favver's fishy humors reside.
    What after some time,
       Like a catch a maena or allec,
    Polyphemus haul up
The Achaean from the chilly brine.
    "All right, vain sir. Be thy name No Man?"
"Ya, ya, ya wrhhhetch," gasped Odysseus.
      "Ye, ye, ye no full well, hu, hu, hu, me name."
"But sir, I can see No Man. For this No Man
      Put a hot lance ta me eye.
But despite the sea's salty brine
      Thee present stench a swine."
    "Whi- whilst. Whilst thou ha-hate me in perpetuity.
Will thee torment me thus while Aeternitas looks on."
      "Lucky we be for the goddess be precise
What me pap, Poseidon, grant us.
    And what a beautiful day for a swim
      And a bit a word play.
Does not thy consider the sea thy first home, No Man.
    Wouldst thou sack the world for the sea?
There. Here allow the likes a me. Here be thee abode."

    And again our hero be plunged in the deep.
What game Athena gaze upon
    And chided Poseidon,
      "Have not thee tormented this man enough

What press and delay him on his odyssey.
Though lost ta reason he be still precious ta me
What by me grace he be prized a
Safe portage ta his dear Penelope
That we may all one day grace her shrewd tapestry.
But love a the hearth be washed away
For lust a the sea.
Ol' Cecrops chose me olive branch,
What be a symbol a peace and truce.
Chose it over the brack
What be earth drawn a ye,
What of another nature pure
Be life ta sustain.
Polyphemus, set Odysseus free.
Nip his torment. Let him go,
As he be dear ta me, an olive a this olive branch,
I swear ta thee."
"Athena, though you goddess be
Sentiment cloud what should be plain.
This Odysseus traffic me oceans,
Builds and plots on me shores,
But have but disdain for our mores
For no blood sacrifice offer he ta the sea
Ta ease his sailin'. What sailor so blaspheme calm
For a gale at his back
What blow his mates ta bitter fates
What for our hero the sea bear some rank curiosity.
Aye. That be a sailor what gets what's comin'
And certain I dashed his ship upon the rocks,
As I would his brains if there be more willin' gods
What garnish me if I takes the pains.
But this be fact, the Ithacans attack me son,
And Polyphemus killed some hence

And as his wont ta devour a few.
But this Odysseus wif a forge fired lance
Not steal me son's life but disgorge his single eye
What torment be not mortal ta dispense.
And there be no knowin' by omens,
And our immortals doth not
Withdraw the moon and stars,
Lest their favors suffer for his wanderin' trifles.
Be I not free ta exact, much less vengeance,
Me own recompense a this man.
As for our ancient enmity there be none.
I be righteous in me wrath
Ta thwart Odysseus impious path.
But ye, ye the object, the goddess a love,
What this man dare leave unrequite.
Nay! More! Betray. And his constant wife.
Yet ye be fond a this pillager,
This lothario, and would me grace his way
What only spurn your labors and blind mine.
For ta plunge keel into me domain,
As it be me heart, the sea,
Me very breast, me beating swell,
What men traverse
What kith and kin a the race I be.
But I swear that bastard's keel be a dagger in me.
What Tiphys, Jason's helmsman see
In a such a prick as Odysseus and
His race's gift a perfidy
At what, I might add, your fawnin' git excel.
Sure! Thy olive trees and their oil
Be close about the Athenian hearth.
But ta prize Odysseus borne as it were a his lies
What be that hearth worth?

165

And what be the cold ash a his abandonment?
And certain me oceans all life bouy
What be a bofe earf and sea,
Salt, for what be ichor ta you and yours,
Me bitter brack remains
Ta tide all creation's pulsin' veins.
This love a yours be a late lot, and none wise.
But this throb, Odysseus, belong longer
Ta a lizard sunnin' on a rock
Than a feathered troubadour in a tailored frock.
Leave off Athena
What only your misplaced heart know.
What by your innocence, Odysseus
Be as ta look upon a Gorgon as ye go."

"Poseidon, thou be a fool upon display?
Does not the Gorgon anchor me aegis
As I attend war?
Did I not spring fully armed and scored
From the head a me favver,
For, blind, Homer saw about me shoulders
The far flung tasseled motto,
What left Troy fraught with terror for therein be
At its apex the head a the dread monster.
I be Minerva ta these
What accompany thy son. This Roman Ictus.
And who be ye? Oh yes, Scabiopilus.
Such renown company, cousin. All blotto.
And Ictus, thy be passable learned.
Doth not me eidolon stand in stone
On the Capitoline;
In chiton and belt and sword such wields
Wif the aegis a Medusa

On her shield and a Corinthian helmet
        Cocked back upon her head?
What be as me wise in the strategies a war.
        And as much as arms and courage,
Be it not deceit what outwit
        And a foe defeat."

Thus so long and loud the god and goddess debate
        The other gods awaken or their labors abate.
"Who pinch me bloody thunderclap," Zeus roars.
        "What loud discourse
        What make ol' geezer Demosthenes grow hoarse.
And outlast the boast and bluster
        A one a them Ciceronian filibusters.
    I take pains in early morning
            What me sheets still be cool
        Ta fuck what mortal me fancy;
    And I'll thank ye take your bloody squall
        From me bedroom window for
    This morn thou fright some Theban nancy.
Sounds the bickerin' of a fishmongers
        Over a bit a cod with the inflate a some eulegy
A dull senator might orate
        A some dead buggered oligarch
What praise his crimes
        Or exotic rheums and cankers what be his estate,
Or what his Insula Felicula wif its 100 flats,
        Or what his Villa Sol wif its 8 sundials,
        Ornate gardens, and 150 slaves will fetch."

And Boreas rouse of a night a horse fuckin'.
        Oh yes, Boreas be a horse fucker true
What sire mares and stallions by the dozens.

But now he thrash upon his palette
   What be a ragin' storm clouds
   And a his most incarnate farts,
He stuff in a old dragon's bladder
    And that be what make his watery bed.
  What cast up winds and waves
    And bones a the dead.
He stretch and yawn
    What make the cumulus toss and billow.
  And bitched wif wine, he wrap his head
    In his dirty, downy pillow,
Against the bloody bupkiss barney
    A Minerva and Neptune.
But the duelin' gods not abate their roar
  Until our cranky Boreas could take na more.
And drawing his arctic dagger
    From his night-table drawer
Rose ta blow down the street and settle the score
  As a citizen might what goes ta slay a bayin' dog.
But still a bit under the weather he be,
    Our Boreas stumble,
  What blunder he pierce the monster's bladder
What rein a storm a violent winds
   What shame what ol' Vergil concoct
Ta threat Aeneas. And in fierce shock it rush
    From Boreas's Aeolian rocky flat,
  The same what Odysseus among his many sins,
    Plunder the god's foul but favorable winds
After Ol' Aeolus saw the Greek's lawless crew
  Abuse his favors and be vagrant a their captain too.
The icy blast what push Ictus and his erstwhile retinue,
  And the godlike farts that seal flights favor,
   Straight through the Pillars a Herakles

As they be but a martio barbuli hurled
　　Likes a Mars hisself
　　　　Out ta the Ocean Sea, ta new worlds
Beyond the sanctions a Poseidon as they be.

Thus our four lads and their bagged and bound hero;
　　Their backs ta luvely fond Iberia and home
And in tatters be Ictus dream a topplin' Rome
　　And havin' Crassus' grizzly head on a pike.
　　And Polyphemus laugh into the grit salt spray
Caught in the cradlin' current a his ma, Thoosa,
　　As took wif joy west as post-Bacchae Boreas
Flail about his larder for the hair of a dog
What might sober up anovver improvident god.
　　As but fickle or evil be our gods over-esteemed.

What they fear not the ocean's edge
　　For Ictus, whilst habiting its cool porticos,
Read a the Aegypti bibliotheque,
　　Where be the Book a Eratosthenes
　　　　What measure the girth a the earth
As a tailor gauge the ambit of a Titan
　　What cinch be at a quarter a million stades,
A reach what take a good, stiff breeze to circumvent.
　　And there be books a Pythagoras and Hesiod
At this lovely place
　　　　What find favor the world be round.
　　And the works a Seleucus and Aristarchus
And Posidonius what Canopus be the captain
　　　　A Menelaus' ship.
And though skin deep Ictus be derelict
　　He possess much grace in learning.

And Ictus shout in the face a the gale,
    "C'mon Scabie. Give us a tale."
And Scabie, "Dun I ever tell the time
    I caught Zeus's bolts
        Clean between me teef."
"Haw!" blast Polyphemus.
        "Good show. A bit a potbellied comic relief."
    "Nay! True it be. For in dreams if it be Zeus
What come a callin' ta me,
    By grace a me honored gods be I not set free
        A this mortal sack a stinkin' jelly
What as be a dreams I be a more appallin' creature,
        What counter a some such esteemed nightmare
    As cranky Zeus set his thunderbolts upon me."
"Ah, dreams," says I. "What afflict but thou doth not so die."
    "Nay asshole. What ta die inta this hell on earf,"
      So say Scabie
        "And you the demon
      What make of a man's terror a muckpit a mirf."
    "And" says I, "What thy carry said compost about
      In thy creases and cracks.
Such our eyes water for what our nose not lacks."

"I give thee a good throb a thy nog, me friend," rail Scabie.
    Such be Polyphemus what say,
      "Kind sirs. Thy quarrel must end.
Doth thy not feel the reverie a god's speed, Mercury,
    What sling us out upon this wondrous sea.
      Gentlemen, put off thy assault.
    Niever by fault nor right ye be.
And forfwif like cod may
    Thy odors be circumscribe in salt."

And soon we pass upon a lush shore,
　　　　What be gabled wif greenery and fruited
Wif ficus and citrum and aliquam galore.
　　Be we push by our rankled gods
　　　　Ta the beggar's door a the Hebrew Eden?
What ta the Sumeez, Edin be an uncultivate plain
　　　　And what before us be the same,
But warrant neither in herbs nor grain,
　　　　Nor leapin' fish nor dartin' game.
And as we ashore assuage our hunger
　　　　Feathered Artemis and the Amazons appear
As from a fable, out a the shaded coast,
　　　　From a glade, across a mighty river.
What our Scabie's teef be chinked a Zeus's bolts,
　　　　Our erstwhile hero upon the opposin' shore
　　　　　　Begins ta strut and promenade
　　And I look about for a cohort what come ta his aid.
What I notice these women be uber less,
　　　　Fittin'a Sparta what they's dames lop one off
　　　　Wif the other breast bound against the chafe
A the bristly feathers a the arrow's shaft.
　　　　But these, these be wifout nary a breast but,
　　　　Likes a us Roman chaps, paps retain.
And bold Scabie a the opposite shore pass again,
　　　　Gesticulatin', wif his hairy arms wavin' about
　　　　　　Claimin' all in sight for Rome and the crown,
　　What sudden a spear a four pedes lengths
And two stone weight graze our guinea hero's bung
　　　　And he go down clutchin' the offended spot,
What be mighty stung for upon witness I cry,
　　"Bloody Scabie, what gods must these be
　　　　What fell wif one blow
The creature what stand Zeus's thunder bolts in his grill.

171

And the bloke live ta tell the tale."
And arrows as rain from the clouds come down.
   And we flee as from a nest a wasps ta our craft
          And pray our nemesis Boreas bear us away.
When Unoculus stretch ta spy above the trees
      And sudden grasp the riggin'
          And begin ta tow our craft ashore.
"Unoculus? What make way wif our ship?"
      And he, "Fear not, me brave cynic.
   For what ta a runty shite like ya self
      Appear primeval bush, wif but one eye
Raised above the greeny welter,
          I espy meself this be a mere spit a land,
   And beyond that spit, ocean what hold our salvation
And what we fair ta bring us ta Rome.
   And straightway he speed out craft
Frough mud and jungle, ta a large lake
          And across another narrow strip,
      Then ta the open sea.
A sea what seem calm. Beyond the reach a the gods.
      And thus forelorn, beyond the reach a Rome be.

"Nay. Buck up," say Unoculos,
          "Doth not your own Strabo
   Cite seafarers what the earth be a sphere,
What mountains hide behind the curve a the sea,
      What their peaks apace appear?
          Put forth as such be this Ptolemy.
And Eratosthenes measure its girth in stadions.
   And Aristarchus and Seleucus even preach
This home a ours be but a ball circlin' the sun.
      Even blighted by ice Captain Salsasferus
Saw fit ta place low the very brute

What rendered his good fortune.
For who knew Artemis held such dominion
         Over birds of the sea
And spied ol' Salsaferus's breach wif splendid ocularity.
         But the ol'd salt wasn't gonna rot in place
Just because he shot some wank
         What appetites manifest an inferior race.
Oh no. As the bird rotted on the bow
         He cried "If this bloody sea won't be tempest tossed,
Maybe if I eat this mouldy albatross entrails and all."
         And thus he dined on the rancid meat
                  Licking the bone and blood.
         And soon a squall
Within his bowels began to stir and froth
         So he lowered his britches and leveled his breach
         And so powerful the blasts
                  That surged from his arse,
That was not only the ship steered
         Upon its watery course, but borne aloft
And soon to home and his wife's soft bosom
         And a foundling cask keen ta chrism.

         So if be you clotted cynics and the like
                  What not forebear such thought.
Well considered passions and beliefs what
                  Might carry even a petty, vengeful shite
         Like thee, Ictus, back ta Rome."

"Beast, what doth thou know a Rome," says I.
         "Certain it carnal be.
And no grace it afford thy moseys and meanders.
         And as sure as the gods be guarantor,
We plunge off the edge a the world."

173

But silent Unoculus remain
As me disdain a his race sting.
    And our one-eyed giants
        Though Polyphemus be dispossessed,
Sail westward what put their broad backs ta the oars,
    And after an arduous trip upon patient seas
What Scabie and I pass the time playin' plats and tali,
        Or bickerin' or sleep
    Appear a sandy shore what we beach our ship.

Soon comin' along the waters edge,
    Be a bloke, slight, wif silk robes
        Leadin' a small retinue,
What me greet wif "Nos romani sumus via."
    Ta what he reply "Domine, tu procul a patria."
Wif what Scabie and I weep what hear
    Our tongue so dear spoke so clear
What in memory the forum and Capitoline appear
    And what by the imperial eagle
        And banner Rome's nose extend even here.
"Sir, whereof ya speak our tongue."
    And he, "Please, I be Liu Xiang, what by courtesy
        Call me Zizheng.
Here upon our emperor Han Yuandi's shore bivouac
        A Romani Legion what instruct our imperial corps
In battle formations, maniples, the gladius, armor,
    Metalurgy and such. What ta me be
        A remnant a Crassus defeat
At Parthia." "Ah what Plinius call the lost legion," says I,
    "What 'til now Rome not know
        Such be settled in this far region.
What we meet wif our countrymen
    That we may feel their tears upon our cheeks again."

174

And leaving behind our two giants wif our bark
      And Odysseus in his sack,
Straightway Zizheng took us to the Romani camp
      What we greet our guinea grunts at mess,
"Lads, I be Canis Ictus what from Rome stray
      And this be me mate, Scabiopilus…"
What a Romani bloke say, "What I hear tell a you.
      Yeah, Ictus what for retribute be cast away,
What be a scrap a that Greek dog Diogenes,
      A big mouf muvverfucker, I hear say,
      What stink up the senate and the forum,
What got no truck wif treasure, the baths
      Or any a us guinea's proper decorum.
What be you here, clown. What ta declare thee unfit
      A emperor's a two continents.
This one as soon take your head
      As see its mouf but twitch."
Ta what I reply, "Spoke like a bloke
      What's naught had his back side ta his betters.
      A maniple wifin a wall. Forgot, destitute
For every mille passus
      He be from the palaces of Licius Crassus
What forsook him at the charge a the Parthian cataphracts."
      "What?" declare this principalis
      What his name be Phineas.
"What dat fuck Crassus be dead, slew at Carrhae,
      What dat Parfian Surena pour molten gold
      Down the ol' miser's gullet
Is what we was tol',
      Separate as we was from our fellows."
"It be true what this Dog Bite old sot tell you,"
      Said their Pilus Prior, one Perditus Gladius,
A ominous name a one a such poise

What plagued me brain
     Led his boys ta the far side a the world.
"Crassus lives. Nay, the old bugger thrives.
     But simple. Ask how I know this."
"Ictus, I would deign ye and Scabie dine wif me men.
     But then again thy stench much less thy wit
          Be better suit of a bloody pikey parged in pig shit.
     And neiver Zhizheng nor his cohort know a such company
          What my mess will feed thee yonder under that tree."
"Much oblige for the grub and the slight, Gladius," says I,
     From the mouf a one what talks like a bumpkin'
Yet pulls and strains the trappings a his rank."
     "Eat Ictus. And pray wif that mouf
     It not make it thy last meal, as unhinged
          As it be from good sense.
You be not in our humble camp 5 minutes
     And do we not hear grumbles for exile.
Exile from exile as we by dire tale be such
     And that thy lack a sense what such be such
And what wif thy tongue
          Sweep filth upon our feet.
What not offend thee, but as thy stench offend us.
     Go bathe first and prove thy metal..."
Says I "Have none put on the kettle.
          I bask a me own sweet stink
     As soon as hot water test me mettle."
"I thought so," thus say this Phineas fellow.
          "So settle in the grove and wither the figs
     Rather what sully prunish our visages."
What Zizheng be privy a this exchange
     Have one a his household take
Scabie and I provisioned beyond the range
     A the nancy nostrils a our new foundling,

Our guinea captain.
And this servant neiver keep his tongue
    What put a physic in the herds feed
        Ta urge its dung,
What some moxie geezer name a Kung hear tell,
    "If you be courteous, you be treated well."
"Well you show me bed
        Lest I show ye the courtesy a me staff.
I not be some such riff raff
    What's mood you may commandeer.
What I be a peaceable sort, I return wif Roman might
        And lay waste a here and, yes,
    All and no more what be but a servant's slight.
        So shut up for I be weary and crave a palette."
"Yes, master. That be all? There be a chill tonight.
        Shall I bring a skin or shawl
        Or perhaps what suit they mood
        Me fetch thee a pall?"
    "Cheeky, fuckin' bastard. Wif likes a you,
        The celestial dome be a lifelong shroud.
So as much, me slanty prick, that will be all."

Canis Ictus's Dream

And weary Ictus lie down, nay fall upon his palette,
        What Ci Ren, as this servant be called,
    After all, for spite no doubt, place a pall
        Upon our hero what be knit wif the zodiac.
And as a dream befall Ictus, his sleepin' body plunges
    As he twists and calls out
        "Speak that I might see," as calm night
Be given over to Somnus squalls and tempests,
    "Speak that I might see," cite he.

177

"Ah. Be thou Marcus Manilius,
      What be that great foster of astrology.
      Speak that I might see thee!"
"Yes be I Manilius what see foretold in the stars
    What be your plan ta lay siege a Rome.
From the heavens I see all, your force a bloody bones
    What by foul temper you have lost.
Your plans dashed with but that wretch Scabiopilus
      And but two giants, one blind,
        And all but one eye between 'em.
I see your gaze scour me soul for answers.
    What your bitter bile and vitriol be favored wif victory.
      What wif no army ta speak of
Like the necromancer, Comedenti,
    You turn for conquest ta spells and sorcery
What have but sharp wit and durities
      And no potions what ta imbibe the stars.
Thou in an instant foster hate among Phineas and his troops
    What if not for love a tyranny they be persuade
      For but share a spoils, a bit a loot.
What for your Sinopean lot, as bumpkin Phineas might
    Say, don't give a bloody hoot.
40 men or so. Nor be they brothers
    Harvested a dragon's teeth.
      Certain less than a start.
   But might they make up for in greed and desperation
    What they lack in kind and heart.
For be it not routed Crassus
    What leave them cut off and desolate,
  Driven east praying fealty ta strange gods and emperors.
    The least among them seasoned,
A breast worvy a contest. Pack up on the morrow,
    Leave this shore, foster this emperor's graces.

Let Liu Xiang guide thee, for what may be in store
    May be fortune if thy have ears ta hear
And eyes ta see beyond the agents affix thy head
        And wit enough ta fear the gods.
As what their sage Kung alarm,
    Before you hatch a plan a revenge,
        Dig two graves."

Canis Ictus and Phineas, allies

And thus I awoke
        As Liu gentle stroke me brow,
What off put as be I a Manilius's words,
        Soaked a sweat as one upon
            Which a fever broke,
    I leap up a me nightmare and flail and shout
        And cast the delicate scholar about
Scalded what wif display me bare backside
        Ta the open portico and door
Where any assassin or debt collector
        Be about their nefarious chore.
    But Liu stay calm and quiet and say
        He be in the countenance a Phineas
What agree if I be a proper temperament
        And wif promise a loot gather willin' allies
            On our way,
He and his company join me cocky plot.
    What Rome and Crassus left he
        And his ta rot on Seres exotic shore
What not see kith nor kin,
        Wife and toddles na more.
"Right. I be general a these
        What me wellspring force prove feckless

Such what dread dragon teeth proof out."
　　"Nay," say Liu "Should not Phineas be thy general
As thee be more suit a ruler a such men,
　　What in your prudence not try his loyalty
But press upon him your surety and
　　　　As one wif his sword in his right hand
Counsel such and accord a plan.
　　　Come I pretext fatigue as what drove thy bile.
Tol' I Phineas a sound sleep and a proper meal
　　Put Ictus in sense ta hatch a plan
What be worvy ta carry you patriots abroad
　　　Ta savage thy homeland."
"Well spoken," Liu. "I do. I do feel a mind ta plot
　　Wif Phineas what best ta overthrow
　　　That corrupt august crew In Rome."

Phineas' cohort joins Ictus' crew

And such some incense be burn
　　And Phineas and I embrace
What I swear the bloke go dick hard
　　A me ol' rotted chub.
Still he bring 40 wif him all horsed
　　A Seres generous rule. And it be set
What we visit this silent monk
　　What a these alien worlds be much revere,
What Liu insist his abode be a direct line a here
　　Ta Rome. What wif little haste our band
Set off apace. Scabie, Polyphemus, Unolocus,
　　Odysseus in a bag and me self. Phineas
And his two prinicipalis, Regulus, a drunken,
　　Ass gaspin', hunchback thing
　　　What only a momma see fit ta style a 'king'

What by irony and abuse his tales a such royal be.
   This ogre what sport red seepin' boils upon his head
And a wivvered hand what double
      The cross a cursed pain what trouble his mortal coil.
Still there do be somefin' noble about the bloke
         What stand at arms the butt
A such a cosmic joke, loved by none but
         His dear ma and hairy singed Vulcan.
And the second principalis be a Gaul
         What be called Aonghas,
      Named a Vergil's Aeneas,
         What hail a that livin' hell, Brittannia,
Though not sport me and Scabie's long portage
      Lay claim a scars a many ports and plots and wars
         Ta claim what he has eyes,
      His bloody eyes done seen it all.
And 38 or so a the Imperium's finest.
      A what fortune place this misspent Linus,
A sagittarus, a Gaetuli, black as Germanian coal
      What could neiver sing nor play a lick on a lyre,
But pluck of a bow string what its arrow
   Be sweeter the tune
      What pierce the savage marrow.
And on this motley host be threat enough
      A what me own hot temper
Tally a lack a 10,000 Spartoi
      What once swear allegiance a my employ.
But, no, nuffin' in it for our miserable immortals
      But ta stave off hangin' about
         And jostlin' for shadows,
Whistlin' at the goddesses what not trifle
      For a package and a Naked Pig.
What be I find mortals more ta me taste

In matters a empire overthrowin' and such.
Weight a man's hand wif a few gold teef,
    And he be eager ta wield the jawbone of an ass,
Or a flail or cudgel what ta make many a muvver
    Wail a her sons mornin' porridge,
What many a feckless god or venal king see fit
    Ta see some toofless hump
        Starve at the war teat.

And dun' that be the in and out a it.
    Phineas and his Roman hoard be on board
What wif booty ta be had
    And sad widows ta be restored.
But first we be off to a great city, Vetit Urb
  What the Seres call it.
    What our guide Liu say be a right peaceful place
Ruled by a monk what but for low grunts and howls
    Observe a vow a silence and but serve his people.
Shaggy red hair head ta toe
      And spastic in his gait
    But strong as ten a his guard.
  Stray and queer a temper
      What breed infinite patience
    Among them what fancy him god.

Sudden what appear in the road
    But a molten lump a dung,
  Snarlin' knarl a foul effluvium .
What Liu say we must not pass
    But roundabout
  Make our way ta Phineas.

"Why?" says I "Must we detour ourselves,"

What this gob a phlegm be wifout legs ta chase
Nor arms ta attach what we not be so sprightly
  As we be bold. But Liu tremble wif fear
"We must not go near. What this demon
    Become immortal if he devour a holy man,
And that be me."
          So Scabie, "Well, I ain't bloody holy.
    So I proceed apace." And riskin' ta furver height
      This creature's wrath he cross its path
Did me luvely Roman rotter and no sooner
        He be utter sucked up
      A this monster what turn viscera ta vulva
        And vulva ta mouf.
And in anovver glance be mouf ta monkey
        Or half-man a some sort.
Lean, hairy, wif a funk
        What be composed a butt filf itself.
And sudden the stench a cookin' fat
      What Scabie call from the demon's inside
        "Shite fellows I be cooked alive."
What Polyphemus and Unolocus
      What grew ta hold ol' Scabie dear,
As brave giants eschew fear and
        Each grip apart these devil's ribs
And what be but Scabie fetal
        In a oven a molten souls hot
Ta render anovver a their kind.
    And out spill Scabie a bit singe and rot
But as Socrates use ta say of his little charges,
    "No worse for wear."
What we mean Scabie
    As we mean him bein' in there.
What we mean bein' in the demon's belly

What more an oven or cook stove be
And our hero giants set him free.

"Still thee not pass," cried the demon
    Be a instant a five hooved lion,
A great fanged carp what swallow villages whole.
    A horned Maidie wif the hooves of a deer.
      A warrior wif a ox or horse's head.
Even a demon a one eye as be our own fond Unolocus
    And as be Polyphemus before that fucker Odysseus
Pluck his midger out wif a sharpened stick.
    These demons a Serica be variously called
Yaksa and Yao Guai and what be many Gui. Si Gui,
    Gui Po, Nu Gui, Shui Gui, Wutou Gui
    And many ovver sorts
        For these be very superstitious folk
What have not enough native torment
      But ta import monsters
    Like us Romans import gods.
And these foreign demons be
    From Pandyas and what land they call Wa.

Liu has fled and Scabie's fat still fizzes
    What I put to our demon we but meet some
Blokes what be from our hometown Rome
    What be encamp just down the road.
"We collect our troops
      And march ta conquer the Romans.
    And you be a substantial geezer.
      So ya wanna come."
And the demon what take the form
      Of a misshapen imp
Pace back and forf as though one wif a limp,

184

And stroke his furry chin and pull on his lip:
"Seems ta me this Rome ya go on about
   Require more than what lot bivouac
    In the gully by the way.
    Whadja say if I tol' ya
   I knew where be 8000 soldiers,
And 130 chariots and 700 horses for the takin'."
"I'd say your daft," what say Scabie.
    "Or Sir," says I, "Mere mistaken."
At what our demon raise our giants in the air
   High 'bout enough wif but our eyes
      They be not there.
    But if thy listen close enough
   One hear their terrific moans and cries.
"Please kind sir, resolve our friends
    Be upon the earf again," plead I.
"Will ya take me offer, ya drivelin' fool,"
    So say the demon.
    "Yes," say I "But first, let's go ta Phineas
    And his troops up the road."
"No," say the demon. "For be your intent as we
   Meet your cohort what they will overwhelm
And make dispatch a me. A what thy be mistaken
   For certain I would kill them. Kill them all."
"But sir," say I. "What march must we make ta gather
    This force. And can we please bring our giants
    Down from the sky."
"March! March! you dumb fuck," my demon say.
   Has thy been away what I eat your fat fellow here
And hurl two mountains into the sky.
   March. What bloody march.
  Just say the word and we be there.
"What word be that?" Scabie ask.

And our demon,
"Can thee make this peon go away?"

The Demon Hunger animates the Terra Cotta Army

Just then, "Here be Phineas," I say
    What are swart Roman principalis
Make his way.
    "Phineas, this demon here…
Demon what be thy name?"
    "No Man," Odysseus called from his bag.
"No, not you. Go back ta your master Morpheus
    Lest be more a your pratt."
"Me name be, Hunger."
    "Herr Hunger here say he manifest a crew
Of 8000. And that these be but meters hence."
    "What say you Phineas?
        Trust we this imp?"
And Phineas, "What takin' down Rome
    On its own shore and all
        Mind ya a treasonous act I deplore,
But willin' ta rule Rome proper. And what be more
    As Dionysius say about cups and cunny,
        The more be merrier
    Also apply ta arms and troops.
What the Roman garrisons be large
    And we be few."
"So that's a yes," says I.
    "What say you creature Hunger?
Perforce, by whatever course,
    Take us to this rough and ready force."
And sudden the air twist in upon itself
    And all encompassed as we be transport

A some tempest a Jove, dark what not be staked
   A what be up or down, or inside or out
What time be naught and we knock about
     What awake upon a narrow earthen berm
At the foot a of a mountain, Mount Li,
     What of our Hunger we soon learn
And a great plain what stretch behind.
       One by one like icy lumps
         We drop from the sky
And lie upon our backs in wonder and fear
   A the manner what we be comin' here.
Hunger form us up and order "Dig".
   "Dig? What you hurl us about and renege
What there be a force a thousands here?
     What be but a sand dune
        Where a thousand vultures loom
   What no doubt intend ta make us a meal?"
Thus Hunger "Ass. I stamp thee
      Under me heel?" What sudden
Shrunk I shelter under the imps' foot me feel
    Me bones crush between his toes.
"You big one-eyed devil", Hunger commands
   "Take up that pine log and dig about the sand.
What soon from me vantage point
    Appear the head and shoulders of figure of a man
      Froze in fired terra cotta;
Then two, and then two thousand;
    What there be a thousand more order and filed
Armed and mailed; all the while Unoculus
   Not be curtail what our giant
     Bring ta light 8000 in all
And numerous chariots and horsemen.
   What I crawl from beneath his fetid feet

And resume me regular shape.
And marvel what our devilish Mr. Hunger complete.
    And ask a me imp master "What we decoy wif these?
What ducks be upon the silent pond?
        Each be hollow as Odysseus's Trojan Horse
What only deceit bring ta life."
    And he, "Shut up ya bloody fool and sneeze."
"What?" says I. "I have not the need."
    "Bloody bounder. I ask a simple thing. Bloody sneeze!"
And pluckin' a vulture's feather he shove it up me nose
    "Nere where I'd like ta put it."
And sneeze I done, whereupon
      What be but clay statue
Move as from a sleep what each warrior the others greet
    And turn and hail Hunger. "These be yours
    What none be less ta me mind deserve.
You amuse me Ictus pitched from thy race
    What a that place rooted
What gods mold bounders like ye a so little faith?
    What god make thee so uneasy
What it be the unease a weather,
    Arrow flight, prophecy or the sorcerer's might?
    Prophets what be wrong, be false.
What ease it be ta shite on thee
    Though I be Hunger such me squats be rare.
General Phineas gather thy forces, new and old.
    We have a journey ahead
    What for men be bold
But for Hunger and his friends be a no consequence
    "What I be ta feed upon a holy man,
This flavor I so cherish,
    A what favor me never perish.
And as pay for breavin' life a the clay army

A Qui Shi Huang, bring me a holy man
Like Liu what I eat him and pass through
   The Immortal Portal birthed into eternity.
What ye likes be birthed into sullen death."
  "But Lord," says I, "Be deference
     Better ta mock and die.
Surely wif thee powers, a holy man
   Be but a rabbit or doe, some easy prey
What wif thy agile wit thy run down and slay.
  What Britannia's naked blue beasts calls coursin'
     Thy do by sheer divinity."
"Nay, nay, nay, Ictus this be not the way.
  A imp got pay special
 What one clear not yet divine be he not a god.
They's rites what by manifest and protocols
    What favored ones, likes a you, must attest.
So no more fuss. Bring me a holy man
    And cast him before me
And then and only then, thee march on ta Rome."
   "Where be these holy men?" I ask.
"What I be new ta this land as much be this task."
   What Phineas say, "I hear Liu tell a legend what say
They dwell in the holes in these cliffs hereabout."
   "Fuck," say Unoculus. "Let's be off
And smoke one a the holy vermin out."
   What grab Polyphemus hand make straightway
A the walls a this wadi when Mr. Hunger say,
  "What be in the bag?"
    "The bag?" I quoth.
"Yeah, the bag. Be it some morsel left a the march?"
  "What bloody march,
    What in an instant the distance yourself secure?"
"So what be in the bag, Ictus?" Hunger again say.

What wif a swipe so sudden
No human eye chart, the bloody imp swipe it away.
        Bold he tore apart the sack
No doubt hopin' there be some exotic snack.
    What be but an ol' man in his bones
        What our imp wifout a reflect swallow whole,
Before Ictus shout out "NO!"
            The crunch a skull, the breast bone snap,
Odysseus prick and balls dangle
            From Hunger's reptilian jaws.
The Greek hero's blood drippin' down
            Leavin' tiny starbursts upon the dusty ground
And churned all way round his foot and calf
        What the imp belch and reel off a laugh
What be the very quake of a thunder peal.
    "Ah, bloody shite a lyin' fuck," say Polyphemus
"If this move us along, bugger the fool.
        Consider Odysseus a gift a me father
            To our little ghoul."
"And this be lunch Herr Hunger?" Ictus say.
    "Nein. This be no Holy Man," the imp say and fart.
"For I but the urge ta take a shite
        Not shake wif the ichor of one a them
            What be a eternal acolyte."
"Off ta the cliffs then," Polyphemus say.
    "To little purpose ol' Odysseus be took away."

"Sides what be this Mr. Odysseus to you, Ictus?
        What he merit be kept in a sack?" ask the imp.
"None ovver," offer Polyphemus, "But this Odysseus
            Usher in a new era a deceit,
        What by his machinations and temper
Forsook his wife and homeland and sunk his fleet.

Also, he insult the gods and they's brood
A what I be one and immortal too.
     Immortal as would be you," say Polyphemus.
    "Go away! You, not an eye ta your name.
 Immortal? How be thee immortal
   What not find the recompense ta heal?
    And I take it ye be done in by this
     Feckless oddity Odysseus"
"What we ta look into it," say Ictus,
    "What upon conquest a Rome
  We bone up on our Discorides and Asclepius
  And set aright our dear Polyphemus sight."
"Who? Be these gods what suffer not such repair
    But it be left ta their starvelings and waystrels?"
Ictus say, "There be Ascelpius
    But I be unaware a any other such."
  "Certain this Asclepius not compare wif the Pandyans
What been drawin' forth darkness from the eyes
  For 1000 years. Sounds like ya need new gods
What always be ready for the takin'.
   Tell ya what, Polyphemus," say Hunger.
"I likes ya. You're a good bloke."
    And wif that he gack up
     Some gob a undigest Greek
And Mr. Hunger stroke it across P.'s eyeless socket,
   And out this Greek goo a new eye grew
Clear, bright, in size and sense worvy of a giant
   And, a course, a gorgeous shade a blue.

And Polyphemus and Unoculus dance,
    Didn't they now.
Shakin' the earf sportin' joy
   Smilin' ear ta ear wif eyes abeamin'.

And Polyphemus laugh, "Huzzah,
     We be ta trap ya a holy man, Mr. Hunger.
And I, ta honor you, lead the way."
     And Scabie lean ta ol' cynic Ictus and say
          "What find his sight lose his mind."

Ictus' cohort search the caves for toothsome Holy Men

And Polyphemus and Unoculus set off
     Ta hunt them a holy man wif Scabie in tow.
And the Roman ask, "Does this holy man be alive
          Thee track? Or will his rotting corpse do?
There be much spoke on this subject in books
     By men wiser than me and you."
"Sure and we forgot ta ask Mr. Humger
     What be his preference," say Polyphemus.
"And more." Say Scabie.
     What be the concourse a the ritual
     Which not done right, what the Hebrews call,
          By the book, what if livin' this holy man must be,
What Mr. Hunger not be took
          A the holy man's commute a immortality."
"And what botched his rite,
     He come to take back the eye,"
          What our giant shudder and cry.
"Quiet down me friend. Nothin' ta fear,"
          Say Urolucus thus.
     "And you Scabie. Shut the fuck up.
Simple we take our holy man alive and if Mr. Hunger
     Like his ascetics poached, we borrow a pot
From Phineas or the Emperor's lot,
     And boil him til tender wif some peppers and leeks
          And chickpeas and kumin a what Apecius speaks

192

And ya see wif your own eyes our Master Imp
  Swallow him down what ta deprive ya seein'
   Your tormenter, Captain Odysseus,
  What but ya hear the sound a the lyin' Achaean
   Ground in Mr. Hunger's jaws."
And the three, they pause,
  Scabie but shrug for fear ta play wif Polyhemus
   Wif Unoculus about what wit be quick
    And cudgel same.
And so silent they be on their way.
   And at nightfall settle at the edge of a lake
At the base of a cliff face pocked with caves.
   And Polyphemus, in new found joyous sight,
Took a giant carp wif his spear. And Unoculus add
  Meat and beer from the forests near
And a hundred a the emperor's terracotta jugs.

And come rosy-fingered dawn
  What the last a the beer and the cook fire be gone,
Polyphemus and Unoculus climb ta a summit
  Above the caves where chased by Boreas, waves
A tall blue grasses weave and dance
  Like flocks a birds what cleave ta their own
Or a quadriga a horses what hasten a chariot.
  Our two giants what wif Scabie kept below
Holdin' Odysseus old abode of a gunny sack
  What ta trap any holy man
What like a mole might scamper from his hole
  And down the hillside when Unoculus and
Polyphemus employ their poles cut a pine
  By pokin' about in the caves
What for ta flush out holy men as so many vermin
  What our patron Mr. Hunger feast upon.

And so the two giants goes about pokin'
    And none ta that a dozen monks flee their burrows
Ta the light a day. And one make right for Scabie
   What our bounder 'pear ta take a monk straight way,
What the crafty devil duck the sack
    What dodge make Scabie stumble
      And the luckless bloke crash upon his back.
"Shite! Shite! Shite," Scabie yell.
    "I can still smell the rancid bastard."
What over Scabie prone anuvver few dozen
  A these holy men flee their homes
What be but holes in the rock.
     And soon wif the giants pokin' a hundred,
Nay a thousand a these holy hermits,
   Scuttle and scurry about the field.
"Fuck, we need but one, and hopes he be holy.
    One a these moles and we set down ta wine."
Says Scabie. Upon what he catch one by the foot
     And step on his neck,
   "Hold on," cry the giants.
And what they rappel down the cliff face and
    Unolocus grab the captured monk
     And snap bofe his legs
What our valiant hunters drag
     Their prey ta Mr. Hunger.
What his holy mates can only watch from afar
    As a Roman pikey and
     Two one-eyed sons a Poseidon
Make their way ta appease their master
    If it please whatever judgment
What this fetid little rat be somehow holy.
    "Gots me doubts," says Scabie
"What this rag please Master Hunger,"

What we shoulda ask for mark or quirk
What by rite or age make these holy.
        Maybe one old. Sage.
    As this be slow, he be younger.
        Master Hunger grow impatient
            And wif demons impatience echo caution."
"Ah fret wif the crones what be doin' your washin',"
        Shout Polyphemus.
"Monk are thy holy." What the wretched monk
        Spit in the cyclops eye."
"Ahhhhh! I be blinded again for the prick a god
        Scorch me sphere. Me one and only."
"I hear it phizz, I does," says Scabie.
        What this be damnable evil
            And such sure qualify as holy.
And for your daring catch
        Certain Master Hunger give you anovver patch."
"Where be he? Where be he what I may
        Kick and beat him about the head and balls?"
Say Scabie, "True. Hunger not divine
        What his meal be alive or dead.
But what relish attend his meal a Odysseus
        On suspect it be livin' flesh he most intend."

And what we return ta camp wif our holy man in tow
    And Master Hunger dance circles
        His rags swirl and billow
Foulin' the air for many leagues
    And bringin' Roman and Serican alike ta their knees.
"What dost thou not just eat the feast thy faithful
        Hath brought thee," Ictus plead.
"Rite be about honor not speed," say Master Hunger.
        What ta join the immortals

I must invite them ta feed."
    And feed they did as awful chunks
      A the nameless holy man be torn away
      As by the wind; as though Boreas had teef
Like a lion or leopard. "See me masters honor me
      Ta me table whilst the hapless monk scream
Bloody murder." And this wind
    Be lappin' at the blood pool
As Mr. Hunger grin and laugh,
      Bone crunchin' in his jowels,
    What the creases a his mouf
   Down flow a froffy, bloody drool.
      His eyes roll back in his head
And he give out a cackle
   And a rapturous groan
What chill me guinea blood ta the bone.

And sudden Herr Hunger's meager bulk
      Writhe and contort,
   What a alien shape ta contrive.
What appear a camel's head wif the fangs
      And tail of a snake.
"And see, Ictus," say Scabie. "See such joints.
    What be antlers like a stag
      And what keep our dear demon Hunger's eyes
    What Muddle wif meek, bovine ears.
Wif scales like a carp and claws like a eagle,
      Wif the soft pads of a tiger.
What there be a broad crown what stretch
    All front ta back a his skull."
"What this be called chimu,"
      Say the Terra Cotta General
    "What lump a bone dub this demon

Be a worvy a heaven."
"But sir," say I. "I have but two questions.
      What be thy name?
            And where be our Hunger
      What be our guide ta Rome?"
So laugh the general, "Me name?
      Me name be Effigy a Meng Tian,
            General ta emperor Qin. And you must be
      Man What Trusts Demons,
            For what it be ta Immortals ta keep their word."
"Yes, yes," guffawed Scabie, "He be
            Homo Qui Confidit Daemonia.
                  Haw, haw, haw, haw. "
"What you sir? What abandon your emperor ta follow
      Us rag tag lot ta Rome."
"I know not emperor as I be but clay
      And so me army
For an effigy owe naught ta man,
      For no man, naught an emperor,
            Can do what a demon can.
Here I be, flesh, what Qin bury me as I be dead.
      A pot more than a warrior.
   No trace a breaf.
And so I be effigy at whim a demons, as I said.
      And the demon what munch upon a saintly monk,
            Mr. Hunger be now giddy wif immortality.
Very devil what breave life inta me,
      Such as it be,
            Simple gratuity or mere afterthought.
      A false reward a instant passage
What compel two cynics and two giants
      What think they have a deal
A instant passage ta Rome

For mere poke about in a hermit hole
    And ta walk a demon his meal.
  Such doth thy gods bring thee ta heel?
      More pity a that.
Better ta be molded mud and stacked in a pit."

And Ictus seize wif despair hurl himself about,
    "How now we get ta Rome
  What our feckless Hunger done run out.
What fools be us ta trust his sort
    What man and demon not be mean ta consort,
Or make oaths, or sign contracts, or shag,
      Or sell his soul or the like.
     Huh? Stout theme for a book!
  Scabie keep mind a me words."
     "Bloody keep your own
What I not be steward a your oral turds," reply Scabie,
  "Recordin' your jabber what be mighty hard work.
Fit for a god. Scribus, maybe.
    Whatever god take account a fools
And what take a plunger ta thy foul rook
    What the arse a poets
      And philosophes be overhung."
And Ictus, "Ah, Scabie. Well said, vile friend.
But in the end what this all before us
    What be banished a the mind a its godly makers,
It be the man what brooding be a least appeal,
    What be his musings what carp pleasure,
Be the bloke what bespoke the truf."
   "Ictus," Scabie say, "Ta be about thy aether,
    Like I be now for a year every day,
Be close ta apportioning the dead.
    See we be ta lead a army a glorified jars

As once are dragon toof Spartoi share the field.
All magic. All fire and brimstone.
Nothing livin' yet heed our appeal."

"Lest it Unoculus and me," say Polyphemus
    Rubbin' a bunion the size of a goat.
"So sorefoot, we march,
    "All the way ta Rome?" says I.
"Yes, ta execute your grandiose plan,
    Doth not it's destiny demand epic proportions
        And a long, tedious tellin' ta boot."

"And no doubt me emperor follow," said Meng Tian.
    "Ta avenge me love a life contra natura.
And certain flesh and blood Meng lead the way.
So not but a march but orderly haste
    For even now Meng's horsemen give chase."

And we pack up camp such as it was
    Ta begin our march ta Rome ta take up our cause.
Though that 'cause' no doubt be deservin'
    A further thought like
    Our road what be rude but clear.
        What the Serican trade wool and silk,
    Tea, porcelain and spices,
For saecula saeculorum pass through here.
    "For if man march ten thousand leagues
        For a wool tunic," say I,
"How much more for an empire a wool tunics,"
        Chime up Scabie.
    What be skunked wif the mind's odor
        A the Cynic what I leave upon him.

And soon our march skirt a desert
      What the Sericans call Han-Hai,
      Gobi ta you.
And there we be put upon
      By a legion a barbarian horsemen
What the Sericans call Hu.
      And from our ranks sudden burst an equites
Upon a tiny paint pony what a mounted Hun
      Rush the reckless bloke and took
His head clean away;
      What our horsemen gallop
      Through the Hun's ranks, headless,
Wavin' his sword movin' toward a sea a pennants
      What encircle their lord.
And straightway scatter that retinue
   And the king and his brilliant horse he did slew.
And circle back ta where his head did fall,
      Pick it up and reattach it ta his neck
      Ta the terror and awe a the Hu
Which we see ranks linin' dunes above us
      Pacin' back and forf on their mounts
         Quite bewildered and circumspect
      Wide eyed wif the betrayal a the cartoons
      The natives tell themselves
   What be a heroes and villains
      And powers reserved for god.
What Polyphemus pull his hood over his head
   And charge the Hu what Unoculus cry.
"Polyphemus, just restored,
      Dost thou again seek ta lose thy eye."
"What if I have no head, I have no eye."
      "No, them pluck it out what see you die."
When the nogless Serie

What one might guess a the headless
What be just for fun for again
   Charge the ranks a Huns head on
And what didn't the barbaries fled.

What we drew ranks and head south
   Skirtin' the Gobi and the Emodian Mountains,
Light a load what our terra cotta grunts
      Need neiver food nor drink,
   Nor rest nor a bit a cunny or the like.
So's Scabie, the giants, the 40 man retinue under Phineas
      And yours truly be well-refreshed;
      And certain we be prudent ta avoid
      The liu sha a the Tarim Basin
   A the Kushan Empire what mass be threat
      Ta reduce our force ta pottery shards.

And what I settlie in and coax a Scabie ta tell
   A tale what ta relate these bleak surroundin's,
   And I ask, dear reader,
      What his answer shock thee
      As it done me.
      "There be none a here worth tellin'," Scabie say,
For this be the Silk Road
   Where ta be is ta but buy and sell.
What the desert leagues drone on
   And Helius what drive his chariot across the sky
Stop direct above wif his pantin' steeds.
   What drive a man ta here traverse be not fancy
Nor the blood rites or odd jobs a gods, but greed.
   What the forge a daylight
      In its utter tedium be antecede.
And this be true a this whole we thus traverse.

For norf there be a lineage a Greek Alexander'
    The same what your Dog Diogenes done slander.
And even now a emissary a the Pandyan a Dramira
    What be received by Rome and Augustus at Antioch
And at this very moment travel ta thy favver's home."
    And I, "My ain't we well-informed a Romulus hearth,
Years away and not a acta diurnal about."
    Says Scabie, "Don't ask for tales
        What but thy mock out of fear.
What though many days in our journey we be
    All realize Rome still be thousands a leagues a here.
We be wary a travails and travel what outstrip
    Herodotus or Strabo in damnable
        Distance and domains."

Ictus' retinue encounters two monks

And as we take pains ta transit
    A swift flowin' stream
What cut Old Tea House Road,
    Appear two monks, one dessicate and t'other fat
As though nature miscribe its mean,
    What their sum be normal
        But what apart be extreme.
And they hang down their arms and hands
    What sway to and fro
 Wif they's toes point inwards and their legs bowed,
    A walk some wit might call lumber.
Scabie draw his pugio, his blood high,
    What Phineas and his legion laugh
And Meng and his 8000
    What Scabie grow purple like a Tuscan grape
And veined like a rose leaf wif the sun behind.

And turn on his comrades, "Thy lot be not friends.
Here I lay thee waste but thee amend thy laughter.
        What I be but goose ta you."
"Dear Scabie," say I. "Do you be whelmed wif fever.
    For you be here slay for a laugh sans anovver thought.
        These monks be not threat.
        But hear that burblin' sound,
It be not stream but the way they pray
        Sure they be here ta receive us in peace and love.
What Unoculus just inform, we be invite ta a feast.
        Time ta fuck and pass on all your milky progeny
    And proper sop thy ample belly
            Honied sparrows and candied doves
        Covered in exotic creams and gravies.
        And no doubt we will soon be a this state;
        Fat, drunk and satiate.
For as Apicius write the greater the height
    The more savory the gravy
            What glory be this!
    These sauces be born a mountains and mists."

And the monks' vacant stares
        Empty no doubt ta bid utter contentment
    Nod in ascent, "We come in peace,"
        And beckon me and Scabie, our two giants,
    Phineas and a the Seres force only Meng
And his lieutenants what leave their troops behind
    For the climb thus be too narrow.

"See, Scabie. There be cauldrons a creams and gravies
    Wif ladles the size a skulls.
And madies what a civility be given
        Where thy nest thy face

What between silk sheets gentle nature hast riven."
And like a beast under his master's soothin' stroke,
    Scabie relent, high strung such he be,
Broke down and wept. What Polyphemus say,
    "What we be better served a our hosts
What our Scabie be in the weeds shittin' out gruel
    Than the drama we see here
What out duel Aeschylus on top a Sophocles
    And Euripides too."
Ta what Unoculus say,
    "And what digest a you guineas
  Be a bloody stool a Plautus,
    What Scabie be his constant fool."

What our Bodhi guides turn us Norf
    Into the mountains call the Himalayas
      What our pass be not arduous
  As it be oft traveled, footworn
    And wept upon by bofe men and gods.
And on the third day two mastiffs
    What sport four eyes each
  Snufflin' among the rocks
    What fright our guides.
And soon follow a figure all blue robed in red
    Three eyes with five flamin' skulls in his diadem
    Wif a noose danglin' a one hand,
  A cinch a hemp 'bout a shufflin' buffalo's neck.
And flush by the hounds from our birch tree privy
    This three-eyed bloke lasso one our guinea boys
And snatch him from the ranks
  What scatter the troop
    As a loosen joist might collapse a roof
  Or a thunder clap a gaggle a geese.

And one the black dogs make for the wounded grunt,
What one a our guides,
The monk what be low and wide.
What the holy bloke pull from his cloak
A rod a silver what mere touch
Upon the mastiff's snout,
The fiend froze mid-stroke and then
Drop ta ground, its flank a rupture
What the bowels stream out.
And me incensed paisan grab their spears
And make short work a the other dog.
Yama as this demon be called retreat frough the brush
Wif his prize, the corpse a one Lucius Tullus,
A lad, oh I dunno, like any ovver
What for a few coppers fill a rich lad's conscript,
What no one but his mum, and I not be sure ere that,
Give a shit a him livin' or dyin'.
But in our histories he a been a brave lad
If it a come ta it. But it did not.
So he be takin' by some barbies' nightmares,
What, if drawin' breaf be naught 'nuff a hell,
The callow confederate in this monster, Yama,
What be the Indoo god a death.
And dispose a Indoo hell
What ere all hell's be trace.
Though we do have a Pluto a home
But we Romans die enough
He don't got ta beat the bush,
Mount on a ox wif dogs.
Too young our Lucius be gone
And we be but 37 Romans strong
Less there be will ta count me and Scabie.
And as for me, I soon as strip the bloody state

A Romulees's patrimony and any memory a it.
How come a man ta hate his homeland?
Let me count the ways.
No, let Pythagoras count and fall wide a the mark.
As I recount the ways
What be these very words before thee.

"A this Yama, friends. We must remain aware,"
Say Badal, a monk a mere skin and bones.
"Beware!" shout Scabie. "Where be this Yama
What that ya brought us here?"
"Sir, this Yama be everywhere
What there be souls ta snatch," Badal say.
"Not in Rome or the dozen years
What I wander the Appian Way."
"Yama prove true so wanton a souls
What he so dog in life
What, weary and chaste with regret,
See his blessings in dyin'
And raise him to a god."
"Now, see. Badal talk a me exile," says I,
What so forlorn I wish ta die.
Not like our Ajax what suffer and moan
A maggot strewn festerin' wound. But I be bitter
A the gash ta me soul me fellows
What regard me not fit ta live a lie."
"Or what contrive verbal knots
'Til thy betters see ya fit ta be tied," laughed Scabie.
"Who be this Ajax a the maggoty wound.
For Yama suffer such too.
Did this Ajax kick his movver?"
"No, worse. He frew rocks at her hearse," smirk Scabie.
What Ictus fume, "What new cynic be you.

What dismiss me cynicism, austere, sincere,
    Wifout sinecure and bane a the rich."
"What them Roman senators hurl thee in a ditch.
    Nay have their slaves or pay some plebes
Toss thee away like so much trash," Scabie say.
    "Or cast a some isle even they not name or covet.
I tire a thee cynic and thy empty rhetoric."
    And the portly monk step to and
        Keep the two guineas from comin' ta blows.
"Peace bruvvers, as our master would wish."
    "Well then let's meet the bugger and share a dish.
Me belly make a rash thing a me mouf," say Scabie.
    "Then this fullness serve thee well
For our master not utter a word
    But speak by gesture, grunts and smell."
"Smell?" ask I. "As you blokes," says he, "Use your 'what'
    For your when, your wheres,
        And your whiches, and whys.
That what stink and a what be a the foulest hole
    Be the most sacred airs a our holiest monk."

Ictus' and Velius' tearful reunion

What after a ten day march the monks
    Point skyward ta a monastery in the clouds.
And what we be meet by a throng in white shrouds
    Followed by the abbott, the curate, the bloody head monk.
        And, here I swear on me mum's chuff,
      As death trumps fate,
This abbott be none over than me dear friend Velius.
    What see me in his portico and I he,
We cleave each ta the ovver
    And weep in his portico, weep so many tears

His people wade ankle deep in our rheumy seep,
    What for the rain and the weary shufflin' a feet,
    It be silent. Not a peep. What our gallant red man
Hold me fair head in betwixt his hands
    And kiss me cheek upon cheek,
As be I so whelmed wif emotion I could not speak.
    So there froze as shadow fell upon the dial,
    And for many days after
All the while bathe in the others love.
    Such affection had I for no ovver being
What me jealous say not this what too be not the first
        But express a some deeper affection
What be beyond man and man, man and boy
    A love of a deeper nature.
For do not us Romans love each other
        Because we can abide in bed anovver creature.
What be me monk the furriest a men,
    I ne'er balk or scruple ta attend his bed again.
And shall honor the feces he daubed in me hair.
    And never wash its impious stink out from there,
What ta show me kinship wif all the world.
    And all livin' creatures we enlight as our concubine
And roll the world over and take it from behind.

Velius' gives his Magician, Tessala, to Ictus

As the very stone a the monastery
    Be me temper a our stay; calm, cool and resolute
        And one day while huntin' with Velius
    And a small retinue
        What include Phineas and Meng,
We come upon that dreadful thing,
        Yama upon his ox.

208

What Velius call his magician, one Tessala.
What bold step forward and
    Face this god a the underworld
    Wif two burnished silver batons
What he scuff together
    And point at the Hindoo monster.
What leap forth bolts not unknown ta Zeus,
    What strike Yama dead, or it seem so,
And cook his ox in its own humors
    What I must abide it smelt good.
And the monastery entire enjoy a feast
    As wif their bare hands
    The monks, entrails and all, fell upon the beast.

Ictus and his retinue bid adieu to Velius;
Velius maks a gift of his wizard, Tessala.

But I marvel at this Tessala's wand.
    "O yes, yes, yes," offer the fat monk
What name be Pang Heshang. "Master Velius
    Be very fond a his magician.
And Velius appear wif a cithara about his neck
    And two large black parchment cones
    Placed either side a his throne.
And Tessala lurk close by twistin' brass nipples
    On a polished box wif clear glass eggs
    What glow through the grill on the top.
    And what Velius shred the strings a his cithar
    A wail went out, plaintiff, dire.
What echo and boom up and down the mountains.
    And Scabie cry, "What the fuck!?"
As a cacophony of raving sound
    Scream across the sky.

"Our Master Velius play the Music a the Spheres,"
    D'un he now," say Pang,
  "A what the Greeks a Bactria teach,
What be harmonious wif the trade roads
        And makin' money. What be sister ta beer
  What too make one forget one's debts.
      What flow east ta west
As do the humors under me skin
      And the slaves what embody there's."

And we feasted there a fortnight,
  A red rice and yak, pork fat and buckwheat.

Note: At this point an exasperated Rastus mocks Jesus in the Garden
of Gethsemane by repeating in the margins his words "Pater mi, si
possible est transeat a me calix iste" ('My Father, if it is possible, may
this cup be taken from me.') The cup being his penance transcribing
the text of Canis Ictus.

    What we bid adieu our gracious host.
And weep he and I in one the ovver's embrace
  What seem anovver fortnight
    For Velius have a most uncommon scent
And a grip what not soon leave thy bones.
    And wif Velius' bawlin' and tearin'
      At his bright red, louse infested, musky hair
  Which offer much for it grow everywhere,
      On his behalf had his minister speak.
"It may be but his heart be slosh wif beers
      What our master here rain a vat a tears
  What watch your scrawny guinea rear
Fade into the mountain mist.
  O shite. It be too much bear.

Wait as our king must take a piss."
What Velius do right there upon the ground.
What stamp his holiness the spot
And bubble up from the yellow mud
A new found spring a the clearest, sweetest water
This pilgrim ever have the honor ta drink,
What Seneca stake be an altar erect and a sink.
And when we all partake a this nestling lake,
The minister continue, "King Ictus or soon ta be,"
At which me blush and scan the ground,
"Please accept me gift ta you
A me magician Tessala what many wonders
And miracles be at his behest.
What we know a Magus, Apollonius and Jesus
The great magicians a the West.
What me Tessala prove out such fakers what
We know a them and they not a us,
Even this Jesus what be tattooed
A many omens and spells and traveled
Ta nearby Zhung and Kirat, what we see such signs,
As a priest, what be this Thoma,
A former slave from the West
What be flogged and expelled as a fraud.
Or this Magus what very now marvel Rome
What he soars above and raisin' the dead
What bofe but be raised a sorcery,
What Tessala ta Rome contest lest this Magus flee,
What be all what save his ass,
Bundle up his charms and potions and cons
And in a puff a smoke vanish inta anonymity."
And a short, gaunt man come forf
Bow before Velius what command him take leave,
What the Master, his magus and

His order a monks grieve.
What I suggest we be on our way
When Tessala wave us round. What I mean
Meng's manikins, Phineas's centuriae, Polyphemus,
Unoculus, Scabie and me.
What sudden we began ta heave and toss
And slow be carried aloft
What the air itself churn
Like watery Karybdis off the shore a Messina
What many ships be lost.
The same what by numbers
Voragus and Procellus reckon.
Whevver water or air, a maelstrom
Contrive ta hold thee under
And what be value needful a its force
Ta wrench a body or a ship asunder.
We now impaled,
Our backs pressed ta the whirlin' wall,
What wif Tessala's conjure
A deep calm fall over us all.
What might be a sleep or trance
What ta be part a everythin'
Ravver than its better part.
What we be embark on a larger dance
Ravver than be tinder
What mere entertain a spark.
Thus, alight in a maelstrom a fire
Ere the calm and still a the mute palaver
A Parmenides eternity
We be given over ta Tessala's spell
And from the hold we be surprised
By the all wise and Bohdi Velius as well.

End of Part III.

Part IV. Rome Conquered

Tessala instantaneously transports Ictus and his army back to Rome

What a sudden as it be said,
    We 'come back ta earf.'
Meng's army. The Roman company,
    Our one-eyed giants even Scabie,
What say "Where be we?"
    "Ask that shepherd, hence."
"Hence? Doth not thou mean there?
    What 'hence' bespeak a time.
And 'there' a where."
    "What yes, Scabie. I misspoke.
Ask a that dear shepherd yonder there.
    And be clear ta take no time in its doing.
What by your lights should a been
    Before ya left here."
And off in the distance Scabie
    Scratchin' his balls and rubbin' his chin
Chat wif great articulatin' cycles
    What find where on earf' are we.
"Damn Ictus. We be in Italy
    What this shepherd speak Latin
      Wif a ol' Volscian accent.
    We be in the shadow a Mount Circeii.
What our shepherd suspect
    We be but 30 leagues from Rome."
What Tessala appear what forgo embrace
    And Velius in full battle gear.

213

"Velius what be here in this place?"
   "Ah, I see me marvel, Tessala,
      Set thee down the perfect spot
     Action at a distance is what we got."
"Also," pant Scabie. "The shepherd say
     A race a monsters wifout flesh
Have laid siege a this place."
    "The Spartoi," I answered.
       "Yes. The very same you affront."
"What? Affront? What be my offense?"
    "Dunno exact," say Scabie,
"But ya call Ekhion, their general, a cunt."
    "Nooooo?" Fend I.
"Aye. Fuck you.
    And all them be cunts by your diplomacy."
"Cunts ya say. And they not abide this?
    I recollect they call you a twat."
"Ah, so what. I be called worse
    And much more since I be cursed wif you."
And Meng say, "How strong be these Spartoi?"
    "10,000," says I "when we parted."
"10,000!" laugh Meng. "10,000!" repeat Phineas
    And the retinue laugh again.

Ictus goes forth to make peace with the Spartoi

Anuvver fuckin' rosy fingered dawn
    What this morn the rose be up me ass
For I be off ta entreat the Spartoi
     Ta rejoin our ranks
What sure ta put a prickle in me crack.
   I, what be Ictus what return home
A few leagues from the devils a Rome,

Crassus, Cicero, Caesar
And a million more content
        Wif their backsides ta their betters.
What cynic, say you,
        What shun his bucket for a sword.
    What I say ambition be a skill best honed
        By one what 'til his late autumn shun it.
What leave the known end ta the hidebound
        When the book be late marked and closed
And the candle wax be puddled and hard.
        What wrapped in the cold
One venture out ta draw near
        The keenin' cry in the dark wood
                And know it.
        Ta kill the wolf cubs in their den
For me tale a exile be me fate
    What I be so endowed wif these armies
    A the dead what empty out Avernus
        And every Hell what for the chance
Ta blot out this earthly hell what be Rome.
        Thus chosen I must go alone
Several leagues ta me comrade Spartoi,
    Ta Ekhion and Peleorus
What a all human content be not fair,
    Such that what be human be all a what's foul.

Note: A desperate Rastus again mocks Jesus crying out in the margins
Christ's plea from the cross, "Deus meus, deus meus, ut quid
dereliquisti me?" ('My God, my god. Why has thou forsaken me.')
Another obvious reference to his intolerable penance.

What a Spartoi lookout see lone Ictus,
    Make way ta the encampment a this bony race

What Ekhion, Pelorus, Chthonius,
>   Hyperenor and Udaeus come apace.
"Well, if it ain't our little cynic shite," shout Udaeus.
>   "What from his direct, take flight a Rome
And abandon all what be fools ta follow
>   And fall, what no doubt, this very day ta Roman gallows.

Ictus: "Fuck you, Udaeus. Save thy temper
>   Ere I tell me tale.
Yonder not three leagues, I bear a force a 8000
>   Warriors from far away Seres
And a company a Centurions
>   Bitter a what be abandonment by Crassus at Parthia.
Plus two one eyed giants, me silent armed monk, Velius,
>   And his most marvelous genie, Tessala.
Poise we be between blandishment, bitterness,
>   Martial impulse, and hatred a empire.
And what give thee now sure be me bald flattery.
>   What wif you stout blokes
What dispatch Hilarus wif a few swipes and strokes
>   Storm Rome
>   And drive the fuckin' guinea lot inta the sea.

Note: Rastus's marginalia reads, "EXCOMMUNICARE ME,
OBSECRO!" ('Excommunicate me. I beg you.')

Us, what spite all possessions,
>   What be not a the manner a spoils,
What but for a few not eat nor drink nor fuck,
>   What so thorough be our natures
>   We drive all such impulse from the earf
What men blindly call their natural lot."

Ekhion: "The same what we be about.
   A few thousand more be not despised.
But one thing: Where be that other blackguard, Scabie?"

Ictus: "He be true and
            At a brazed hog's kidney or two as we speak."

Ekhion: "If we join your gang.
            May we see him hanged,
Even as we spare you
   What be ta wield the noose."

Ictus: "What be your natures so prickly
            What want a nothin'?"

Ekhion: "What pricks be ta know such folly
      What that filfy noxious, glutton, Scabie embody
         And put forbearance beyond the light."

Ictus: "Ekhion, what know thee a forbearance
         What not desire what be forborne?
      Join us. Perhaps we hang Scabie.
         Perhaps we strip him and paint him blue
Like one do a that barbarous isle, Britannia,
      And wif bow let him hoot and howl
         And ovverwise defame Crassus name.
Until the Romans send some legion out
      Ta cut him down and like Hector drag his corpse
         About the city walls
Whilst we whoop wif laughter
      At our dear Scabie's final stunt
Anovver greedy cunt
      Bouncin' behind a chariot at the end of a rope."

Note: Here Rastus cries out in the margins "Tantum ut interficias me." ('Just kill me.')

Ekhion: "Here we thought you two be close."

Ictus: "Not so close I slit his throat.
        But ta improve me run at empire
What so zealous the gods and fate me cast."

Ekhion: "Counter ta thy former state.
    Give us ere our nature
        What in mere words we debate.

Ictus agrees to hang Scabiopilus

Ictus: "Alright. Agreed. You join our avengin' army
    And in return I'll hang Scabie."

    And thus say Ekhion, "We shall return."
Now, Scabie be no patriot what be eager
    Ta take one for the cause
When the cause be but vengeance and coin.
  What such tales not be endless lies
    What might give the shite infinite pause.
He lend a lad a spear ta fall on
    What we might pontoon his body
        Across a frosty creek,
And naught the inheritance a the weak and meek
    But ta dip their purses as they queue.
Besides I canna' think a one such sacrifice
    For good a fellow man
What facts don't make me laugh

218

When fallacy and fantasy get its due.
So I return wif the Spartoi in tow,
   10,000 more what a silent cheer resound,
Suspicious a comrades what be wifout flesh
       By one's what be but clay
And certain the ovver way around.
    And Phineas's forty what be overwhelmed
And a Roman philosopher and certain no king,
   What echo a civil mutiny, at the helm.

But Ictus be not deterred what he be little aware
    Such be power close his mind ta earthly things
What so singular and celestial be his desires
      What he be king.
"Scabie," Ictus call. "There be news
    What noble act what be thine ta choose.
'Pears the Spartoi here can't stand the sight a ya,
    Nor thy spittled harangues and swinely sack."

And Scabie "What these ta speak a discomfit mien
    What be but foul death o'erweaned."

"Scabie listen. They propose thee be hanged
     And I concur. As what appear ta the audience
     A casualty a casual barter
   For future king and cause make thee a martyr."

"Certain Ictus," say Scabie.
     "Thee be a con and a cur.
   Constant ta spirit a con
    What I be aim and mark."

What Velius hearin' this barney

Amble the midst a the three great armies
Wif worvy Tessala in tow.
And what silence restored, Velius's genie
Begin ta speak: "Me master, Velius, and I
Care neiver for this Scabie.
No greater brigand and bounder there be
Since that Achaean shite Odysseus ply the sea.
Less Crassus and his venal ilk
Have mocked the gods and
Cast the world a their own folly,
Lest the righteous muse a their lust for lolly."

"Right but be not I what crack the Greeks head
Like an egg dashed in a sling," said Scabie.

"That not be the ways I remembers it,"
Say Polyphemus.

"See, Scabie," says Ictus. "That be the very thing
What by hangin' thee might atone.
And when I be king, I pardon thee as
But petty rogue or misguided quisling
Such that songs be wrote
And schoolchildren sing
A the lessons a probity
What thy sins contravene."

And Scabie say "Nay. Bloody fuckin' nay,"
As a noose be wrapped about his neck.
"What be ye treat me this way, Ictus;
What be comrades through many trials."

"Nuffin' personal," says Ictus.

"One what need these 10,000 armed
But one drunken, feckless thug.
    Though every tale be made stout
        A one or two."

And Scabie's body drop and for a bit
    Wriggle like fish on a line.
And a great huzzah went up among
    The attendin' troops
For out a tedium of a soldier's life, any murder
    Be the occasion a music, meat and wine.

However, at this point in the margins this remark made by Tessala
appears in decidedly corrupted Latin. "Tessala dicit; 'parci tamqua
muta ilum dimittae exercitus.'" Which presumably should read 'parce
tamquam muta illum dimittam exercitus' or 'spare this brute as with
him I will spare your armies." What's odd is that the further plot of
the poem follows the note in which Scabiopilus is spared, not the
original text where he's hanged presumably followed by a protracted
war between Ictus' forces and the forces of Rome. Scholars such as
German paleographer Dr. Hans Frederick von Lockinkopf and
French mystic and appeasiologist Madame Constance Sifflet
Pourchien surmise that Father Rasmus, saddled by the Pope with the
penance of transcription and bored with his task simply destroyed the
original lengthy ending by the decidedly long-winded Canis Ictus
himself and wrote a shorter ending forging Ictus' hand. He then
made a copy to appear to be the original on some corrupted sheets of
vellum and then transcribed his forgery. Since no one ever read the
text, over the centuries none have been the wiser. Also note the bulk
of the rebel force partakes of neither 'meat nor wine' perhaps a
contextual error on Rasmus' part."

What step forth Velius and his wizard Tessala.
What set forth, "Hang not this cutpurse Scabie
What be a use ta me as Ictus' giants be ta Vulcan."
What Velius shook his arms and danced about
And in show a good will gather Scabie inta
His arms and legs,
What Meng lean ta Ictus and whisper,
"Vos scitis quod est simis?"
And what all wrapped ta listen ta
What this Tessala give voice
What by conjure transport this mighty force.
"A thief like Scabie be wed ta stealth.
What we take this device and make six more
And bring down the Roman aqueducts
What they no longer thirst for conquest
But ta see the days end.
And this wizard held forth a simple rod
No longer nor thicker a the grip on a hod,
Wif a pendulum attach ta one side
And a hammer ta the ovver.
What the pendulum swing the hammer pound
And when Tessala set this engine upon the ground
Soon the earf beneath our feet commence
Ta tingle and quiver and the stonework sway.
The piston keep its swing as our balance give way,
And the plain begin ta hum and dance
And the music a this sphere be of a tune
What the earf quake
What leave naught standin' but in ruin.
And startle our armies a clay and bones.
And as sudden wif but a touch
Tessala stop the quake
What his rude machine did make.

222

"Here be me plan," Tessala say.
    "Rome's aqueducts have their origins in the East
Where the snow melts and springs are born.
    Thus Meng and Ekhion lead their force
Ta the West what this Crassus think
    Be the nature a your attack.
While Phineas and his forty be wif me and Scabie
      What hurry east what Roman set upon Roman,
  Tallyin' any guards, or patrols or messengers
    Wif arrow, knife or garrote
Whilst me and me cutpurse lay me engines
    Against the aqueduct walls
What all them fall and leave
    The bloody Seven Hills high and dry.
Among skeletons and painted pottery
    There be no spies."

"What we engage the Romans on the plains
    Southwest a the city?" ask Ekhion.
"What thy will," say Tessala.
    "But as little blood be shed a either side
If you have your forces balk
  And keep a distance whilst me crew
    Plant these vibratin' rods
  What we leave ta do their work
    Whilst Rome wilt like a daisy a these labors
And their fields and cattle die
    And their mills fall silent.
  Lest they drink a the Tiber
    Or foul springs,
Then what be sent ta repair
    In the cloak a night creep from the city

What thee in their hunger and despair
Fall upon wif or wifout pity,
   Whatever thy custom and temper be.
But recall Roman hills be prowled
     By those predatory by nature.
       Raised by wolves.
So beware what be any incline ta spare such."

When a rock becomes a rocket, or the trajectory of conquest

And enamored a Science's plan,
  For what mean this Sun Tzu rubbish ta them
   What a whim a some bloody emperor
They be by a bellows blast cast and cooked
      A Avernus inta clay men
   What Tessala like the pneuma a the Hebrew god
    Shock this dirt ta life again.
    Meng and Ekhion move their main force
Northwest toward Ostia along the coast
  What have Crassus surmise we strangers
    Lay siege a that great port
   And cut off supplies ta Rome.
And immediate a large force gather ta our Norfeast
   Intent on drivin' us inta the sea,
What as we plan set up camp
    And Tessala prepare many engines,
Several planks wif gut and holes
    What the Seres fire 2000 arrows
     Wif the flick of a single lever
And missiles wif cylinders a black powder
     What explode the deck of a Roman merchant
And a couple a catapults and trebuchets,
   What monstrous devices we possess,

Made a their own fine Roma pine
    And bronze what keep the guineas away.
What Ictus prance before this force
      What be clear ta the Roman view
And infuriate the aristocracy
      What merely exiled
What they coulda, wifout censure or outcry,
         Slew.

The Wizard Tessala brings down the Roman Aqueducts

And meanwhile a hundred clay pot Seres
     And another 100 gaunt ta a fault Spartoi
Wif Tessala and noxious Scabie
     Made haste a the aqueducts
   And their springs ta the east;
The Appia what most lie underground
     And fed the Forum Boarium;
Old Anio what be raised on crutches;
     And Marcio what tower over the countryside
Ta flow ta the Capitoline; and Tepula at Subiaco;
     And Julia; And Virgo; and Alsietina what at Trastevere
    Mock battles were fought upon its lake.
  At each a machine what make the earf rumble
Be placed wif pendulum wif perpetual swing
     And soon the countryside around began ta heave
And shake, rivers flowed backwards
   Or changed their course. Lakes emptied
    As though mere mug toppled in a tavern.
And indeed all of the aqueducts came down.
   What because a the interconnect a stone
     Some plunge many leagues and beyond repair.
So Ovid, "carpite florem".

But Ictus be not that
What means the maid in your poem
What pluck Rome's rancid flower,
    Before of its wicked nature
        It fall a its own accord.
And what be accord by discord
        Be discord and ne'er accord.
Rome itself, pox and all, be the maid
    What forestall old age
    By fallin' victim ta this venomous cynic's
        Raging tutelage.
And what soon a mob turn on the Senate
        And bring bleedin' down the whole lot
    Upon the concourse and feed 'em ta the dogs.
And what first be but a trickle
        Come ta surge souf upon the Appian Way,
What we deny the people water
    What slivverin' from the sea our kind be spared
        For anuvver day.
    And the troops lay down their arms
Made familiar wif the natural order
        What put water ahead a war
That such be fought over the former.
        And the prattle what be Laotze's undermindin'
    What be all ta proverbial and the like
        Ta the army a Meng's clay shards
            What they be animate as flesh and blood.
What those be deprive a water be lowest
    What be bleak and rash ta seek it.
        Not in BEIN' it,
    What our philosophers boast they be
        Ta beguile us what be our betters.
What instead the simple relish bein' in it

Like the beasts.

Polyphemus farts

Polyphemus say ta Unoculus "All this war
      Wearies me. This bloodlettin'
Parches me heart and be scant by me soul.
      What say we abandon this carnage
I be a mind ta eat every clam
         What sponge off the Tyrrenean Sea
And take what prescribe a that Roman sawbones,
      Asclepius, by way a remedy,
        What it be a genial cure,
What the old crow scrip say "Be no healf
      But ya stuff your belly."
    And drive force downward the bloody ennui.
   But, second thought if such be thinkin',
      Leave room for a vat a poached figs and honey
   And a good mead or ale for drinkin'."
And our two giants sat a pub
      On the shore at Ostia
What port be the call a every exotic food or drink
      Came a empire,
Such our one-eyed heroes feast
    Upon every fruit and fish, legume and beast
What walk the earf, organ and sinew a what be left
      A days slaughter a the coliseum.
What if ya not be their ta see 'em
    Some bloke down the road a grill up its kidney,
Pan fry its liver or braze its heart in garum.
   Honey up its toasted balls or deep fry its bladder
No matter what the wild bugger be
      Or what the gods call 'em.

So our giants feast a week,
　　What turn ta two,
For the goose liver be so sweet
　　As the wine cut wif defrutum.
And doth there be a cosmic rumble
　　From the portage about Polyphemus' middle.
"Fuck! And just the cakes come off the griddle.
　　I fart soon and it be a mighty blast,
For, and take this fair warnin'
　　I not rise ta shit the mornin' two weeks ago
　　　　What we, like our kin Herakles,
　　Take up the labor a this repast."

But Unolocus say "For certain,
　　Not yet a blow be struck."
　　"No, me friend. But both sides be in lieu
A raised arms a which me belly anticipate the blow.
　　Doth it not strain and growl
　　　　Like a siege engine's gears and riggin's.
Doth not me breath stink a death
　　So long it be strangled wif nourishment.
　　I fear for these Romans what not err a me,
　　　　But serve me wine wif defrutum, onions
　　And turnips and clams and eels from the sea."
But sudden and sure as be a Cumae augury,
　　What fortune like his eye he have but one
　　His giant's asshole shudder like a thunderclap
　　　　Wif a foul and savage thrust,
　　His galactic repast in such violent strife.
　　　　Garlic fall upon the garum,
　　Calamari dispute the honeyed dormice,
　　　　And turnips antagonize the figs,
And there still be bits a gladiator in that bear's belly

And the pottage be a month old
So the pork therein be oft bought and sold.
So hard be just the blast it mock Aeolus.
But a smell. A green gaseous vapor fell
Upon Latina and Caserta and Neapolis in turn
Ta man, woman and child and livestock all,
Wif the wild fish and fowl fell down in a swoon.
Some do say ta this day the sun turned away.
And the Tyrrenean Sea in its entirety
Turned to a fetid lagoon
What every creature under its auspice
Bear the settlin' stink, and thus be afflict
And soon swoon and what be its life blood cease.

And as the gas be release a his paunch
The great greasy bands a sinew
What line his haunches give way
Ta a turd what art compare ta
What Mons Vesuvius convulse
Wif such force noble historians
What be Sallust and Livy confound
The two what I mean the volcano
What smuvver Pompeii
As though she be but a recalcitrant slave
And our one-eyed giants monumental shit
What destroy the commonweal souf a Rome
And norf a it.
And poison the Tyrrenean Sea all about wif
Festerin' matter, compost a the noblest quality
Bussed many leagues
From the four corners of the earf
Or whatever angles your ancestors judge its girf.
And such the myf grew what

This Corsica and Sardinia
　Be but fertile lumps a the giant Polyphemus' shite
What the latter namesake be a the tiny fish
What nibble their own in the cyclops's foetid dish
　What the giant imbibe in oil by the barrel
What put the bloody Roman people in such peril.

Without the Aqueducts Rome withers like Crassus' ballsack

And what ta watch the woe bestowed an empire.
　What such great baggage ta unhook and dislodge.
What histories ignore and gods false.
　　A pitiable poison what seep the dissolute
Ta waste a culture ta the root.
　　　For lack a water the empire wither away,
　　　　What might give some future pause,
　As these what flow ten abreast outta Rome
　　And down the Appian way
　Like so much human muck out the Cloacina.
What, red cheeked, witness blandishments and flatteries
　A the empires splashing fountains
　　And bait a bread and games.
All gone a the bile a one little man,
　Meself what offer nuffin
　　But what destiny choose ta take.
So I be a me Spartoi or Seres band
　Not a your race but of some ovver grand
In his turpitude, coddle wifout creed or statute
　In the fist a fate.
And all these great Roman men
　Can go fuck themselves what they banish me.
For I claim not their stature
　But say I come ta mock it.

And do tell, who have the fickle gods heard?
　　　　Today we march on Crassus and a small hoard
What hope the charred flesh a the Ara Martis and
　　　　The Aedis Martis and the Circus Flaminius
Steal some a me thunder what err they beset
　　　　　As the thunder be given ta me by Jupiter hisself
For I be naught this nor that
　　　And live ta not know what thunder be,
Nor be of them what airs its presence.

Velius slays Crassus' mastiffs

And on the field Crassus, all bronze armor
　　　　And flanked by four huge mastiffs.
What face Velius in an open copse a spruce,
　　　What Crassus loose his curs upon Velius
What wiffout shield or sword attend the bloody hord
　　　　What one dog be he take upon by his tail,
What Velius slam against a tree severing
　　　　　Each from each midbody. And a second catch
By its open jaws and snap it twain
　　　　And rip and tear the bandy sinew
What anuvver wretch fall again.
　　And third mutt what Velius dislodge a spruce
And struck it about its flanks crushin' bofe its legs
　　　　What his dung and bile steamin'
　　　　　　Collapse upon the ground,
　　　What mewin' crawl ta Crassus feet and die.
What the fourf turn tail and run
　　　　Abandonin' his master ta exile upon Velius's field.

231

Velius slays Crassus

What Crassus launch a fierce attack
    And Velius at his lorica
        Wif ease snap the Roman's back.
What Crassus lay upon the ground
    Hands up at the elbows shakin' out,
And fright a death in his eyes.
      And Velius stomp his legs what Crassus howl.
  And this all the while what the Roman
    Lord a lands, frothin', wild eyed
What Velius pluck out the same
    And swallow them whole
And dig about the landlord's entrails
     Ta raise up gobs and partake a the smell.
And snap off his jaw
   And fling it ta the vultures
     What broad wings flail akimbo, jig nearby.

And as Velius pick skull from brain
    There be no rage
But innocence lookin' about and perhaps a toss
    Or what semblance a kiss
  Upon a scrap a Crassus' mangled flesh
Or pound the muck a his breast
    What by blows had been throw open
  Like the Ancient Gates a the Hebrews
What let the King a Glory enter
    And splash around a bit.
What Velius lift up poor Crassus' entrails
    Like a washer woman at her tub
And press back his lips and smile, all toof,
      At his handiwork

What be a remedy for the rich
What any just god be high ta recommend.

And the Spartoi and our clay funerary
    Barely flex their wares
  In this most uncommon of foreign wars.
Both born a death deliver little
  What possess no earthly hunger.
This be irony what test Agathon or Andronicus,
  The weepin' and fallin' hair sot wif tears
    What send Telos reelin'.
For what be gods
  But ta betoken our burlesque,
Baubles what shape our duress.

And what the war sated guinea royals
    Still thirst for battle;
  On the right flank be the Spartoi
What evoke a their very visage, the rattle a death.
  And upon the left our clay Seres
What myfs make animate a god's breath,
  And in between be Phineas
    And his enlightened crew.
And pinch as I be on exile's shore
    In crush a hungry cancer's claw
Many foul Romans form up ta be slew
  Such that all that day and that night
A blood torrent a Rome supplant the Tiber,
  A brew what one here
    These new Jews see fit ta drink
    And ere their ichor be a one well.
But these, these Romans be a fever
    Ta occupy their own hell

What for mum ta tell their toddles.
What this day don' the numbers swell.

And what a me, Canis Ictus Cynicus,
    What be ta walk the fine line
A moral austerity and what Rome must hope
      What I discover simple charity
    What be customary most false
        And by action mocked
For citadels in heaven be drawn
      A lusts and desires a minded earth;
  Sicut in caelo et in terra.
What I cannot vow for what be before me
      What be found undone a me mazy fate.
No ease a me minds palaver
      What Lucretius abide Epicurus by dint
  A his many associates and vast estate,
What allow for endless jabber
    Amid leisure what ovvers be pained ta provide
    What a these powdered fools
      But pleasure and pain coincide.
Counter dwell inside the most pampered
    What such be their ease a materiel.
As The Dog might say, wealf be nuffin'.
But be this nuffin' but the Dog's way
What not seek it so much as step
      On one's own turd in the thoroughfare
And so by declare oneself the Son a Jove
  Or Imperial Rex, such be whimsy's power
    What a us what set aside ambition
And be forfright in our poverty
    So as ta be true ta fortune
Beyond the fix of a Saturnalian lottery

Or Crassus' team on the rail at the Hippodrome
But ta cast the world by the bones and abide.

Ictus mocks the beheaded slumlord, Crassus

Who's head me dear comrade, Velius,
　　Bring me now, this lantern of greed gone out,
　　　Struck through wif a Roman pugio,
　　　　What be heavy as me take in hand.
Crassus' nog what aim his fate
　　Wif the darts a avarice and ambition,
What his aim be true for a time
　　And what blaspheme Nature
And none require contemplate,
　　　For not ta take his life be the crime,
Whevver by pox or pugio he be dead
　　Ta what Gaia sigh.
How odd, Crassus, me fortune be
　　Mintage a me exile.
What yours be ta attend the Senate,
　　Wif the heads a state on a pike
No wonder we marvel a the gods
　　What whimsy be omnipotent
　　　What we allow anarchy what lie
　　Beyond our understandin'.
Behold your troops, a few cut down,
　　A the perimeter, and returned ta the earth
What most be joyous ta once again
　　　　Till the same.
No longer the alumentum a empire be blood
　　　And its engine, slaves.
What this wizard so easy overturned
　　It not appear such and desire be diminished.

Even thy head find a body
    Perhaps of a swine or a Gaul
    For Tessala's magick not seat thy marrow.
You'll always be a pompous shite, Crassus,
        Even be there but pox and pall,
    When the outcasts sweep their bloody harrow.
And I delight ta entertain thee here
        What a theft and lies, greed and murder
    Thy be queer a thy countrymen only in degree.
And this pugio be your last podium
        So speak as our portion be in thee ta hear.
What no account a the bargain?
        What be the Esquiliae
    What your thugs torch
And your brokers callous broach
        Before the bloody flames die out
And the charred children be wept upon?
        What we philosophers dissect the world.
What even attend killin' ta suss out your kind,
        Ever wonderin' what the populace
What every day in the Forum hear your name cursed
        And curse it in turn
        Become anatomists a your kind.
What acolyte a the cult a Asclepios,
    What couch your rheumy eye ta let in some light
Or lean over your cadaver puzzle
        Ta find the organ, the unerring tumor
        A your blindness.
What evil allow thee celebrity
        What so rash be mistook divine.
What be thee now but
    The wealthiest severed head in the Empire.
What thy kin crawl over the corpse a thy estates

Ere the worms and maggots
What pluck thee from the stars
And bring thee back ta earf.

And soon I join ya for beyond dung,
    What curious some crone a Cumae
        Calls her shite Ni-Tro-Jun,
        Earf have little need a the likes a us,
But what our bloody estate leave,
        A race cast a dragon teef.
Clay puppets what by some magic
        Be blown wif Ares' martial breaf,
What these o'ertake us
        What sprung a our very head.
And took down Crassus what speculate
    In what only short sighted mortals call real estate.
        And martial his spoils
Ta cut short Spartacus' revolt
    And share the consulship wif Pompeii the Great.
And what be politics in money
        Be a patrone a Julius Caesar
And join him and Pompeii in the First Triumvirate.
    So the richest a the Romans be a slumlord
What accord his own citizenry
        No comfort or security
    What not be ta his own gratuity.
Why say thus I? For historians, his historians
    Will write no doubt he not die at an ape's hand.
What they ferret of his body
        Ta his imminent campaign against the Parthians
And claim he perish at Edessa, Babylon or Carrhae.
        Though a herdsman a one eye
Smash their divine Odysseus in a bag;

Impair him ta mash and chips a bone
Ere the bloody Greek cunt
        Abide the gods and stay the fuck home.
What not these wander and betray good hosts
    What neiver need of invite
        The guinea swine upon their coast.
Certain Crassus by fire raze burnt
      The Roman tenements a the poor,
    Ta buy the ruins on the cheap
        And rebuild what remain wif slave labor.
What Plutarch call 'fire and rapine'.
     What now learn this be no slave rebellion
A Spartacus kind, but a force a terror minded
     Bloodless hordes a Spartoi and Terra Cotta fiends
What care not a the affairs or desires a men,
    Their omens and evil eyes and bewares.
For what a man kinds as superstitions,
        They be them what know
They be none such in their fathomless being
    But some over what mankind cannot annunciate.
     So what be they ta regard a men
But the most unconstrain and curious among them.

Such I be and as such they follow me.
    For what be a dog
      But what the dog be in man.
Nothin' a what all be transgress,
    So dog be furthest away as it be nearest.
What me smell be strongest
     I be standard a me kind
For what better demark than sense,
    Eyes, ears, nose, tongue and touch.
But what sounder fortune

What sense not mistook
       A bear's scent for a ponce.
Nor a bears' nose for a Roman's
       No matter bofe be proper large,
One what reach not sense as far a its end
       What the monster be leagues off;
Ta what stink sure still be morsel,
       Even the filf and grime of a cynic's crack
What we know a bein' ta hunger a that.
       Dun' this be what raise the riches' shank?
What very polis be brought ta ground,
       What I be ta favor a bear.
       What by its nature,
Its golden nose be so attuned
       A milky virgin's cunt vie
              Wif the most festerin' pocky crotch,
So sated be our slicks and darbies.
       What banish a man
              What not be on your tether,
Be ta mistook that man for a dog.
       A most ennoblin' gesture
       Amongst present company
What I look you square a your rheumy eye,
       Me foamin', gory cabbage, Crassus
       A lantern fit only ta test Avernus.
Your mercs and slaves rush to splash
       Your face wif their spittle
Such it run its glory down me forearm
       And pool upon the earf
       What we now know be Lake Albano.
I be willin' dog what awake thee from thy swoon.
       So loud Fortune not shunt me aside,
       A tremor Rome not feel.

239

For why magic cling ta me
    But the vine what strangle out the tree?
      For Jove and Hephaistos and Poseidon saw
    I had no love for thee,
      If such be tempted
    Be met wif contempt.
But among these pilgrims
      What come ta defile thee
Need but little what in thy infinite charity
      Could not give.
For what be your love but to embrace all.
    And what be your curse but ta be cursed by all.
You guineas what make the world an arena.
    Damn you Rome and what may follow!

We be not ta loot and rape and burn
   For among the Spartoi
     What about their bones hangs no flesh
   Be no need a victual and frivolity
And be no virtue counter their slaughter
    What be pure as a tigers.
Nor our clay men a Seres
    What as babes be not ta know
What be but what accoutrements
     They be carved in.
   So it be left ta Scabie, Velius
     And the two one-eyed giants,
What ta loot and rape and provide
   What Rome recognize as victory,
Lest some patriot mistake what transpire.
   And behind us and leagues off,
What be source a Cicero's trucklin' praise
   Rome blazed such that at last his triflin' books

Be read of a proper light,
For sentiment does violence
    Ta the heart of experience.
  And our four and Phineas' men dance
Shadows against what them be shy a sense
    Declare a thee ashes the birth of a new age,
What so much smoke be mirrors
    A what clear be norf from souf.
What gods when such sift
  Through the ash leave clues,
    They be hereabout.
I revel in me polis' destruction!
    Revel? Nay I dance!
What the vermin go up in flame
    Squeakin' their virtue.
  Their novel right ta live.
What be in bloody nature
      Not have the sobriety ta die
  What live passed spawnin'.
I be named mad for what me shite in the road,
  What I be an old mange hugged by toddles,
What mum warns off lest there be dog bite or fleas.
    What they cheer Crassus mastiffs
      What tear apart a slave
And leave a load or piss upon his agony.
  Trained as such by Hilarus
    What me Spartoi gladly slew.
So this be you, Crassus, what be precise,
    A head upon a stick.
And this be me, me hand in inward gesture,
    Your impaled head a me left hand,
And a wineskin a me right,
    Your bloody empire felled

By an alien magic what trump Simon Magus
    And Paul a Tarsus and all what canker your polis.
But this Tessala what serve an ape.
   Lest I forget what he befall upon Rome,
And some indisposed god take notice,
     And put a sickle ta me head
Or brand me an ass what I not so much mind
    As an ass be ta a dog, as a ox be ta a housecat.
I pour a libation ta this Bhodi
      What leave Rome wifout water
And me drunk a uncommon victory
    Wif bofe Rome and Hades a one frontage.

As Homer beckons the gods
    By klesis to his immortal hymns,
Or as here, a drunkard sings of destiny
    Bestride a mongrel cynic's whims.

EPILOGUE

Epilogue or how Plinius came ta write his Naturalis Historia

And what in me leisure and dotage
   I take up some abandoned villa a Ovidius
What that fat fuck not recall he be deeded
   So much land be secured in his name
As the hoi polio cherish their songs and shibboleths,
      And ta toss a coin at pretty words
         And charming dillies,
     As ta toss a bear a grape.
What the gate be locked a ringlets a iron,
     And so the garden there be
        An Adonis wif a mane a stone.
O fuck, let this ol' dog strain his yardie chain
    What splashed about in the fables a blood
       A what be said and what be claimed.
Words what led away in shame the likes of Ovidius,
      Under Augustan guard in these self-same chains.
    For what demon then what I held aloft
The head a Crassus what owned a thousand villas,
    What, ta pun Heraclitus, in his current state
     Not be disposed ta claim a one.
And a this place one Gaius Plinius make his way
    What ta hear a me travels
       And ta who I freely speak
So whatever come a his books, first cross me eyes
    Certain me name be the sun and the moon a his text.
And much I say ta him what be in jest
      Such that Polyphemus and Unoculus and their kind
        Ate Roman flesh what make him squirm
What he, me and the giants take our repast.

What the kittim eat a man
What just be imbibed by a lion or a bear
      And not fear human flesh what linger there.
Or a joke what creatures wif 8 toed feet
            What grow backward,
And Plinius "Who be ta report these?"
    And I say, "Very reliable source. Megasthenes,
        What travel ta Milus where these folks dwell."
          Or me hoppin' one foot blokes.
And the blokes wif no head and a eye in their chest.
          All a joke, a bagatelle,
What ta see the silly git publish any a it.
      Or the earth be round like a grape
What have it stem hole, the world's navel,
        A the southern pole.
      And Deucalion what saw Atlantis wash away
What Helios forgot ta turn on the day.
      And they be dogs what speak
          And men what bark.
Wif what nonsense me lick the ear a this Pliny,
      This tumult from me lips,
            Be but the scat of a skylark's song.
And so it be with any tale.
        Be it wive's or be it whale.
A hot focaccia decoco,
        Or cold and swallowed whole.

ABOUT THE AUTHORS

Professor H.C. Earwicker was the Porcus Dementious Scholar of Classical Languages and Antiquities at London's Wandsworth Prison from 1990 to 1998. Formerly a don at Cambridge where he was a Distinguished Lecturer, Professor Earwicker split his long teaching career either in the British pedagogical penal system or, alternately, England's prisons. It was in the latter he made the acquaintance of Carlo 'Ubatz' Parcelli, an autodidact who had fled Sicily after embezzling 10 million lire from various joint Mafia/CIA/Vatican held banks in Messina. In England, Parcelli was charged with impersonating a priest for the purpose of hearing confessions and extortion. A local magistrate denied Parcelli's claim that he was actually impersonating Lenny Bruce impersonating a priest and sentenced the classics scholar to 14 months in prison. It was there that Professor Earwicker sought the services of Mr. Parcelli in the translating of *Canis Ictus in Exsilium (Dog Bite in Exile)* after the latter shivved a fellow prisoner over conflicting interpretations of line 17 of the Homeric Hymn 'To Apollo'. "I saw a high seriousness and devotion in Mr. Parcelli's approach toward the classics," commented Dr. Earwicker at his collaborator's sentencing hearing. Professor Earwicker has published numerous titles, most notable his classic 'Those Inscrutable, Beautiful Naked, Oiled Greeks and How We British Envy Them' and 'The Margites: Homer Meets Fatty Arbuckle'.

Mr. Parcelli is widely published and has authored several books of Poetry. He was named Beat Poet Laureate of Maryland for the years 2017 and 2018. He has been abundantly praised for his dramatic performances of his texts especially monologues from *The Gospel According to Simon Kananaios*, and is generally considered to be one of the greatest poets of his generation.

www.ingramcontent.com/pod-product-compliance
Lightning Source LLC
Chambersburg PA
CBHW071139260626
47162CB00003B/854